ANTHONY GAGLIANO's
STRAITS OF FORTUNE

"*Straits of Fortune* is a smashing debut thriller, evoking all the magic and mystery that modern day Miami has to offer, its mile-a-minute storyline etched in prose as finely chiseled as a body-builder's six-pack. This guy could end up making the rest of us South Florida crime writers look like 98-pound weaklings."

Les Standiford, author of
See You in Hell and *Havana Run*

"*Straits of Fortune* is a ripping good Florida yarn, part Carl Hiassen, part Randy Wayne White, and first-novelist Gagliano is quick with a good, hard-boiled simile. It's a safe bet that Jack will be back—and that the many fans of Hiassen, White, and the rest of the Florida crime pantheon will add Gagliano to their list of must-reads."

Booklist (* Starred Review *)

"Gagliano is a welcome and powerful new voice in the Florida crime scene, deftly gene-splicing Mike Hammer and 'Miami Vice' as he takes the beach by storm. Only complaint: I'm left hanging for the follow-up."

Tim Dorsey, author of *Hurricane Punch*

"[A] great summer read."

Contra Costa Times

"Although Florida is awash in top-notch mystery writers . . . there is always room for more good storytellers who find inspiration in the state's vagaries. . . . Anthony Gagliano makes a most welcome debut in the well-plotted, gritty *Straits of Fortune.* . . . . [An] exciting story. . . . Gagliano infuses *Straits of Fortune* with an energized plot reminiscent of early Lawrence Block and Robert Crais. . . . Gagliano also nails the South Florida background. . . . This new series is off to a fortunate beginning."

Ft. Lauderdale Sun-Sentinel

"A hot, impressive debut thriller. . . . There are double crosses galore. . . . Gagliano's dark, pulse-pounding, action-packed tale is tough to put down; it's an accomplished tale by an exciting newcomer."

Lansing State Journal

"Anthony Gagliano has re-invented Florida noir with fresh humor and lovely writing. Hard to believe this is a first novel—it's got all the right moves. A crime-lover's dream cruise."

April Smith, author of
Good Morning Killer and *Be the One*

"The author takes what could have been a cookie-cutter whodunit and twists the genre to craft a contemporary action-adventure novel well-suited to the summer movie blockbuster crowd. *Straits of Fortune* begs to be enjoyed with a cool drink at the beach."

St. Petersburg Times

"Gagliano is a welcome addition to the Miami noir all-stars."
Florida International Magazine

STRAITS OF FORTUNE

ANTHONY GAGLIANO

HARPER

An Imprint of HarperCollinsPublishers

This book is a work of fiction. The characters, incidents, and dialogue are drawn from the author's imagination and are not to be construed as real. Any resemblance to actual events or persons, living or dead, is entirely coincidental.

HARPER

An Imprint of HarperCollins*Publishers*
10 East 53rd Street
New York, New York 10022–5299

Copyright © 2007 by Anthony Gagliano
ISBN 978-0-06-087810-8

First Harper paperback printing: June 2008
First William Morrow hardcover printing: June 2007

Printed in the United States of America

Visit Harper paperbacks on the World Wide Web at www.harpercollins.com

10 9 8 7 6 5 4 3 2 1

To Lana

STRAITS OF FORTUNE

ONE

IT WAS LATE AUGUST when the Colonel called me, one of those hot, humid, interminable days when you search for a new adjective for the heat and end up with nothing for your trouble but the taste of salt at the edge of your mouth. I was surprised to hear from the old man. For one thing, anyone with the money for a personal trainer will generally use some of it to leave Miami in the summer, a fact that had left me time for some casual fishing. I had just come back from the pier at Haulover with my catch of the day—a pair of yellowtails—when the phone rang. The plan had been to fry them up in a little olive oil with a few slices of lemon for company. But after my conversation with Colonel Patterson, I put the fish into hibernation, took a quick shower, and then drove out to Sunset Beach. After all, that was where the money lived.

Strange, now, that I used to call the Colonel's place "the

house of light," but light was so much a part of the architecture it was as though it had been written into the plans. The mansion was all mirrors and white steel and the audacity that comes with great fortune. It was all about math and money and inhuman precision, and at night it was magnificent, especially when the moon was full. But at the same time there was something about the place that worried you. I can't quite describe it except to say it was not a place where the birds would land, but it had cost $10 million to build, and with that kind of money you can buy all the birds you want. Funny, though, that with all that glass it was impossible to see inside.

By the time the diamond mansion was halfway built, property values within a quarter of a mile on either side of the inlet where it sat had tripled and the movie stars had begun showing up with their eyes and wallets open. So, all in all, Sunset Beach had been a good place to have a client, and I liked the Colonel well enough. If anyone asks me if I'd ever met anyone of true genius in my life, then I would certainly offer up Colonel Andrew Patterson as my contribution to the conversation. He had been a Green Beret who served in Vietnam in the days before anybody had ever heard of them, but that was only the soldier part of the story. Then there were his years as a military scientist and the top-secret experiments for the government. There was also Professor Patterson, the West Point graduate with the doctorate in chemistry who later started his own biotech company, Pellucid Labs, which is where he had made his fortune. You can imagine that the Colonel was a very interesting man to spend an hour with.

But as great as it had been to have a wealthy client with a beautiful mind, it was even better to have such a client with a beautiful daughter—a rich girl I had ended up training for free. (And why not? Who's to say the rich have no need of charity?) So as I drove out there that hot day in late August, it was neither the mind nor the money I was really thinking about. Though if the truth be told, when it came to Vivian Patterson, thinking wasn't something I usually brought along with me, but I'm not ashamed to admit that. You can't stay tied to the mast of reason all your life, and Vivian was as good a reason to become untied as any other woman I had ever met. You just had to know how to survive her company. With Vivian you rode an unsteady wave of excitement, always in imminent danger of crashing, but it was a wave you rode with a smile on your face, although maybe it was a stupid smile.

The guard at the gatehouse took one look at my car, realized I didn't live anywhere near Sunset Beach, and so came out with his clipboard and wrote down my name and license number along with the time of day. That way if any Picassos went missing, they'd know where to start looking. I glanced past the guardhouse and up the lane that led to the Colonel's house, its slanted roof leaning in the heat as though it had melted down from a previous altitude. When the guard was done checking me in, I drove very slowly past the corridor of super-tall California palms that flanked the hard-packed road of white gravel, then on through the second gate. As I drove, the car kicked up a cloud of dust that hung in the air for a moment before the breeze pulled it apart, and beyond that the man-made brightness of the Colonel's mansion.

I parked the car and walked past the flagpole that didn't have a flag that day and up to the door and rang the buzzer and waited. The black Bentley was parked slantwise on the grass, but even though the red Porsche I remembered so well was nowhere in sight, my heart beat harder in anticipation. Waiting there at the door, then ringing again, I felt a sense of trespass, as though I weren't supposed to be there, like I had gone back on my word in returning here and was in violation of something sacred, something personal, a promise I had made to myself. I half wanted to leave, but when you're that close, it's already too late. You've already committed yourself, even though you may not know it.

Dominguez, the family's chauffeur, came out of the four-car garage at that moment and spotted me waiting by the front door. He waved but didn't come over, which I found odd, because we had been pretty friendly at one time. He had come from Santiago, Cuba, even before the revolution and had worked at every kind of job imaginable before joining up with the Colonel back in the seventies. We used to talk baseball like it was Esperanto, and the only person he had hated more than Castro was George Steinbrenner. In fact, he had a theory the two of them were related. When no one came to the door after a few moments, I walked over to say hello, thinking that maybe he hadn't really recognized me.

Dominguez had lifted the hood of the Bentley and was staring down at the cleanest engine I'd ever seen outside of a car show. He didn't look well. His brown eyes had lost their shine and were surrounded by a sickly looking yellow haze, like a pair of beetles floating in pools of spittle. When I had seen him last, he still possessed the stubborn, wiry physique of an old lightweight fighter and at seventy had looked as tough as the bark of an ancient tree. Now he was downright thin except for a slight swelling of the gut beneath his jacket that didn't match the thinness of his arms and legs. We shook hands, but then he went back to staring down at the engine.

"Cómo estás?" I asked.

"Good."

"That's a nice-looking engine," I said. I could tell he didn't want to talk to me, but I pressed on anyway, thinking that maybe he was just in an off mood that might break with a joke or two.

"I never thought you come back here anymore," he said without meeting my eyes.

"Neither did I," I said. "The Colonel called me."

Dominguez slammed the hood down and turned to me. He was definitely sick, but there was more than illness in his expression. It was something, I thought, akin to disappointment. He took a white cloth from his back pocket and wiped his hands.

"Nice to see you, Jack." He turned and walked away toward the garage. I didn't believe him. I didn't think it had been nice to see me at all.

I have a fairly thick skin about things like that, and snubs don't cause me much loss of sleep. But there was something off about it just the same, and I wondered if maybe he'd been body-snatched by aliens. I watched him walk away, then went back and rang the doorbell again.

There was a brief flurry of footsteps, and then the maid opened the door and led me wordlessly through the acreage of the living room. The house was as cool as a meat locker, but it would have seemed cold at any temperature. The walls were bone white, and the extra-wide marble tiles looked as though they'd been cut from a slab of glacial ice. There were vases and sculptures and paintings on all the walls, some of it Mexican, most of it Asian. On the wall above the fireplace was a portrait of his first wife, Vivian's mother, a beautiful half-French, half-Vietnamese woman he had married against the advice of his superiors back in the days when we were still advisers over in Saigon.

Seeing the portrait reminded me again of Vivian. His first wife had had the same oval-shaped face and high cheekbones, the same liquid black hair. She had died in a car crash during the evacuation of Saigon. The Colonel brought Vivian back to the States while she was still in diapers, and a few years late married a wealthy socialite whose family had made its money in publishing. It was the family who'd provided the seed money for Pellucid Labs, the Colonel's biotech-pharmaceuticals company. That marriage had also produced a son, Vivian's half brother, Nick, a guy I had spent a long time trying to like before giving it up for easier hobbies.

Colonel Patterson had never spoken much of his second wife. The only thing I knew was that her name had been Mona, that her family owned Vermont, and that she was buried in Palm Beach County. If there was a portrait of her hanging anywhere in the house, I had never seen it. Maybe the Colonel kept a snapshot of her in his wallet, but then again, probably not. He was about as sentimental as a gang-plank on a busy day. It was hard not to suspect that the marriage had been mostly about the money.

I turned for no particular reason and saw Rudolph Williams peering down at me from the second landing. He was the Colonel's man, had served with him in the army, before and after Vietnam. He came down the winding staircase, moving with the ease of a man who knew very well how to move. Not once did he take his eyes off me. There had been few times during our previous meetings when in some way or other he hadn't tried to intimidate me—in that half-friendly, overblown macho way of his. To him I was an intruder who didn't belong anywhere near the family that had practically adopted him, and that fact hadn't changed even when I was seeing Vivian, and everybody knew it.

Williams—no one but the Colonel ever called him Rudolph—had never understood why the Colonel had elected to work with a personal trainer instead of himself, a man who looked as though he'd been raised in Gold's Gym, but the answer was simple: The two of them had been together for so long that the Colonel had decided he needed some variety in his life, someone with a new batch of stories, and he liked having an ex-cop for a trainer. And yes, he'd had me checked out thoroughly, and by the kind of people a man like the Colonel would know. By the time I showed up for the first appointment, he already had a file on me that went back to kindergarten, and he let me know about it, too. He also knew why I wasn't with the NYPD anymore, but he never brought it up, though we had talked about everything else.

Williams looked about fifty, and the book on him was that he'd been too crazy for even the Green Berets, which is scary when you think about it. So the army stuck him on long-range reconnaissance patrol to keep him out of mischief. He would go off into the jungle for weeks at a time, cut off people's ears and noses, then use them as receipts when he got back to base. The more ears, the more money he made. He was six-four and went about 260 or so, but without the 'roids he would have only been 240 at the most. He had a shaved head, the bright blue eyes of a Viking on a raid, and a red handlebar mustache flecked with gray. It wasn't hard to imagine him wearing a necklace made of human ears. He'd been bred for war and was wound way too tight for civilian life.

He stared me up and down, then sneered. "You look soft," he said. "What happened? You take up yoga or something?"

"Origami," I said. "I'm a black belt now."

We shook hands. His were so callused that if my eyes had been closed, I might have thought I was holding a piece of sanded-down driftwood. He squeezed a bit more than was necessary, but that was Williams for you: He never let an opportunity pass to show you how much more of a man he was than you were.

"I can still break five boards with either hand," he informed me, regarding his own hands as though he had just found them again under the bed.

"You should have been a lumberjack," I told him. "You could have saved a bundle on chain saws."

"Is that supposed to be funny?"

"Where's the Colonel, Rudolph? I didn't come out here to go down memory lane with you."

He frowned at the sound of his first name. "Out by the pool," he said. I followed him past a wall of windows toward the French doors that led out to the patio. After the air-conditioned chill of the house, hitting the August heat again was like walking face-first through a box of invisible cotton.

The sunlight was shining on the surface of the swimming pool, and it gleamed like liquid turquoise. At the far edge of it, the Colonel sat at a table under a green-and-yellow-striped umbrella. He was looking out at the ocean through a pair of binoculars. I followed the line of his gaze and saw a white yacht anchored about three hundred yards out. The sea it sat on was as blue and as flat and as calm as the water in the swimming pool. The sky above it was a tourist's dream of permanent summer. The only thing in it was a small plane dragging a banner I couldn't read in the sun's perfect glare. The Colonel stood up as I approached and tightened the sash of his black silk robe. I knew he didn't like to shake hands, so I didn't bother with the gesture.

The Colonel was nearly my height but as lean as a fox and looked as if he hadn't gained a pound since college. He had a widow's peak of straight white hair smoothed back over his narrow head like a skullcap or maybe one of those latex hoods some sprinters wear. His eyes were light gray and penetrating. He had a million-dollar tan, skin so taut it looked shrink-wrapped, and the ultra-high cheekbones of an ex-model—though he would have died if you'd told him that. I knew he was seventy, but he looked at least ten years younger. We nodded at one another and sat down in a pair of teakwood chairs without cushions.

"Well, Jack," he said in a jovial tone that didn't suit him, "how's business?" He looked up at Williams. "I'll take it from here, Rudy."

Williams nodded, then walked back along the edge of the swimming pool like a tiger very sure of his footing. The maid appeared and filled our glasses with orange juice from a crystal decanter, then set it down on a place mat at the center of the table and went quietly away.

"Business is fine," I lied. "For this time of year."

"Training anybody interesting these days?" the Colonel asked.

"Just Elvis, but he's missed a few appointments lately. I'm starting to get worried."

He smiled and set down his glass. "It's been a long time, Jack. I've missed your sense of humor. I'm still working out, but it's not the same without you. Of course, considering the circumstances, I understood why you elected not to keep me on as a client. It would have been awkward."

"What happened to the trainer I referred you to?"

"Raul? Oh, we get on fairly well; he's a nice fellow, really. But you know how it is. I was rather spoiled by your company. Raul is a good man and all, but not much of a conversationalist—other than on the subject of progressive resistance, which, as you know, has its limitations as a topic of interest."

"Not for Raul," I said.

"We had some rather interesting discussions, you and I, wouldn't you say, Jack?" Something seemed to come to him. "By the way, did you ever finish reading Gibbon?"

He was referring to the leather-bound, hand-sewn, three-volume set of *The Decline and Fall of the Roman Empire* he had given me as a gift soon after he realized, once we'd worked together for a week or two, that I could actually read. He'd bought it at an auction in London. It was without a doubt the single most valuable thing I owned, and there was no sense at all in telling him that I'd be pawning it in a few weeks if business didn't pick up.

"I finished it," I said. "But I think they should make it into a movie, like *Star Wars*."

But the Colonel hadn't heard me. He was still looking out at the yacht. He shook his head and sighed deeply.

"Nothing ever changes, does it, Jack? The greed, the corruption—the inflated egos of the politicians, almost all of them afflicted with third-rate minds. Have you ever noticed how rarely it is that ambition and ability are proportionate to one another? Take Caligula, for example: stone cold mad, and there wasn't a thing to do about it. Of course, they killed him in the end, but by then Rome was ruined—at least from a moral standpoint. Ambition and madness make for disaster."

"That's no doubt true, especially for emperors, but then there are different kinds of ambition, aren't there, Colonel? Take yours, for instance. You don't really care that much about money. It came your way as a kind of by-product. Now you're rich and bored. That leaves politics or suicide. Why don't you run for mayor, or maybe even city commissioner? That way you would get to go to all those fun meetings they have every week."

"Do you honestly think I have the tact for that? For listening to a bunch of cretins argue for hours on end about whether or not to put up another one of those dreadful condominiums on Collins Avenue? Or about how best to suck the dollars out of the tourists each winter? You know me better than that."

"That's just the point, Colonel," I told him. "You don't have any tact at all. You never developed it. It's like a muscle that never got used."

"My children often tell me that very same thing, especially Nick. They think I lack warmth. Perhaps they're right."

At that moment two kids on Jet Skis came out of the sun's glare as though they'd been born from it and roared toward the yacht at full speed, their bright orange life vests lifting behind them like capes as they rode. The Colonel stood up and watched them through the binoculars. The riders circled the yacht a few times, then went back the way they'd come. The Colonel seemed to relax after they were gone. He sat back down, but there was a frown on his face. He rubbed at his eyes with his thumb and index finger. His eyes looked tired, his face drawn.

"I've never been good at maintaining relationships, Jack," he said, again staring out to sea. "I'm sure my daughter informed you of that. The military is poor preparation for the demands of family life, and there are times, quite frankly, when even my own children seem like strangers to me. I can easily imagine not knowing them. Isn't that a horrible thing for a father to say? But at least I'm being honest about it. I'm cursed with the mercenary's mind, Jack. I tend to think of people in terms of their utility, and my children—Nick especially—seem to have damned little of it."

"Don't give up on him," I replied. "He may come around yet."

"Not as long as there's a dollar left in his trust fund, he won't."

He looked out at the yacht again and shook his head again.

"I wish I had kept in touch with you, Jack," he said after a moment. "I flatter myself to think that you and I were friends."

"Don't worry about it. I don't send out too many Christmas cards either."

"Still, if we had kept in touch, what I'm about to ask of you might be easier, or at least more appropriate."

"That's a mercenary's expression of regret, Colonel," I told him.

"Yes. Yes it is. I suppose it comes through no matter what."
He studied my face for a moment. I had no idea what he was
looking for. "Well, Jack, what do you say? Are you up for a
bit of adventure?"

"What did you have in mind?"

"Despite what you said a moment ago, I understand that
your business is rather slow in the summer."

I didn't say anything to that. I took a swallow of orange
juice and put the glass down on an orange coaster with a
black dragon printed on it.

"I thought that as a fellow mercenary you might be of a
mind to make a lot of money in very little time."

I took another sip of orange juice. It was freshly squeezed,
with an inch of pulp floating on top, but it was a bit too sweet
for my taste.

"That's a reasonable thought," I said. "Can I ask you a
personal question?"

"Go ahead."

"Why do you keep staring at that yacht?"

The Colonel turned and looked at me. In profile his face
was thinner than I had remembered it.

"Whatever happened to you and Vivian?" he asked.

"We came to a parting of the ways."

"In other words, it's none of my business."

"I wouldn't say that. It's just that there's not much to talk
about."

"You thought she had too much money for you to keep up
with. Was that it?"

"That was part of it, but there were other reasons."

"Such as Mr. Matson, for instance."

"Among others."

"You're looking a bit edgy, Jack. I'm not offending you,
am I?"

"Not really. I just never thought you were all that interested in the matter."

"I understand it was you who introduced her to Matson. Is that correct?"

"That's right."

"Maybe in retrospect that turns out not to have been a smart move."

"They call it networking."

"She would have married you, you know."

"We must be talking about two different people. Who told you that?"

"The only person who would know for sure."

"I never got that impression."

"She was using Matson for leverage. You saw it happening, and you let it continue. Then when the thing got to a certain point, you became indignant and walked away."

"I introduced her to a client of mine at a party, Andy. That didn't mean she had to sleep with him."

"That's the first time you ever called me 'Andy.' Despite all the times I asked you to. It was always 'Colonel' or 'sir.' Now it's 'Andy.' Are we friends now, Jack? Should I be flattered, you distant, hard-nosed son of a bitch?"

"Why be flattered? It's a lot better than me calling you 'Dad.'"

He laughed. "Would that have been so bad? I always thought we got along rather well."

"Why don't you tell me why it is you asked me out here today? I don't mean to be rude, but it's getting late, and I don't like to keep Elvis waiting. You never know. He might show up today."

"Vivian got into a rough crowd after you left."

"She was with a rough crowd when I met her. She was living in Tattoo City for quite some time before I came along."

"You added Matson to the population, a cheap pornographer."

"There were a lot of people I introduced her to: doctors, a

few politicians, some lawyers, even an anthropologist. She picked him out of a fairly large bunch. It was her choice, not mine, not yours."

"You let him take her. You didn't even bother to fight. He had money and you didn't, and so you just surrendered Vivian to him. I would have expected at the very least that you would have kicked his ass. I was disappointed in you, Jack."

"I guess that's why you got me out here today. So we could sit around and be disappointed together. Is that it?" I stood up. "I usually get paid for my time, Colonel. It's the only thing I have to sell that's worth anything. But that's okay. This one's on me."

"How would you like to make a hundred thousand dollars?"

I hesitated for a moment and studied the fault lines in his forehead. Then I sat down again.

"I know you can't be bought," the Colonel said. "But I was hoping you might be for rent, at least for a few hours."

"What's this got to do with Vivian?"

"I suppose I played that card too early."

"No. Not too early, but you did play it. And you played it hard. You can't put it back in the deck now."

"You see that yacht out there?" he asked.

"I see it."

"There's a dead man on it."

My heart leaped at the wall of my chest and fell back, ready to try again. I stared at the Colonel for a moment; then I lowered my shades and looked out at the yacht.

"A dead man," I said. "And who might that be?"

"Matson."

"Matson?" I took a deep breath, not moving my eyes from the yacht.

"Walk with me, Jack. I get stiff if I sit too long."

We took a narrow path that followed a break wall until it curved around toward the gazebo where I used to sit with Vivian and then on past the long-neglected tennis courts with their nets hanging limp and exhausted in the flagrant heat of midday. Beyond that was the Japanese garden the Colonel had had installed at great cost when he purchased the property. But not even the Green Giant could have made the project a success. The climate was too humid, the soil too salty, the sun too relentless. The gardeners, imported like the bonsais they had planted, had been forced to use native species for the project. All but one of them had returned home, broken, bitter, but a lot richer for their troubles.

The Colonel stopped suddenly and looked at me. I was thinking about Matson dead on the boat. I stooped, picked up a small stone, and absentmindedly tossed it into a fish pond where bright orange Japanese koi were swimming around frantically, looking for a way out.

"You never told me why you quit the police force up in New York," the Colonel said, apropos of nothing.

"I never told you because I knew you already knew. What difference does it make now? Let's get back to Matson."

"You know," he said thoughtfully, "it's a sorry fact that at least fifty percent of men engaged in combat never fire their weapons, even when they're being shot at, even when people are trying to kill them. Hard to believe, isn't it?"

"History proves I'm not one of them."

"No, I suppose not. But sometimes when a man makes a mistake—let's say he shoots the wrong man—it can make him timid. He doubts himself. The next time around, he hesitates, and that's the end of him. I've seen it. I know."

"He wasn't just the wrong man, Colonel," I said. "He was a cop. He was a cop just like me."

"We call it friendly fire, Jack. It can't be avoided."

I started to say something, but instead I turned and looked

out at the water. What's that the kids say? Shit happens. It occurred to me that I'd been in Miami too long. Too many people knew who I was. I had lost the sacred one-time-only gift of anonymity.

"That scar on your cheek," the Colonel said. "He fired, too. Would you have preferred that it was you who were killed—or worse, crippled? Is that why you insist on slumming as a personal trainer, Jack? Is that your idea of repentance? Wasting your mind teaching old bastards like me how to do push-ups?"

Now I turned to face him. "What's this got to do with Matson?"

The Colonel stooped and picked up a pebble of his own and tossed it underhand back into the fish pond.

"Why did you come out here, Jack?"

"You invited me, remember? You're not getting senile on me now, are you?"

"You were hoping to see my daughter, weren't you?"

"Stop playing me, Colonel. You think I don't get what you're doing?"

He smiled. We kept walking. I had given him the satisfaction of knowing just how badly I wanted to ask about Matson. I was as hooked as the two fish lying frozen in my freezer, and the Colonel knew it.

A winding, stone-lined brook gurgled alongside us as we walked. The lizards danced and flirted with our feet, and the wind carried the smell of the ocean from beyond the dunes. Neither of us spoke for what seemed a long time. I was thinking of Matson. I was thinking of Matson and Vivian. The Colonel walked beside me with his hands in the pockets of his black silk bathrobe. A gardener carrying a hoe and a bucket of dead plants stood up from behind some weather-beaten bushes. The Colonel spoke to him in Japanese for a few moments as the lizards skittered through the ferns like little fugitives. While they talked, I thought about Matson some more and tried to work myself around to caring that he was dead, but I couldn't seem to find the right frequency. The gardener took one last forlorn look at his work and shook his head like a doctor who's just seen a bad set of X-rays. We watched him shuffle away.

"He says everything is dying," the Colonel told me. "Too much salt."

"What did you expect out here by the ocean?"

"Expect? It was more a gesture I felt inclined to make. Something you do. I didn't expect anything. Let's go back by the pool."

Soon we were sitting by the pool again. "Can I assume Matson didn't die from natural causes?" I asked.

"He was shot."

"By whom?"

"I think you already know the answer to that question."

"Let me have the short version."

"There is no short version."

"Be creative."

"After your abdication, Matson used to come around here a lot. I never much liked him. He was all money and no class. That's not a particularly original phenomenon in this city, of course, but it's also not one I cared to indulge now, at a time in my life when I'm no longer forced to by business pressures. Even so, I was always polite." The Colonel looked at me. "He was a sorry replacement for you, Jack."

"Too bad Vivian didn't think so. Why'd she shoot him, and, better yet, why are you telling me all this and not the police? I work with the living, not with the dead."

"She did it to protect me."

"From Matson?"

"From Matson and the people he worked for."

"He made porn movies. What does the director of *Hitch-*

hiking Bitches and *Lesbian Gymnasium* have to do with you?"

"On the face of it, nothing. But things aren't always what they seem, and neither was Matson."

"You're being mysterious, Colonel."

"Matson was a blackmailer. Did you know that?"

"He had money. Why would he want to waste time getting yours?"

He waved the question away with the back of his hand as though it were irrelevant. "He managed to talk my rather delinquent daughter into helping him steal some very important research from my files. Work I had done years ago while employed by the government. He was going to sell it." The Colonel cracked his knuckles and flexed his palms out and away from him, his fingers locked. Then he cracked each knuckle individually using the thumb of either hand.

"You are wondering what he stole, perhaps."

"No, I was still wondering why you called me out here."

"I need your help."

"As in?"

"I want you to take that bastard's yacht out there and sink it down to the bottom of the sea."

I thought about it for a moment. "And for that I get a hundred grand. Is that what you're telling me?"

"Well?"

"Let me think about it."

"There's no time to think about it, Jack. That yacht has been anchored there in the same spot for over a day now. It's only a matter of time before the coast guard takes notice. Then it will be too late. It's not just a question of Matson. There are certain sensitive items belonging to me on board that I do not wish to be found. The sooner the boat disappears, the less chance of that there will be. So the time for thinking is rapidly fading, Jack. This is a time for action."

"What did Matson have on your daughter?"

The Colonel glared at me with an expression that was an ugly mixture of disgust and rage long contained. "It would appear she inadvertently starred in one of his films when she wasn't thinking straight. When she went out to his boat, he took the ransom and my research, but he reneged on the film. He taunted her. Told her he'd made copies. That turned out to be a mistake."

"So she shot him over a film?"

"There was a bit of passion involved. She felt betrayed." He lifted a copy of the *Wall Street Journal* from the table. Beneath it was a blue videocassette. He picked it up and held it out to me. Then he reached into the pocket of his robe, brought out a key, and tossed it at me. The key took a bounce on the table, but I caught it on the rebound as it came off the glass.

"That's the key to Vivian's room. I assume you still know the way. Why don't you go upstairs and make use of the VCR and watch the film? It might fuel your ambition."

"I don't have any ambition. Not as far as your daughter's concerned."

"You did once."

"Once is over."

"Think about the money, then."

I looked at the film cassette and put it down. Then I thought about Matson and looked out at the yacht, so white it could have been a shape carved from ivory. It had lost all its innocence, like the Trojan horse on the morning after. The Colonel sat watching me. After a few moments, I took the cassette and stood up.

"This orange juice is too sweet," I said. Before he could answer, I had turned and gone back through the French doors and was bounding up the winding stairway that led to the bedrooms.

Even on the second floor, the place was still more of a museum than a place where people lived. It lacked the warmth of occupation. There were no toys scattered in the hallway, no family dog or cat stretched out on the marble tiles, just a lot of style and no air of comfort. A computer program with the human touch deleted. There was a painting by Botero of a family of refugees from Weight Watchers and another by Modigliani of a boy inside a blue balloon floating over a bombed-out city. There was a statue of a woman carved from onyx lounging on a pedestal inside a recessed section of the wall. There was more, but even if there had been twice what there was, the hallway still would have felt empty. It was way too well lit for a corridor that led to rooms where people slept and dreamed and wore pajamas.

I hesitated at the door, and for a moment it occurred to me that I could simply go quietly down the stairs, out the front door, and back to my car without saying good-bye. A man I had once thought of as a friend was dead on a yacht, and in my hand was a film he had made of a woman I didn't want to see. I had come here half hoping I'd run into Vivian again, though, in one of those strange, schizoid acts of self-denial, I hadn't allowed myself to think about what I would say to her if I had. Now I was going to get my wish. I was holding it in my right hand.

I opened the door and closed it behind me. Nothing had changed, and yet to call it her room is misleading. She'd had her own place down on South Beach for years now, ever since dropping out of Smith College. But in a house with eighteen bedrooms, most of them empty, there had been no reason to change anything, and now, whenever it became necessary, she used this place as a refuge from her new life.

It was the room of a woman in her late teens. In one corner sat the bronze Buddha I recalled, still wearing the Santa Claus hat she had stuck on its head and still sporting the cigarette she'd left dangling from the edge of its metallic mouth. Around the statue she had built a miniature temple of flagstones stacked in a progression of shelves. The two incense holders on either side of the Buddha were empty now, the last stick burned to a nub at its base.

She hadn't been here in quite a while. The stems of two dozen or more dead flowers leaned from their vases like bony fingers, and everywhere on the floor before the shrine lay the petals of red and yellow roses, all as dry as doilies. I stood there looking around like a voyeur stranded in his own memories.

There was an enormous teakwood dresser imported from Cambodia that four strong men would have had trouble lifting, and on top of it, in front of the mirror, ran a row of old-fashioned atomizers, some of them still full of perfume. There were photographs of her family taken in Vietnam: one of Vivian and her mother, both in white dresses, and the Colonel, then a captain, much younger, with darker hair, in his uniform. They stood poised and smiling in front of a large white split-level chalet that looked like it belonged in a French suburb. In the driveway sat a battered army jeep that went with the Colonel's uniform but not with the house it stood before. They were like two disparate dreams merged by memory, war, and accident.

None of this, of course, went with the Aerosmith poster on one powder blue wall or with that of Hendrix, Afro high and guitar in hand, on the other, any more than the plush, white teddy bear wearing a red ribbon around its neck went with the woman I recalled. Only a dead man or one not long for the living could have failed to remember at precisely that moment the first time I'd laid eyes on Mr. Bear. Why the first time had to be here with her father asleep and not at her apartment on South Beach, I never figured out, except for realizing I was about to enter a drama whose intricacies I didn't care to decipher.

I had driven at midnight through a jungle rain, my companion heart keeping time with the wipers swiping away at the falling flood of water on the windshield. I remembered the expression on the guard's face as I pulled up to the gate, how he emerged from his booth like a specter. The hood of his poncho covered all of his face except for the white of his teeth as he smiled and waved me through, not bothering this time or any future time to record on his clipboard the odd fact of my lucky arrival. *The bastard's hit pay dirt,* he must have told himself. I knew then that I was one of the chosen. It is a good feeling while it lasts—that is, until you find out what it is you've been chosen for.

What I remember next of that night was opening her door without knocking, just as I had been told, and seeing Vivian sitting naked in her bed, casually smoking a cigarette and cradling the teddy bear between her legs as though it were a child, Edith Piaf crooning softly in the background like a sad ghost trying to exorcise her own memory, and the lingering flying carpet of marijuana exhaust floating over her head as I closed the door behind me. It was an opium den with a naked girl and a stuffed bear, both of them waiting just for me. A night, in short, for the record books, and when I drove out before dawn, the guard was asleep in the chair in his booth and a thick fog filled the space between earth and sky, but not nearly so thick as the fog in my mind.

And now here I was again, not really believing it. Everything came back a little at a time, like the pages of a diary thrown into a fire, then retrieved from the ashes. I went over to the shelf with the stereo and television and slipped in the videotape. I was aware of the element of self-torture involved with what I was doing, aware that I was having my buttons pushed and pushed hard, aware of the yacht silent and white in the sunlight, aware of the money, aware that I was being foolish. I switched on the television and the VCR, then sat back in a yellow beanbag chair that absorbed me like a giant sponge.

Several times I was forced to turn away from what I saw. There were no trailers to sit through, certainly no cartoons, only a brief, ragged fence of static that morphed into the view of the room. Matson and Vivian sitting at a table in what looked like a hotel room, judging by the generic furniture. They were talking, smoking cigarettes, and there were glasses and two bottles of red wine. I turned down the volume. For some reason hearing her voice was worse than seeing her face.

Then a second man entered the frame, and I jumped as though he had burst in on me. I didn't know him. He was well tanned, well groomed, dark-haired, handsome in that perfect way. He seemed to be in his late thirties, a medium-size man in a beige sports jacket and black slacks. He had a military-style crew cut. He walked over to the camera and leaned down and placed his face close to its lens and grinned like an idiot. Then he went over to the table and poured himself a glass of wine and sat down across from Vivian and Matson. Matson held up a hundred-dollar bill to the camera and winked devilishly; then he rolled it into a tube. Each of them did a line of coke off a mirror laid flat on the table.

After a while they got into it. Vivian slipped off a periwinkle-colored silk dress, and the men began taking off their clothing. Vivian and Matson kept up their chatter as she removed her bra and panties, but the other man looked nervous and uncertain. The cameraman, whoever he was, panned in on his face so that I could see him sweating. Vivian's eyes looked glazed, and I gave in to the merciful thought that she had to be on something.

Matson went first. He was tall, rangy, with a hawk nose and a shock of straight black hair that made him look like a rock star. I remembered the times I had trained him, taught him a little tai chi and tried to get him off the coke. He had the arms I had given him, but also the puffed-out gut of a skinny, full-time drinker he had given himself. I watched him and tried to understand that he was dead.

He was very thorough with her, as was she with him. Then the other man came over, looking shy and tentative and trying to hide it with the fake smile of a man who would rather be elsewhere. Matson went and sat down and drank his wine while his pal took his turn. The other man was trying extra hard to look lustful, but all he managed to do was look sad and pitiful, like a man who has reached some previously unexplored limit in himself and does not like very much the new territory he's discovered there. Matson drank his wine and watched them like a man at a movie, like me watching him. But only one of us was a masochist, as far as I could tell.

I watched far more than I should have. I fast-forwarded until I came to the part where Matson and the blond man dragged the couch away from the wall and bent her over it. The quality of the film and lighting were both very good, but I would have paid money for a few shadows to hide the obvious pleasure I saw on her face.

It was ugly and degrading and enthralling, and by the time I shut it off and was standing by the window looking out at the yacht, I was feeling like a man who's roasted himself over a fire while turning the spit himself. I went back to the night when I had walked into a bar after a long drive back from Gainesville, where I'd gone to see an old friend who was dying from cancer. It was an out-of-the-way place, and I was in an out-of-the-way mood. I had gone there for the specific reason of having a solitary drink without having to talk to anybody I knew. The chances of my being there at all on that or any other particular night were so slim as not to be calculable, but I was only there a short while when I saw her and Matson swapping spit in a booth. It was just a month or so after I'd introduced them.

I don't remember how I got over to Matson. Possibly I levitated or passed through the ether like a ghost. But I remember well enough how the bouncers there pulled me off him. I remember the shock on Vivian's face, the livid embarrassment that held for a moment, then collapsed into tears. The bouncers were only doing their jobs. I didn't want to fight them, but one of them hit me in the side of the head and drew blood, and from that moment on, as far as I was concerned, they were on Matson's side.

Then the cops came, as cops will. One of them smacked me over the head with a nightstick and took me away. I had to call the Sheik, another client of mine, to spring me from jail. The only good thing that came out of it was the community service I had to do. I spent the better part of a month showing some retarded kids how to throw a Frisbee at a Jewish recreation center. Those kids were all right, even if their parents were a little leery of me at first. When the administrators realized I wasn't a complete maniac, they even offered me a part-time job. The pressures of the marketplace didn't allow me to take it, however, but I still went back once or twice a week or when business was slow, even after I was done with my atonement.

I was standing by the window staring at the yacht and thinking about all this when I heard the door open behind me. Williams was standing there. I would have known it was him without having to turn around. He was easily the tensest man I'd ever met, and the steroids weren't helping much either. His eyes had the jaundiced tint of someone who'd been on the juice for way too long, and he was retaining so little subcutaneous water that the muscles of his massive forearms had that telltale snakeskin tautness I'd noticed a lot of down on South Beach.

"I see you've been at the movies," he said, glancing over at the television screen, now filled with jittery horizontal lines of static.

I reached over, shut off the set, and popped out the cassette.

We stared at one another. I am six feet one and weigh two hundred pounds, but Williams had me by three inches and enough muscle to make a difference, plus he'd been trained to fight by the best. Even with the age difference—I was thirty-four—common sense told me I should have been afraid of him, but I wasn't. At that moment, staring into his grinning face, all I wanted to do was hit him, hit him hard. He knew it, too. He smiled, turned sideways, tugged at the legs of his trousers, bent his knees, and assumed a fighting stance. He cocked his head to one side and then the other. There was a cracking sound you don't hear much outside a chiropractor's office.

"You in the mood for a wee bit of a workout, Jack?" he asked in a fake Scottish accent.

"When I am," I said, "you won't have to ask." I wondered if, like me, Williams realized how stupid we were being. Then he threw a punch that stopped an inch from my nose. He smiled when I didn't flinch. He looked offended, disappointed, as though I had refused a gift. I shook my head and walked past him out the door. I had nothing to prove to him. Williams tensed when I passed by him. He followed me as I went down the stairs, but not too closely. The bad vibes followed us both.

The Colonel was swimming laps in the pool when I walked out onto the patio. Williams trailed me, a few feet back, still not getting too close, as though he sensed my mood. I wasn't the same man who had arrived here a short while ago. I had switched tracks halfway through the film, and I wasn't so sure I wanted to switch back. Still, despite my frame of mind, something didn't jibe about the blackmail angle, at least not as it pertained to the video I'd just watched. My gut feeling was that it was just a ploy to distract me. Unfortunately, it had worked.

The Colonel saw me out of the corner of his eye, swam past me to the shallow end, and walked briskly out of the blue chemistry of the water. I waited off to the side for him. Williams handed his boss a black silk robe, which the old man promptly wrapped himself in, tying off the sash at the middle. He said a few words to Williams, who glanced over at me with a grin, then turned and headed off toward the garden. The old man went and sat down again at the table, and I went and sat across from him. A bottle of Johnnie Walker Black had appeared on the table, and he poured a bit of it into a glass and drank it straight down in one shot.

"Williams doesn't like you very much, does he?" the Colonel asked, looking at his empty glass.

"No," I said. "I don't suppose he does."

"I wonder why."

"You should ask him," I said.

"What did you think of the film?"

"That's a stupid question."

He thought that over for a moment. "It's been a very long time since anyone referred to me as stupid."

"You'll need to get used to it if you think I believe that your daughter killed someone over a film, even one like that. I suppose you've seen it."

He shook his head. "I've seen enough ugliness in my life, Jack. I took her word for what was on it, hers and Williams's. I told you. She did it to protect me."

"If she really did shoot Matson," I said, "then protecting you was probably only part of it. I'm betting she just lost her temper and popped a cap into him. I'm not buying this loving-daughter crap."

"He was going to send copies of his little masterpiece to everyone I know, people in Washington, people who matter. She didn't want that to happen, and she took the matter into her own hands before I could stop her." He looked across at me. "Do you want her to go to prison for killing that scumbag?"

"She might get off. It's happened before, and you've got the money to make it happen."

"I don't want to take that chance, and I don't want the publicity. I just want the whole thing gone as quickly as possible. A hundred thousand dollars, Jack." His eyes brightened, and his voice rose into a tone of false triumph, all for the benefit of my proletarian perspective. He made that much while brushing his teeth.

"Why not get Williams to do it?" I asked. "He works a lot cheaper than that."

"There's a slight chance that if you're careless, you'll be caught. If that were to happen to Williams, I'd be drawn into it. I can't risk that."

That didn't sound quite right for some reason; then it hit me. When it came to moving quietly through the night, there wouldn't be too many people better at it than Williams. Compared to him, I would be an amateur. The Colonel would know that as well as anyone. It was early, but I poured myself an inch of scotch to cover my thinking time. I could almost feel him trying to read my mind.

"Williams could've been out there and back a half dozen times by now," I said after taking a sip of my drink. "And you and I both know it."

"I need Williams here," the Colonel said. "With me."

"Why? Sure, he's cute, but you could spare him for a few hours, couldn't you?"

"Matson had friends, and I have reason to believe that the house is being watched. Williams is almost psychic when it comes to things like that. He refuses to leave my side."

"If that's true," I said, "then Matson's friends must also realize that something's wrong on that boat. It's been there long enough. Why haven't they gone out there to investigate?"

"It may be that they already have, possibly at night. If that's so, they're probably waiting for my next move, see whether I'll call the police. They may be expecting me to send Williams out to take care of things, in which case I'd be here alone."

"I'll tell you what," I said. "I'll stay here with you while big bad Williams goes out and does the dirty work. How's that sound?"

"You're good, Jack, but you're not Williams."

"Funny, but for some reason I take that as a compliment."

"Are you afraid?"

"Not yet."

"Williams stays here. As I said, if Williams were to be caught, it would lead back to me. That's not something I can afford at this stage of my life."

"And if I get caught? They'll think I killed him."

"Your alibi is that I called you here to ask if you knew where my daughter was. I told you I thought she was on the boat. You went out there and found the body and decided to sink the boat and spare an old man the trouble of bringing the police into it. They'll dig the bullets out, but they won't match with any gun you own. We won't mention the film, of course. That would give you too much of a motive."

"So who killed him, then? That's the kind of question the police tend to ask."

"A man in Matson's business makes plenty of enemies. The Russian mob has moved into the smut business in a big way. Matson ran afoul of them. I know a lot of judges, and I'll get you a good Jewish lawyer. You have no record, and you used to be a cop. On top of that, I'll double your fee."

"How do you know I can even drive a boat like that?" I asked.

The Colonel smiled. "Let's not be obtuse, all right? You know damned well I had you checked out long before you showed up here. You used to work for Captain Tony, right? Taught you everything he knew about repossessing boats.

You have a captain's license—expired, but I'll overlook that, considering the circumstances. You and he even got shot at a few times. Once, down in Veracruz, you even got locked up for a few days. It seems the Mexicans thought you two were thieves."

"Coming from them, that was pretty hard to take."

He was talking about the time Captain Tony and I had been asked to return a thirty-foot sailboat that belonged to a stockbroker whose numbers had gone bad. The broker had sailed down to Acapulco to get away from it all, but he hadn't gone far enough. Now he was in a prison up in central Florida, doing time for insider trading. After the FBI caught up with him, the Mexicans wanted to keep his boat. The bank had disagreed with that and called in Captain Tony. It was good money, but we had almost gotten killed.

"I understand you have a kayak," the Colonel said.

"That's right. So?"

"You'll need it to get back once the boat sinks."

"I'd have to take that boat out at least five or six miles, into the Gulf Stream. That's a long way out."

"You're making excuses, Jack. We're wasting time on all this. Are you going to do it or not?"

"The thought of jail fails to intrigue me, Andrew."

"I don't see why. You'd be able to lift weights all day long. Now, look: We can bullshit here all day, Jack. Yes or no?"

I looked across the table at him and shook my head. I stood up. The Colonel seemed crestfallen, deserted, as though his best hope had left him. All I wanted to do was get out of there, away from all of them, but the look on the Colonel's face ate into my resolve.

"You don't expect me to believe the blackmail story, do you?" I asked. "And don't give me that crap about your friends getting the video. First of all, you don't have any friends, and second of all, if you did, you wouldn't give a rat's ass what they thought. Besides that, nobody who knows Vivian thinks she's been in a convent the past ten years, so why don't you tell me why she really shot Matson?"

The Colonel looked me over carefully and nodded approvingly.

"You're a good man," he said. "I'm sure if you hadn't shot that other officer, you'd be a detective by now. You're right, the smut wasn't the only reason, but it's the only one I'm prepared to provide you with right now—that and a hundred thousand dollars."

"Where's Vivian?" I said. "Maybe she'll tell me what's going on here."

"I don't know where she is."

"I hate calling you a liar twice in the same day, Colonel, but I'm kind of getting used to it. Save your money for your daughter's lawyers. By the time they're through, a hundred grand won't even pay their bar bills."

I stood up. The Colonel gazed at me and shook his head slowly. Then he stood and, despite the fact that it was not his habit, extended his hand. The gesture caught me off guard.

"Sorry I brought you out here, old friend. No hard feelings," the Colonel said. He wore the faint smile of a man who is trying hard to be brave.

"What will you do now?"

"That's no longer your concern."

I thought for a moment. Something he'd said earlier was bugging me, and I'd almost forgotten it.

"You mentioned that Vivian had stolen some of your research," I said. "Supposedly for Matson. He used the film for leverage, is that it?"

"Yes, that's right."

"What would Matson want with your work? The closest he ever came to chemistry was working behind the bar at Monty's."

"Good-bye, Jack. It was nice of you to come. I hope I haven't wasted too much of your time."

Suddenly I was the one who wanted to protest. My curiosity was winning out over my common sense. I wanted to know more, but I knew damned well I should get out of there. The trouble fuse had been lit, and it was just a matter of time before the whole thing blew. I knew it, and yet it still took considerable effort to walk away.

"So long, Colonel," I said, forcing the hollow words out. "I'm sorry I couldn't help you out."

"I was a fool to think you would."

I started to say something, but he had already turned his back and was staring out at the yacht. I watched it with him a moment. Then I turned and walked toward the house and left him sitting there with the sunlight, the yacht, the bottle of scotch, a lot of money, and no way around the fact that he had a daughter who would probably have to go to jail. I was walking away from a lot of trouble, and I knew it. I only wished that doing it were easier than it felt.

Williams was outside standing by my car when I came out. The sun was in my face, and I lowered my shades.

"I told him you wouldn't do it," he said.

I went around to the driver's side and unlocked the door without answering him. He took one step and placed his hand against the window.

"You're a piece of shit, mister. Don't let anybody tell you different," he told me.

"You better have your blood pressure checked, Williams," I said. "You're about to explode. Now, get your hand off my car." I pulled the door open, and he stepped away, watching me. I got in and started the engine. It was so hot I had to immediately roll down the windows.

"Look," I said to him through the open window, "you know I used to be a cop, right? So listen to me: Have her go to the police. It'll be loud and it'll be messy, but eventually it'll be over. That's the best advice I can offer you."

"There's a lot you don't know. The old man's in trouble."

"He's not the only one," I said. I gave him a salute and hit the gas.

As I drove away, I saw Williams standing in the center of the driveway still watching me, getting smaller and smaller as I approached the gate. Like me, I'm sure he sensed that there was something left unfinished between us. I just didn't know what it was. One thing I did know was that I didn't owe the Colonel anything. I didn't owe Vivian anything, and for sure I didn't owe Williams anything, but the feeling of incompleteness remained, made me restless. I turned on the radio and began working the dial east and west, wandering through the songs. Nothing sounded good.

I listened to the rich baritone voice of a Baptist minister, but his words on the nature of sin and salvation drifted past me like birds finding no place to land. On a channel far to the left, a woman talked at great length on the many benefits of tofu and other soy products. Around the dial again and Howard Stern was interviewing a man who had become a woman and a woman who had become a man. After a while I turned off the radio and listened to nothing, and I liked that a lot better. It was one of those days when the only thing that makes any sense is silence.

I drove south on Biscayne Boulevard until I reached the Kennedy Causeway up on Seventy-ninth Street, then turned east toward the beach, my usual route, past the crab place and Mike Gordon's with its big steaks and redwood waitresses. Two years on Miami Beach and the sight of a pelican still made me stare like a tourist. The wingspread of a pterodactyl; the focused, unblinking eye; the steady flight and the sword thrust of its long, gray beak into the bay. Then I was on the main bridge with Biscayne Bay flashing north and south, the sailboats placid and going nowhere.

In a place like Miami, there is always the ongoing battle

between the paradise visions of the past and the nightmare prophecies of the future. Depending on where you were at the time, it could be hard to tell which was winning, but today my windows were open and the sky was endless in all directions, and it seemed to me that paradise, my paradise, still had a few more good years left in her. New York was another life, crowded with memories, like a love affair that had been good while it lasted but you wouldn't want back again, even if it could somehow be arranged.

I had come to think of my life here as the "Miami Years," both words capitalized and in quotes, like the heading of a chapter in a memoir I would probably never write. After the troubles in New York, I had headed for Miami because of Gus Santorino, an old cop who had broken me in on the force and then taken his savings south and opened a nightclub on the beach just as the party crowd began crowding the old folks out of "God's Waiting Room," as the beach used to be called. Come on down, Gus said, and so I did.

So too began "The Uncertain Years." Gus made me chief of security, but I was really just the king of the bouncers, battling with machos at three o'clock in the morning, and wearing a black bow tie and a tuxedo shirt that more often than not ended up with blood on the sleeves by the end of the night. The violence was part of the music, and it came in waves, rising through the pulse of the dancers like a tsunami. Someone would be given the old heave-ho, and the dancing would go on. The broken glass would be swept away, and the hips of the Cuban girls would start swaying again on the dance floor. Endless free drinks from the bartenders who watched my back and who never stole enough from Gus to get themselves fired. That, too, had been another life.

I avoided the cocaine that was everywhere at the time, but I drank too much. Then one night I got into a footrace with a purse snatcher outside the club and wound up doubled over, out of breath, out of shape, and sucking wind big time. That was something I couldn't tolerate. I found a gym owned by an old-timer named Cal (a friend of Gus's) a few blocks from where I lived and slowly started on the road back. I lifted weights and I ran. I took kickboxing classes and yoga. My social life was a series of workouts. I trained alone and didn't make any friends, and then one day when I was on the treadmill, I noticed Cal looking at me from where he sat behind the counter selling memberships and protein shakes. Our eyes met, and the old man nodded.

Then he offered me a job.

And so the segue from cop to bouncer to personal trainer was complete, and I became a gym rat for hire. I took a test and got a certificate, and Cal set me loose on the clientele, but I knew what I was doing. The biggest problem was the amount of talking required, and I was not in a talking frame of mind back then, but there was no way around it. Clients, especially the women, expected you to talk, but, being a cop, I was a lot better at listening. It got so that I became some kind of damned hairdresser or psychologist. I could write a book with the stories I heard. If you ever want confirmation that most of the people in the world are crazy, then my advice is to set up shop as a personal trainer. Fifty bucks an hour minus the split with Gus, and a new nut every hour.

It was an unexpected life, and there were many times when I felt that it was the wrong life. Not a bad life, mind you, just a sidebar to the main story, the threads of which I had somehow lost. A year turned into two years. I made money, but that didn't help relieve the feeling that somewhere out there my "real" life was waiting for me to come and live it. I was wrong about that, of course. There is no other life besides the one you're living in the here and now. To think otherwise is just another brand of self-pity, and remember: The speed bumps are there for a reason, and it's not the one you think.

More than once I found myself on the verge of becoming a police officer again. Even Gus and Cal thought it was a good idea. As trainers went, I was good, very good. I spent a lot of time in the library studying exercise physiology, nutrition. There was a lot to know. I even thought of going back to school to get a degree, but my heart just wasn't in it. Finally I gave in and took the cop test for the city of Miami, but when they called me down for an interview, I decided not to show. The truth is, I just couldn't see myself in a uniform again.

Then one day in the spring of '99, Cal calls me into his office, and sitting across from him is this beautiful, black-haired Asian woman—about twenty-five or so—whom I had never seen before. She had a bold look in her eye, I'll tell you that much. She stood up and offered me her hand, and suddenly I was facing a lot of leg. She was wearing a pair of white shorts that in Kansas City would have been scandalous. Fortunately, however, my brothers and sisters, we were not in Kansas City. Down here those little white shorts made perfect sense. Like a pith helmet on the banks of the Zambezi River. They were even a bit on the conservative side—not by much, though.

"Vivian Patterson," she said. "You must be Jack Vaughn. Cal was just telling me about you."

The vibe that came off of her was different from her appearance. That happens with the beautiful sometimes. You're so busy looking at them that you don't see them. You miss the extra glint in their eyes, that extra burst of life and the gift of mystery some people have. She had it.

The legs had thrown me off for a moment, but that was understandable. Impeccable manners and the voice were not what I would have expected. Another surprise to sweep away the veil of her appearance. She could have passed for a Valley Girl, but the accent had a trace of England mixed with something else that brought it home again.

The boldness in her eye was not sexual in cast or in intensity of expression, just appraising and self-assured. The sex was there, though, lounging in the background like a black cat on a Persian rug. You know what I mean. It was blended in, natural, nothing artificial, no need to force it.

We sat down, and Cal got called out of the office for a moment. There was the usual awkward silence that hangs in the air like an invisible piñata waiting to be broken. I let it hang. No sense saying anything stupid until it was absolutely necessary. Besides, if you're quiet, you can feel people. I caught a lot of people that way when I was a cop.

"Cal said you used to be a police officer," she said.

"Yeah, in New York."

I was a little pissed at Cal for having told her about the cop thing. I understood why he did it, though, especially with the wealthy, the famous, or the nervous. People figured that it made me that much less likely to haul off a Hummer or talk to a tabloid. Maybe they were right, but I didn't think so. Either you're honest or you're not. I wasn't a thief, and I knew how to keep my mouth shut, but I hadn't learned that at the academy. My father had beaten it into my head with his shoe and other sundry objects. Plus, I read the right comic books.

"I'm looking for someone to train my father," she said. "You'd have to come to the house. It's quite nice there, really. Would that be a problem?"

I was glad she was talking to me mainly, because it gave me an excuse to look at her without being impolite. She had the glossy black hair of a Chinese, but she looked mixed, maybe Eurasian. Everything about her seemed to come from someplace else.

"Mind if I ask you a question?" I said.

"Not at all."

"That's almost a British accent you have, but not completely."

"I went to school in England when I was little. I guess I haven't lost it yet—the accent I mean. Well, what do you think?"

"About what?"

"Training my father. What did you think I meant?"

Cal had come back into the office, and I was conscious of him sitting back in his swivel chair watching us.

I laughed. "I thought you were asking me about your accent. I mean, what I thought about it."

"Well?"

"Keep it. It's nice."

She smiled. "Thank you."

"Let's stick to business, okay, kids?" Cal said mercifully. "I'm trying to make a living here."

"Where does he live?" I asked. "Your father, I mean. We have to tack on a bit for the travel time."

"Not a problem. He's out on Sunset Beach." She studied me to see what effect the address was going to have on me. I wasn't surprised. She had the look of money without being obvious about it. Everything top-shelf but inconspicuous— Cartier watch, small diamonds. Was it old money? I didn't think so. It didn't have that musty, old-book smell to it.

"Sunset Beach? Sure, I've been there," I said. "Except they always make me leave when it gets dark."

She looked at me for a long moment, as though I'd said something strange or more revealing than I had intended. Then she laughed.

"I think my father will like you."

"Really, why so?"

"You're in disguise. You have secrets. He likes that. People look at you, but they don't see you. But my father will see you. And I see you."

"I see you, too."

She looked around. "I guess smoking in here is out of the question."

"I don't think Cal would like that. He smokes his cigars outside."

She studied me for a moment. "I've seen you before," she said. "Do you go to the clubs?"

"I did when I worked at one."

"Which one?" she asked. "I've been to all of them."

I told her.

"Let me guess: You were a bouncer. Don't take it personally, but you're the type they'd stand by the door."

"Really?" I said. "I thought of it more as public relations. The darker side, of course."

"You see?" Vivian said triumphantly. "I told you, another disguise," she said. "Tell me, who are you really, Jack Vaughn?"

I decided to give her a serious answer. "I don't know," I said truthfully. "I really have no idea."

"Jesus Christ," Cal said. "All this talking is killing me." He sprang out of his chair and stalked out of the office. I was glad to see him go.

Something in my tone must have convinced her that I was telling the truth. We stared at one another for a moment. I sensed a certain hunger in both of us to keep up the conversation. She was the kind of person you could really talk to.

"I know what you mean," she said, looking around the room. "Sometimes I think that perhaps I've traveled too much. After a while everything seems foreign." She looked at me earnestly as though to see what I would make of her statement.

"I think I know what you mean," I said.

"Yes, I think you do."

Then Cal had come back. I know the three of us talked, but I don't know if I made any sense that day. She wanted someone she could trust to come out to the house and train her dad, a Colonel Patterson. It didn't matter, though. I would have buried dead mules in her backyard with a tablespoon if she had asked me to. We had known each other for a thousand years. It was just a question of getting reacquainted. No need to rush.

When she had gone, Cal frowned at me for long moment. He twirled a pencil around in his gnarled fingers and shook his head.

"What the hell was that all about?" he asked in that gruff voice of his.

"What? You heard her," I said. "I'm going to train her father."

"It's not what I heard, shithead; it's what I saw."

"I don't know what you're talking about."

"My ass you don't. You two really hit it off. I about expected her panties to fly off when she stood up."

"You're crazy," I told him.

"I've been crazy, and I'm going to stay crazy, too, but there was something pretty jazzy going on between you two." He looked more worried than pleased when he said it. "You know what they say about business and pleasure."

"You're telling me I should stay away from her? You don't have to tell me that, Cal. And you're forgetting one thing: I am a certified personal trainer. That has to mean something in this crazy world."

"It means shit. Look, wise guy, I didn't say you had to stay away from her, not necessarily, but you've got to play it right. And sometimes that means not playing it at all. Can you grasp the subtle fucking mystery of what I'm telling you? Sometimes you just got to grin and bear it. You got to stand like Cary Grant with his hands in his pockets. You're smart. You know what I'm saying. Don't give me that certified bullshit."

"I know what you mean. I've got to stand like Cary Grant."

"Is that right? Say that when she's sitting by the swimming

pool, wise-ass; when it's hot and you're thinking, What the hell? When she's asking you to put the suntan lotion on her back. What are you going to say then, Charlie Chan? What? 'Cal, I fucked up. Her father's on his way over here with a flamethrower. Save me, Cal.'"

I laughed. "What the hell movie did you get that from?"

"No movie, real life. I been in this business for fifty years. Right after the war. I was real cute then, muscles and everything. Not out of a bottle like Raul. He's on the juice again, by the way. You know how many women have tried to kill me? Go ahead, guess."

"All right," I said. "Ten."

"Actually, it was nine. Then I got old and retired from being stupid. You're still on active duty in that department. I'm thinking of making a comeback, though. I can still get a boner you can hang a mink coat on. Hah! I bet you never heard that one before!"

I had an apartment that year near the beach up in Surfside, not far from the old movie theater that some friends of mine had leased and converted into a gym. I trained a few of my clients there. I had moved up there after the northerly migration created by the hurricane back in '98 had driven up the rent prices down on South Beach to the point where I had to either buy a condo or spend the rest of my days resigned to the task of helping send my landlord's kids to Harvard. In the end I moved north.

The boom hadn't reached as far as Surfside, and the rents there were still reasonable. The place I lived in was a twin-level apartment building on Byron Avenue, called the Lancaster Arms. The neon sign out front didn't work, and the blue-and-white building looked faded against the relentlessness of the sun. An octogenarian named Sternfeld owned and managed the place, and he was nearly as surly as Cal.

He liked to stand on the stoop of his building behind his walker like an old admiral at the prow of his ship, and he had the crazy, wispy, white hair of a conductor in search of a symphony.

The day I came by to see the apartment, Sternfeld looked me over with the expression of a man attempting to calculate just how much trouble you were going to be to him. He was delighted when I told him I had a job, as though I'd accomplished something remarkable. He was even happier when I told him I was single, without even so much as a goldfish for company. In the end he promised to chop a hundred dollars off the rent if I would walk with him three evenings a week.

So for four hundred a month, I got a one-bedroom apartment with two entrances, and if you left both doors open on a hot day, a nice breeze would blow through. You had to be careful when you did that, however. The neighborhood was not all that safe and secure. One day I came out of the shower and caught a sun-fried crackhead with a glass eye trying to download my laptop out the back door. The lesson there was that while the rents were reasonable, the people around you might not be, and after that I was more vigilant.

A quiet man who minds his own business and who doesn't own a stereo with too large a set of speakers will, in general, get along with his neighbors, and so I did. On my left was a family from Ecuador. They had a twenty-year-old son whom the police came for one night because he had decided that parking people's cars wasn't quite as profitable as selling them. His parents knew I had been a cop, and so they asked me to counsel him. I did what I could. After that he decided to raise pit bulls for the dogfights over in Hialeah, but the police hadn't liked that idea very much either, and so now he was back in community college, trying to find another way into the economy.

Billy Shuster lived in the studio on my right. He was a transvestite who worked as a postman by day. It sounds clichéd, but he really did like show tunes, particularly Ethel Merman's rendition of "There's No Business Like Show Business," which for some reason he never played all the way through to the end. It was very anticlimactic in an annoying way. It got so that I could even predict to the second when he would lift the stylus only to set it down at the beginning again.

Sometimes, when Billy left his door open, I'd see him standing at the ironing board in his bra and panties, ironing the clothes he was going to wear that night, his sand-colored Twiggy wig perched on the end of the board like a depressed cat. Billy told me once that he liked me because I brought stability to the building. In his own way, so did he. He had been a tenant there for fifteen years. Sometimes, on cooler evenings, he and Sternfeld played chess on a little tiled table they'd set up in the shade on the small patio behind the hedges. It didn't seem to matter much to Sternfeld whether Billy was dressed like a man or a woman, though he didn't curse nearly as much when Billy was in drag. He just didn't like the fact that his partner usually won their matches.

Later that afternoon, when I pulled up in front of the apartment, Vivian's red Porsche was parked at the curb, just past the spray of purple bougainvillea that was overwhelming the hedges in front of the building. Sternfeld was sitting in a lawn chair under the eaves, his aluminum walker off to one side. He shielded his eyes from the sun as I came up the three steps that led to the first landing. I looked down the walkway at the closed door of my apartment.

"Where is she?" I asked.

"I'll give you two guesses," Sternfeld said. "And it's not my place."

"You let her in?"

"She had the key, asshole."

"You're right. I forgot about that."

"You told me she was history," Sternfeld said.

"She is."

"Well, I guess history just got reincarnated."

"We'll see about that."

"When are we going back to the Rascal House?" Stern-feld asked. "I'm overdue for a corned beef on rye."

"Soon," I said.

"That's what you said last week."

When I opened the door, Vivian was sitting at the small table in the alcove next to the kitchen. She stood up and walked into my arms, and I held her to me. She was trembling with fear and relief, as though in great distress she had arrived at a place of possible deliverance, and I knew that I had been waiting a long time for exactly this moment, when every absence and betrayal would be canceled out by a simple embrace—at least temporarily.

I took her chin in my hand and turned her head. There were tears in her dark eyes. Despite myself, I was glad to see her.

"You cut your hair," I said.

"I hate it," she said petulantly. "They took too much off."

"No," I said. "It looks good."

I asked her if she wanted anything to drink, then went to the fridge and brought out two Diet Cokes and poured hers into a clean glass. When I came back, she was smoking a Marlboro. I went into the kitchen again and found a lid from an empty jar of mayonnaise and set it down in front of her to use as an ashtray.

"I thought you quit those," I said.

"I started again this morning."

"A killing will do that to you."

Her face lost its tan, and for a second she reminded me

of one of those scared, desperate people you see sitting in a holding room at the police station who are at the beginning of a new kind of trouble. Her dark eyes quivered, then stared straight through me.

"It seems like a nightmare," she said.

"It is a nightmare. What are you going to do?"

"I don't know. My father said you were out to see him this morning."

"He asked me to get rid of your boyfriend's boat, but I had to turn him down."

"I know."

"Then why are you here?"

"I'm not sure. I suppose it's because you're my friend."

"It's strange you picked today to remember that. I haven't seen you in more than a year."

"You didn't want to see me."

"Why do you think I want to see you now?"

"Should I leave?"

"So you shot Matson. I guess things didn't work out between you two."

Mentioning Matson's name had summoned up all the bitterness I had felt toward both of them. I watched her impassively, as though her weeping were an accompaniment to the dark, righteous mood I was sealed so tightly into. But it was no fun being in command of a shit situation.

Her cigarette burned down, and the ash tipped backward onto the scarred surface of the table. I picked it up and snubbed it out, flicked the butt over her head and into the sink.

"Do you have a tissue?" she asked.

"No. You should have called ahead."

"You're not going to help me, are you?"

"I'll help you call the police. I'll even go down there with you, but that's about all I can do."

Vivian looked at me as though she were searching for

some sign that I was still the same man she had known before. I wasn't. I felt a great coldness toward her. My mouth was clamped shut to the point that my jaw began to hurt, and I took a sip of Coke to ease the pressure, but it didn't ease the coldness that held me like a man frozen in an iceberg.

"I know I hurt you," she said in a soft voice.

"Don't worry about me. Worry about what you're going to tell the cops."

"I'm not sure I'm going to the police." She hesitated. "What do you think would happen if we just left that boat out there?"

I smiled. "Right in front of your father's mansion? Very convenient. Well, it would go something like this: They'll dust for prints, and they'll find yours because you didn't wipe the place down, and even if you did, they'll find something somewhere. You don't have a record, so the cops will sit on things for a while. Then they'll ask a few questions. Your name will come up, then your father's. There will be a few wrong steps here and there, but eventually they'll get around to you. I give it a week after they board the boat. What's the matter?"

"I was arrested once. Drunk driving, after a party. I went through a stop sign. I was seventeen."

"Well," I said, "that does it. They'll be able to match your prints. That doesn't give you much time. Maybe you should leave the country, save yourself all the bullshit. You've got money. Go to Switzerland. You used to live there once. I may even visit you from time to time. Personally, I think you should talk to the cops. Just show them that film Matson made. Who knows, you might get off—or maybe they will."

"I told my father not to show you that."

"But you knew he would."

"Why would you say that?" she asked.

"Because I know you and I know him. You're both first-class manipulators, and even though you know I know it, you can't help yourself. Besides, he was trying to make a point, but it may have been a tactical error now that I think about it. Maybe he thought I'd get overheated and chew a hole in the boat like a shark. Anyway, whatever you do, you'd better do it fast. I'll even drive you to the airport—no charge, of course."

She reared back and threw the can of soda at me. I waited to gauge the trajectory of her arm, then moved only slightly. The can went over my head, and I heard it hit the wall and then the floor. I took my Coke and placed it closer to her.

"Here," I said. "Try again."

She reached for the can, but I grabbed it first and threw it over her head. Like the first, it hit the wall just beneath the clock and fell and rolled and spilled itself across the brown tile.

"Get out," I said. "We're all out of drinks here."

She stood up. She wore a yellow sundress that clung to her hips and fell into the curve of her thigh and stayed there long enough for me to realize she wasn't wearing any underwear. Even through the coldness, I knew I was going to miss looking at her, so I took as long a look as I could, and I let her see me doing it. It was my last drink before the lifelong desert of not seeing her anymore, and I wanted to fill up my cup for the endless time ahead.

I held the door for her. She seemed shocked. "You're just going to let me go. I know you won't sink the boat. You have . . . what, morals? Okay, but what about me? You don't have anything left for me at all?"

"I have plenty left for you, but it isn't anything that's going to help you with Matson."

"Oh," she said. "So it was just the sex?"

"You're shallow; you're not very bright, and you're a liar of the first magnitude. What else could it have been?"

That rocked her, and I had the morbid pleasure of seeing the hurt spread across her face until all her exquisite features seemed to be pulling away from each other. What was I doing but killing myself by saying things that I didn't believe? It was only when I'd said them that I realized how long I'd been imagining just this moment, just this time. It was my big scene, and I'd played it the way I had dreamed of playing it. I'd gotten the knife in and twisted it big time, but what I couldn't understand was why it felt like I was the one who had been stabbed.

Vivian turned, and I held the door and watched her walk past Sternfeld and out to her car. The birds were singing back and forth across the street to one another from out of the palm trees. She walked away slowly, holding her head a little to one side as though listening to something, and I remembered that was the way she held her head when she was upset. There was something in my chest that wanted to come out, but I couldn't interpret it into any known language, and so it stayed there waiting like a blood clot until the Porsche let out a single, distinctive roar and drove away.

I had two clients scheduled for that afternoon, the Sheik and a singer from Germany named Tamara who lived down in South Miami. I didn't feel much like training either of them, but it was too late to cancel. I picked up the Sheik around noon at his house on Pine Tree and drove him over to the beach, where we ran along the boardwalk in the very hottest part of the day. The heat was, for him at least, part of the challenge. Where the boardwalk ended, we pounded down the wooden stairs and out onto the hard-packed sand and ran south toward Government Cut, where the big pleasure ships entered the ocean.

After the run we went back to his house and spent another hour or so practicing kendo, in which he was an expert and I was not. It wasn't the first time that I'd found myself playing the student rather than the teacher with a client. In fact, I sometimes wondered whether I hadn't learned as much from my clients as they had learned from me.

His name was Anwar, and he was by right of birth a prince in a country I won't name, but he had spent almost all his life in American schools, including Johns Hopkins, where he had received his degree in restorative plastic surgery. When I met him, he was thirty-five and had already practiced medicine in Somalia and Cambodia under the auspices of Doctors Without Borders. As far as I could see, he had responded to the challenge of nearly incalculable wealth as well as anyone I'd ever met.

It was our ritual after we put away our staffs and padding to sit in the Sheik's Jacuzzi and drink a patient glass of his thousand-year-old scotch. His wife, Rhonda, was not there that afternoon, and so my pensive mood was less easy to camouflage once the sweat had dried and I was boiling my feet in the bubbles of chlorinated water.

"Something's not quite right with you today," he said.

"I saw Vivian today."

"I guess that means you'll be losing your mind again shortly. Too bad I won't be around to witness your madness."

"Where are you going now?" I asked.

"My family is having a party at our hotel in the Bahamas—a reunion, you might say. Would you care to come?"

"I'm not family."

"Not technically. My father would like to see you, though. Why don't you come? He's not so well, you know."

"I have some business here to take care of."

"With the woman?"

"And her father. Possibly. They made me an offer that I refused. But now I'm wondering if I did the right thing. Seeing her kind of rearranged my brain."

"Her father? You mean the scientist?"

"That's him."

The Sheik said nothing. He was looking down into the bubbling froth of the hot tub with a thoughtful expression on his face. "You know," he said, "I met him once at a party down at the Biltmore. I think I told you. Some kind of charity function, I forget which. There was something about him I didn't like. I never quite put my finger on it."

"I know what you mean."

"Have you ever found yourself playing a game of chess with someone—even though at the time you thought you were only having a friendly chat about the weather?"

"It was that way every time I trained him," I said. "I always got the feeling he was looking for an opening, probing. I think it was almost a habit with him."

"Do you think he found your weakness?" the Sheik asked, smiling.

"Probably."

"Have you ever thought about my offer at all?" he asked.

"Not recently."

The offer had been to get rid of all my other clients and become his personal assistant, duties to include some body-guarding, personal training, and whatever else came up.

In any case, I had never taken him up on his job offer. I didn't like the idea of having only one big, rich boss. The money he offered me would shock you, so I won't even mention it, lest you think I'm nuts for turning it down. But look at it this way: You have multiple clients, you have multiple options. That means you can always tell at least one person who gets on your nerves to kiss your ass, without going bankrupt. Anyway, there's more to life than a great dental plan and a 401(k)—at least until you get old and your teeth start falling out.

Later, after I got dressed again, Anwar walked with me

to my car. Neither of us said very much, but I could feel his concern. He had a depth of presence that came through most strongly in his silences. They were like the atmosphere inside an empty church. He was my age, and yet he seemed much older. Sometimes it seemed to me that I had known him forever.

We shook hands in front of my ride. His dark eyes were solemn. I slapped him on the shoulder, hoping to bring on a lighter mood, but he wasn't buying it.

"I'll see you when you get back," I said. "Tell your father I said hey."

We embraced, and I got into the van with a completely different mood from the one I wanted. I wanted to be breezy, cavalier, but there was no changing the climate in Anwar's expression. He stood back listening as the engine of the Ford sputtered, then caught.

"You should know when something is over, Jack," he said. "Sometimes it's dangerous to go back once the dance is done. Even if only five minutes have passed, it will not be the same."

"Yes, I know," I said. "But what if the music is still playing?"

"Then it will be a different music from the one you heard before."

As I drove away, I glanced at the rearview mirror. The Sheik was standing there, watching, just as Williams had.

Nothing went right after that. The Ford died as I was going southbound on the Don Shula, and I had to push it off to the side of the road in the middle of a rainstorm that lasted just long enough to soak me to the bone. I used my cell phone to call Tamara, the German singer, to tell her that I wouldn't be making it that afternoon. Then, as I was calling for a tow truck, the battery in the phone died, too, and the spare in the van didn't work either. It was lucky for me that the rain had stopped, because I had to walk half a mile to the nearest call box.

By the time the tow truck dropped me off in front of my friend's garage in Overtown, the afternoon, while still hot and bright, was all but gone, along with any hope of profit. And by the time the traffic started crawling the other way, I was sitting in the thrift-store clutter of the garage's office, sipping a cup of coffee and talking to Paul March, the owner, who sat across from me cleaning one of his guns.

March liked to clean his guns at his desk so his customers could see that he was a serious person. In the past he'd had trouble with some folks who wanted their cars back but couldn't afford to pay for the repairs. It was Paul's opinion that the timely appearance of a firearm in plain sight brought a new sense of reality to such negotiations and was worth a lot more than the sign on the wall that said NO CREDIT.

"That car of yours needs a new transmission," he said. "Whoever sold it to you must have seen you coming."

"I think his name was March."

"Never heard of him." He had finished putting the gun back together and was reloading it. "Come on out back with me," March said. "I got something you might like."

We went out to the lot behind the garage and walked toward a row of beaten-down-looking old cars parked near the fence. A tag team of Dobermans ran out from under a white truck and raced at me, their teeth bared, their small brains charged with inbred malice. Then they recognized Paul and started prancing around him as though he were a one-man party.

Paul, who had the same manner with animals as he did with people, smiled and kicked the male in the ribs. The bitch sat on her haunches and looked bemused. Paul made a sweeping gesture with his arms, and the hellhounds slipped back under the truck, where they lay watching us from the shadows, the two of them as quiet as a pair of snipers.

"What about this one?" Paul asked, patting the hood of a black 1977 Thunderbird with a bike rack bolted to the roof. "It's only got a hundred thousand miles on it," he said.

"Was that before or after you turned back the odometer?"

"After, of course. Hey, man, at least you can't say I'm a liar."

"I like the bike rack," I said. "With this ride I'll probably need it."

At that instant a rat sprinted out in front of us and ran behind some stacks of retreads outside a rusted corrugated shed. We both saw it at the same time. Paul frowned at me and, with a stern expression on his face, placed his left index finger vertically across his lips.

"Time for safari," he whispered. "Be right back."

Paul crept behind the row of dilapidated cars and disappeared behind the shed, his gun barrel up and next to his ear. I was just thinking that I had to find a new mechanic when I heard the shot. The three men bent over the open hood of a car by the garage straightened up and looked in our direction. They stared for a moment, then went back to work. All of them knew their boss very well.

Paul came back a minute later. The gun was stuck into the waistband of his blue jumpsuit. From the look on his face, I knew that the safari had not been a success.

"Did you get him?" I asked.

"How the hell should I know?" he retorted. "You think I got the time to look for the body of a dead rat?"

It was six o'clock when I drove my "new" black Thunderbird out of March's lot, and I hadn't gone very far when I realized that, like the last car he'd sold me, this was one I probably wouldn't be driving for too much longer. They had cleaned it up and given it a shiny new paint job, but it was nothing except war paint on a steel hag. The engine coughed at every stoplight, and I had a pretty good idea that there was something wrong with the carburetor. By the time I got home, I was glad just to have made it. When I shut off the ignition, the car kept making noises for the next thirty seconds, like loose bolts in a steel bucket.

I took a shower and drank a beer, then turned on the news and sat in my black recliner with my feet up, listening to the day's calamities and scandals, but if you had tested me on any of it ten minutes later, I wouldn't have been able to recall a single thing. After a while I got tired of the anchorman's handsome, self-assured expression and shut off the set. I was in a strange mood that is hard to describe, except to say it was as though there were a neon Vacant sign blinking over my heart like a permanent question I didn't have an answer for. Maybe I'd been living alone too long. Maybe it was time to get a cat.

I thought of calling Barbara, my ex-wife, but she lived up in New York, and I couldn't afford very much long-distance. I liked to tell people that we were on good terms, except that it always sounded as though we'd had some kind of business relationship rather than a romance that had petered out like a flower that needed more watering than either of us could agree to. She was a stockbroker and I was a cop, and never the twain did meet, and even now, after five years, I had yet to figure out how it was that the longer we were together, the more like strangers we became.

But I didn't call Barbara, and it wasn't just the long-distance charges either. We were both too far gone from one another, and I didn't feel like hearing about the Dow Jones or about her new boyfriend, whoever he was this time around. There were times when she dropped hints to the effect that she wanted kids and I might still be in the running for sperm donor. It seemed that in that overheated Barnard brain of hers the baby clock had begun to go tick-tock, and I suppose it was to be taken as a compliment that she still thought I had good genes.

But it was clear from the way she put it that what she had in mind was in no way to be mistaken for a possible reunion. I got the impression that her idea was for me to fly up, then make like the Lone Ranger, leaving behind a silver bullet. It was not the worst offer I'd ever gotten, yet there was a certain chill to it just the same that failed to move me. But maybe that was just me being old-fashioned again.

I took off my shirt and lay on my bed and looked up at the ceiling fan for a while. That didn't help much either, though. An egg of an idea was trying to hatch itself in my brain, but it needed a little nudging along, so I got up, went over to my desk, opened the bottom drawer, and took out the last letter Vivian had sent me. I popped another beer and sat down at my table with its two undersize chairs and read it again for at least the hundredth time since she'd sent it to me. I knew it by heart—right down to the freaky line breaks, but I read it again anyway; it was like sipping from an empty glass.

The letter was written in plain English, but as usual I went over it slowly, lingering on each word like a sun-dazed archaeologist deciphering obscure hieroglyphics. She was right. I had backed down, or rather I had backed away, and it wasn't because Vivian hadn't been worth fighting for. I had fought harder for much less. At the time I had seen Matson's incursion as a test of loyalty on her part, and when all the signs made it clear that she had failed that test, I jettisoned them both, girlfriend and client, in a flash of pride. To hell with the both of them, I'd thought.

The part about the money was also true, though I had refused to think about it. America might be a classless society, but there was a hierarchy of cash that could be overlooked only until the first time the waiter handed you the wine list.

The economics of the romance started dawning on me after the first couple of dates, when I began to realize that I was going to have to train half of Coral Gables in order to keep up with her. I came clean with her on the subject, and she laughed and said it didn't matter. But it does matter. And while her father treated me like an equal, most of her friends thought that she was slumming, that she would come around once the shine wore off my charm.

My self-esteem had never been based on the gold standard, but Fitzgerald was right: The rich are different. Their feet touch the ground only when they want them to, but mine were there all the time. In the culture of money, I was a definite outsider with little chance of conversion this side of winning the lottery. It was all right for a while, but I couldn't see the thing working for the long haul. I just didn't want to go through life feeling like one of Elizabeth Taylor's poorer husbands.

Over the course of our affair, I gradually talked myself out of being in love with Vivian. I was like a man trying to rescue himself from a cult he had started. I told myself I was being realistic, noble, that I was doing her a favor, but I couldn't deny the hurt I saw in her eyes when she realized I was pulling away. I went from being too available to being too invisible, and when she pressed me on it, I gave her that old bullshit answer that I was too busy. I knew exactly what I was doing, and when Matson came along, he became part of the exit strategy. Judging from my reaction in the bar that night, however, it had worked a lot better than I thought it would.

And now Matson was dead, but nothing was finished. In fact, things seemed less finished now than when he was alive. If I closed my eyes, I could see the white yacht with its perilous cargo sitting quietly in the water as the sky darkened, the sun now far to the west and set on setting. Then something that had been trying to surface finally did, and all of a sudden none of it made sense. Matson had money, but the boat I'd seen would have cost at least $3 million, and that much he didn't have. Sometimes people become more mysterious in death than they were in life, and that seemed to be the case with Matson.

Then I started thinking about the money the Colonel had offered me; five zeros after a one, and don't forget the comma. I kept thinking about the yacht out there, inert off the coast with a dead man on board like a thing waiting to be done. I began to feel a strange tension come over me, as though I were being held back, and I knew then that I would do it. I knew in my gut that I had a rendezvous with that boat that I would keep for better or for worse. It was only then that the tension eased and I could relax.

I t was seven o'clock when I picked up the phone and called the Colonel's house. I was half hoping that it was too late. The maid answered, and a moment later the Colonel picked up the phone. It annoyed me that he didn't sound at all surprised to hear my voice.

"Did you call to say you've changed your mind?" he asked.

"No, I called to ask what your sign was."

"A dollar sign," he said, laughing heartily at his own joke. We were good friends now, fellow conspirators. "I knew you were a mercenary at heart, Jack. You were starting to worry me."

"Send your daughter over with half the money, and send her soon."

He didn't laugh at that one. "You think I keep that kind of cash around the house?"

"I don't care where you keep it," I said. "I get the other half when I get back." I listened to the sound of my own voice as I said this, and I didn't particularly like what I heard.

The Colonel must not have liked my tone either. I listened to him breathe for a few seconds. "What time?" he asked. "What time should I send her?"

I thought for a moment. "Make it midnight."

"She'll be there."

"Groovy."

"I'd like to ask you a question."

"Ask."

"Are you doing it for Vivian or for the money?"

"What do you think?"

"Mercenaries often lack heart, Jack. But love and money aren't mutually exclusive."

"So long, Colonel," I said. "You'll be seeing me soon." Then I thought of something. "Oh, and one last thing while I've got you on the phone."

"Yes?"

"How did Vivian get out to the boat, and how did she get back? Don't tell me she swam."

There was only a brief hesitation. "She went out on her Jet Ski, and that's the way she got back." There was another pause. Nothing in his tone indicated that he might be lying, but it's harder to judge a thing like that over the phone. With the Colonel, though, it would have been difficult even if I'd been staring him in the eye.

"Anything else, Jack?"

"If there is, it'll have to wait."

I hung up and sat for a while staring at the phone as though it were a crystal ball, but it wasn't. I stood up and looked around the room. Something about it seemed foreign all of a sudden, like I was standing in a house that belonged to a man I knew only vaguely, someone you meet once at a party and never see again. Eventually I got restless, so I went down to the Cuban place on the corner and had a double shot of espresso.

The first thing I did when I got back to the apartment was get my gear ready for the trip. I got the kayak out of the storage room and waxed it so it would slide through the water like a greased-down barracuda. Then I loaded the compartments inside the hull with the things I would need. It was not going to be a particularly long excursion, but I made sure I packed two bottles of water, a flashlight, four flares, a dive knife, my spare cell phone, and two protein bars. I took my life vest out of the closet, dusted it off, and laid it across the kayak where it rested, very much out of place, on the living room floor.

Then a sudden thought darted into my mind with the urgency of an unexpected warning I couldn't ignore, and I went to the desk and got out the Glock 9-millimeter. I didn't much like the look of it for some reason, and I had that feeling you get when you meet an old friend you're not quite sure you want to see again. I put in a full clip, felt it click into the handle. A sensation of dread rippled through me and passed on. I put the gun in a plastic bag, sealed it, and stuck it in a pocket inside the kayak. I was glad when I didn't have to look at it anymore.

I was watching the *Tonight* show when I heard the Porsche pull up. I peeked through the slats in the venetian blinds in time to see Vivian crossing the street. I listened for her footsteps, and when they got loud, I opened the door before she could ring. I didn't want to wake Sternfeld. It was a little late for kayaking, and I didn't need any questions.

Vivian walked past me, and I closed the door behind her.

She was wearing a black, sleeveless, leather dress that showed, I thought, a bit too much leg for the neighborhood—not to mention for my better judgment. She went over and looked down at the kayak. Her body was as hard and as dark-bright as a candied apple, and I caught her scent as she went by me, brushing my chest with her shoulder. She leaned over the kayak and caressed the smoothness of the fiberglass hull as though it were the flank of a racehorse.

Both her dress and the kayak had the same shine, like ripe fruit stained by the light.

"Did you bring the money?" I asked.

"Nick's bringing it. He should be here in a moment." She had seated herself in one of the wicker chairs and was lighting a cigarette.

"Why'd you bother to come?" I asked "Your brother's the one with the cash."

"Why do you think I came?"

"To wish me bon voyage, I suppose."

Vivian looked up at me and shook her head. "You're taking a chance for me. I thought I should be here."

"You're forgetting there's a little money involved."

The doorbell rang, and I let Nick in. The first thing I noticed was that he had dyed his closely cropped hair platinum blond, but the darker roots had already begun to appear at the scalp like a row of fresh quills coming in. He wore a black T-shirt over a pair of black Levi's encircled by a black belt with silver studs, like a gunslinger's livery. He was very tall and thin to the point of emaciation, with the wary face of a fox for whom the hounds will always be just around the last bend and closing fast. There was a Louis Vuitton knapsack on his back. He gave me his usual condescending smile, as though I were a fool for reasons beyond my philistine powers of comprehension. Considering the night's main activity, he may have been onto something.

In the beginning, when we first met, I'd tried hard to be his friend, but from the start he'd never missed a chance to let me know he considered himself my superior in every realm except the physical. He had attended Columbia, the University of Chicago, and the Sorbonne and had managed to escape from each of those august institutions without a degree, but it wasn't because he lacked smarts. On the contrary, he spoke Spanish, French, a little Italian, and was extremely well read and knowledgeable about art. He just thought that everybody in the world except for himself and a few of his friends was ineffably crass and stupid, including his professors.

Nick stripped off his backpack as though it were on fire and threw it on the floor at Vivian's feet.

"Do you have any idea how hard it is to get fifty thousand dollars in cash at this time of night?" he demanded furiously, turning first to me, then Vivian.

"Relax, Nick," I said. "It's for a good cause. You want a beer?"

He looked at me as though I had offered him a turd. "No, you idiot, I do not want a beer. I don't suppose you have any white wine. That would be too much to expect." He looked around the apartment. "How can you live like this?" he asked.

"I keep my eyes closed," I said.

I picked up the backpack and opened it. There was a lot of money inside. I closed the bag and held it in the palm of my hand. It was heavy. "That seems about the right weight. You done good, Nick," I said. "Real good. I'm proud of you."

I carried the bag into the kitchen and put it in the cabinet under the sink, burying it beneath a hoard of plastic bags from the supermarket. Then I went into the fridge and found half a bottle of white wine. It took me a while, but I managed to dig up a mismatched pair of wineglasses with a layer of dust on them. I knew Nick wouldn't appreciate that, so I rinsed them off in the sink. I went back into the living room and poured each of my guests a glass. Nick took a very suspicious sip, held the glass away from him, then set it down.

"I hope you like it," I said. "It cost three bucks."

I watched him take another cautious sip.

"You were overcharged," he said.

Vivian drank her wine down in one gulp. "Nick," she said. "Maybe you should go now. I'll meet you back at the house."

"Why can't you go with me?" her half brother asked. "I'm not about to leave you here. Look at this place!"

"I want to talk to Jack."

"You don't need to talk to him. Talk to him when he gets back."

"Finish your wine, Whitey," I said. "I'm getting tired of your attitude. Tell your dad I'll be in touch."

"Who the hell are you to give me orders?"

"You know who I am, Nicky. I'm the one who's pulling your family's collective ass out of the fire, remember? You could do it yourself, of course, but I know that would be beneath your dignity. You might get your hands dirty, and we couldn't have that, could we? Now, get up and get out."

Nick glared at me, but his heat vision failed to melt my head, so he tried it on his sister. "I'll see you back at the house," she said.

Nick stood up. He looked around the room. "You and your men," he said. "You'll drag us all down before this is over."

He bumped the edge of the coffee table as he went by. His wineglass teetered, then spilled over. I didn't move. The glass hit the floor but didn't shatter. A moment later the door shut. I got up and put the chain on. Vivian sat watching me. I went into the kitchen to get some paper towels to wipe up the wine Nick had spilled. When I came back from the kitchen again, Vivian was on her feet.

"How much time do we have?" she asked.

"Not much," I said. I knew what she was thinking.

She turned her back on me. I don't remember moving, but suddenly I was standing right behind her.

"Unzip me," she said.

"Is this my going-away present?"

"It's whatever you want it to be."

I pulled the zipper down slowly and watched as the two halves of the leather dress came apart. Vivian pulled her arms free of the straps, and the garment, unsupported now, collapsed about her waist. Her back was brown. I ran my index finger from the nape of her neck down the trail of her spine, feeling the knob of each vertebra until I reached the bottom. Her skin was feverishly hot, as though the leather had sealed in her body's heat that was now being released. She arched her lower back toward me. Then I put my tongue on all the places where my finger had been a moment before.

TWO

AN HOUR LATER I sat on the edge of my bed fully dressed, watching Vivian, just out of the shower, drying off with one of my tattered beach towels. If trouble had a body, hers was it. Then I zipped up her dress, and she slipped on her pumps. It had been a great show, but I was feeling impatient. A part of me was already out on the water doing what had to be done, and I was anxious to get going. I rechecked my gear and tried to think if there was anything I might have forgotten. I felt like a drawn bow, poised, ready to fire.

It was time to go. Vivian sensed my mood and was very quiet. I lifted the kayak up and balanced its weight over my left shoulder. Vivian carried my life vest and held the door for me while I maneuvered the eight-foot-long craft through the door as noiselessly as possible. As usual, I had some trouble on the stairs and had to turn and reposition either the kayak or myself several times, but that was the only hitch with the going-down part. The street was quiet, empty, and Sternfeld didn't poke his head out as we passed his door. It was the time of night when he turned off his hearing aid and let the silence and the sleeping pills put him to sleep.

As quietly as I could, I got the kayak up onto the roof of the Thunderbird I'd bought that afternoon from Paul March and lashed it snugly to the bike rack with some bungee cords.

"Where'd you get this ghetto cruiser from?" Vivian asked.

"From a friend."

"I'm not so sure I would call him that."

"You'd better hope it lasts one more night," I told her. "You'll have to come back for me in it. The kayak won't fit on the Porsche."

"I've never driven a car this old," she said doubtfully.

"It's not old, it's an antique."

"Antiques usually go up in value."

We drove in silence. I was trying to work myself into a state of mind that was matter-of-fact, calm and confident, cut and dried, with no room for conflicting emotions concerning the task. The fact that it was Matson who needed burying made it easier. I could still see the leering delight in his eyes and the elfin whiteness of his skin, his pale cock curved like a tusk, but I rejected these images as they arose. I needed clarity now, not conflict. I needed to be alert, not paranoid, a fairly tall order considering the circumstances and the people I was working for.

"I never really thanked you for not telling my father about Williams and Nick," Vivian said suddenly, and apropos of nothing. "I never thought you would, though."

She was referring to something that had happened at a party at her father's house a long time back, before Matson, when I was still very much in the picture and walking the rapidly vanishing line between hired help and new boyfriend.

Out behind the house on the wooden deck, with the Atlantic Ocean as a backdrop, three hundred people in formal dress were beginning to act informally, men and women naked in the swimming pool, the training wheels of civility getting looser and looser with every glass of champagne.

I went upstairs, made a wrong turn, and opened what I thought was the door to a bathroom. It wasn't. If not for the music from the deck below, I might have heard the telltale low moans that always mean the same thing. I flicked on the light and saw Williams lying back on the couch and Nick on his knees, his head bobbing up and down like a monk praying. A moment of surprise and I shut the door, but not quickly enough: They both had seen me. I went on my way, not really caring, but from then on, Williams treated me like an enemy, and Nick, who had never liked me to begin with, had reinforced his air of determined belligerence whenever I was around.

"Williams was mortified," Vivian said. "You know how he likes to play that macho thing. He was so worried you'd tell the Colonel that he honestly considered killing you. Can you believe it?"

"What made him change his mind?"

"Nick talked him out of it."

"That doesn't sound like the Nick I know. I was never his cup of tea, you realize, especially after I started in with you."

"Nick thought you'd probably blackmail them. He thought he could buy you off."

"Why did he tell you about it?" I asked.

"I'm not sure. I guess he thought that I might be useful in the negotiations when the time came."

I laughed.

"What's so funny?" she asked.

"You guys," I said. "You're not exactly the Partridge Family, are you?"

"You wouldn't have lasted so long with the Partridge Family," she told me. "Anyway, it's not like Nick and Williams were ever an item, you know. It was just something casual at a party that people do when they're drunk. Williams just didn't want the Colonel to find out. You can understand that, can't you?"

"You honestly think your father doesn't know about Williams?" I asked. "After all these years? Come on. He doesn't care. It probably works out better that way, at least as far as your father is concerned. No family, no wife and kids, on call 24/7—what would he care about Williams being gay or not? And I know he knows about Nick. The kid's been out of the closet since he was twelve. Your father doesn't care because he doesn't care about Nick—or about you either. As for me, who gives a shit? It's South Beach, baby. Williams is just paranoid, that's all, and believe me when I tell you that the steroids aren't helping his mood much."

I pulled into a small lot just south of Sunset Beach and found a space behind a row of scrub pines that couldn't be seen from the street. I cut the headlights while the car was still rolling. I wanted to get going as quickly as possible, and I was out of the car and unlashing the kayak as soon as I put the car in park. It was just the kind of secluded place where a policeman might be inclined to take a cigarette break while filling out a report or two, and I didn't want to have to explain why I was there at that hour with a one-man kayak and a pretty girl for a send-off party.

I got the kayak off the roof of the Thunderbird and onto my shoulder again and began walking toward the ocean across the fine white sand, Vivian walking in uncharacteristic silence beside me. As we crossed the dunes, the sand got soft and I nearly tripped, and Vivian grabbed my arm to steady me. At the shore, just above the breakers, I set the kayak down on the sand and did a little stretching to ease the cramp in my shoulder. Then I slipped on the life jacket and handed Vivian the paddle.

"I figure it will take me four hours, maybe more, maybe less," I said. "Somewhere around then, I'll call you and tell you where I'm at. The current runs north. Depending on where I dump the boat, I'll make landfall near Fort Lauderdale. I'll call you when I get close. That way you won't have long to wait. Just make sure you keep your cell phone handy, all right?"

Vivian was watching with an expression of confused wonderment, as though resigned to some unforeseen and unwelcome conclusion. She seemed very far off. I put my hand on her arm and gently shook it.

"Did you hear me?" I asked. I was eager to go. Already the muscles in my back and shoulders were sending me over the water, through the creases of light. I could feel the kayak, a Burns Hell Chaser, gliding across the sea like a strange and quiet amphibian made of fiberglass. Vivian put her hand on my cheek. A single tear broke loose and fled down hers.

"Why is it that when I'm with you, it feels like I always have been, that I should always be with you?" she asked.

"I have no idea."

"But do you know what I mean? Don't you feel something like that, too? Or is it just me sounding crazy?"

I looked over her head, across the sand, to where the scrub pines, lonely in the night air, were waving at the stars. I knew exactly what she meant. I thought of all the times before when I had studied her face, trying to recall where I'd seen it before, as though some clue, hidden in her dark eyes, might be discovered there. At any rate, I'd never found it, whatever it might have been.

"I know exactly what you mean," I said. "It used to bug the hell out of me."

"And it doesn't anymore?"

"No, not anymore," I said. "You better get back to the car now."

"I'm going with you into the water."

I was going to object, but I didn't have it in me. Another mood had claimed me, and suddenly I was in less of a hurry to leave. I wanted to linger and study that strangely beautiful face with all its secrets. A few more moments and something might have come to me, but there wasn't time.

"You'll get your dress all wet," I said.

"I don't care."

She kicked her shoes onto the sand.

Together we walked the kayak into the surf, until the water was just above my knees. I got myself into the kayak, and Vivian handed me the paddle. She stood beside me, steadying the Hell Chaser, the dark shine of the water merging with the even darker shine of her dress. I looked up at the sky and saw the faint glow of the moon hidden behind the clouds. There was no wind, and I didn't think it would rain.

"Why didn't you fight for me?" she asked suddenly. "It was no contest."

I smiled. "Maybe I couldn't take a chance on winning."

"You know," she said, "sometimes I hate you."

I found my balance and took a few strokes to get going, then turned around in time to see Vivian walking through the breakers toward the shore. I waited till she looked back. I lifted the paddle over my head. She waved at me with one hand and pushed back her black hair with the other. She yelled something out to me, but the waves smothered the sound.

I jockeyed the kayak around again and got it pointed north and east into the current, the unchained blood singing in my head with the reckless joy of release, the unmitigated thrill of the doing of the thing at last, the muscles working and rolling like willing slaves. What I wanted. A hundred yards out, I turned the kayak parallel with the beach and saw the headlights of my car plowing through the dark. I watched her make a right out of the lot, and when she was gone, I turned again myself and headed out to sea.

The sea was calm, the breakers rolling lazily into shore as I pulled through the water with slow, even strokes. I hadn't been on the ocean at night for a long time, and I'd forgotten how quiet it could be. I was grateful for the distant company of a cruise ship gliding across the horizon far to the south. There were other, smaller craft as well, but not many. Most of them were fishermen, heading out for deep water where the big fish ran, but I was sure that at least one of them was the Marine Patrol. Several times I had to wait and drift while they crisscrossed in front of me, unaware of my presence. I felt their wakes lifting beneath me; I heard their engines and smelled the diesel fuel. None of the boats came close enough to cause me any worry, but I stayed very alert all the same.

Two hundred yards out, I turned north and headed for the yacht. I had nixed the idea of leaving directly from the Colonel's mansion, though it would certainly have made for a quicker trip. There was no particular reason for this decision. In fact, it didn't make sense, the shortest route between two points being a straight line, but that was true only in geometry and not necessarily in the realm of human affairs.

I was acting on intuition and could not have explained why I was coming in so far from the south, except to say that I didn't want anybody to know exactly where I was or the exact time I'd started out. Vivian, of course, would know where I had put in, but even she wouldn't know exactly how long it would take me to reach the yacht. Nobody had shown all of his or her cards in this deal yet, and there was no reason for me to show all of mine.

The lights from the condos were on my left as I paddled north with the current. The quarter moon had slipped free of the clouds and was on my right. It gave off very little glare. The water was pale dark, enlivened by minute flashes of brilliance. When I was perhaps a half mile from the mansion, I began angling in toward the shore, pointing the kayak's nose at the spot where I estimated the yacht to be, though it was still too far off to see. Then the row of condos ended abruptly and there was no more light from the shore, just a gap of blackness filled with the outlines of trees and their billowing shadows. I paddled past it, and soon, beyond the gap, nestled in a cove, I saw the subdued lights of the Colonel's house pulsing faintly against the dark sky and beyond that, at the edge of the light, the vast shadow of the yacht, my silent, looming prey.

I laid the paddle across my lap and surveyed the scene. I stretched my arms above my head, then out in front of me. I drank some water and chewed my way through a protein-carbohydrate bar that tasted like vanilla-flavored bread dough and followed it down with some more water, most of which I spit out. I was just about to start for the yacht when I heard the sound of an engine, but it was not the engine of a boat. The faint roar came from overhead.

Out of the deep silence of the sky above and just ahead of me to the north came a subdued droning. I looked up and at that moment saw the pontoons of a white seaplane skim the blue-black surface of the sea, sending up a spray of foam before gliding smoothly into the water. Almost immediately the plane wheeled and taxied in my direction, its twin propellers still churning but with less of a roar from the engine. I was about to aim the kayak toward the shore and out of its way when the sound of another engine stopped me in mid-stroke and a red light shot out to sea from the dock at the far edge of the cove that cradled the mansion. It was a speed-boat, wedge-shaped and ebony black, racing toward the sea-plane, skipping and hopping across the ocean, as much out of the water as in.

The plane had slowed and was now completing a wide circle, so that it was no longer coming in my direction but curving back out to sea, and as it did so, one of its lights grazed the side of the yacht, briefly illuminating the hull before passing on. The speedboat swung wide and intercepted the plane as it came to a full stop, the two shadows merging. The sounds of their engines overlapped in a muted rumble that quickly faded and then, after a moment, quickly flared again. The seaplane gathered speed and lifted slowly into the sky. It flew very close to the surface, not more than fifteen or twenty feet above the water, like a gull hunting for food. Then the engine of the speedboat roused itself. The long shadow that was the boat itself fishtailed violently in the roiling water. The pulsing red light at the helm gained speed and moved rapidly away from me, then vanished around the cove's northernmost shore.

The kayak bucked gently beneath me, then settled. The water settled down, too, but not so my thoughts. I tried to understand what I'd just witnessed and how it pertained to what I had to do. There was one major question: Where in this curious night had the plane come from? A plane isn't a car; you just can't just jump into one and take off and fly any distance—not without a flight plan, not unless you're in a crop duster in the middle of nowhere, where no one gives a damn.

Of course, you could fake a flight plan, then fly low, but not for too far. You would have to get up and get down fast before the radar caught you and the coast guard sent the drug helicopters out for you. Drug dealers did it all the time, but it was risky. You would have to be desperate, daring, or lucky. But it could be done—for a reason, and there was no reasonable reason for a plane to pick just this evening for such a maneuver.

I thought about turning back; I thought about the money. I thought of Vivian and the yacht and Matson still being dead off the coast in the morning. I didn't much like either the plane or the speedboat. They were a complication, a pair of high-speed variables that shouldn't have been there. All I knew was that one small section of a very big ocean had, for a few very intense minutes, gotten very overcrowded very fast in what should have been a tight, compact drama, starring two men, one of them dead, one of them me, and a yacht that needed to disappear from sight. In the script I had written, there'd been no plane, no black boat, but there they were, a couple of loudmouthed actors without parts, their engines roaring, demanding to be written in.

I decided to keep going and hope that neither the speedboat nor the plane made a curtain call. Enter and exit in the first act, and stay that way. I could see the yacht now, a massive silhouette about a hundred and fifty yards ahead of me and off to the right. I began paddling toward it, stopping every so often to listen, but there was nothing to hear, and so I listened to that.

The closer I got to the yacht, the more nervous I became, all my senses on high alert, my heartbeat pacing my every stroke. And then, all at once, I was right beside it, like a solitary bird flanking a behemoth. I moved around to the stern. I intended to keep the boat between me and the mansion, because I suspected that either Williams or the Colonel might be watching out for me with night-vision glasses, and I didn't want them to know I was aboard until the time came to take her out to sea.

I grabbed my flashlight and played the beam along the hull. *The Carrousel* was written there in gold italics, each letter outlined in black. I touched the white hull the way you might touch a sleeping stranger.

I paddled back to the dive deck and used two tethers to lash the kayak to the aluminum ladder, and when I was sure I was in tight, I put the flashlight in a pocket of my life jacket and got ready to haul myself up and out. I grabbed for the middle rung of the ladder and twisted my legs and pelvis until my feet swung free. During the ride my legs had stiffened up considerably. The moment I lifted my right knee, the hamstring cramped up so badly that I had to spend a few moments pumping my leg until the blood broke through and I could begin climbing again.

I went into a crouch the second I was on deck and looked back at the Colonel's place from behind the door leading up to the cabin. The back of the place was well lit, as usual. The two tall towering spotlights that flanked the property glowed like miniature moons, but the house itself was dark.

I listened to the darkness for a moment, then opened the cabin door. It was too dark not to use the flashlight, but I kept the beam away from the windows. The light revealed a large stateroom furnished with black leather couches hugging the walls and a comfortable-looking red leather recliner that had toppled over onto its side across the rose-colored carpet. Next to the central couch sat a long, low, irregularly shaped coffee table made of burnished driftwood that looked like it might still be capable of giving someone a bad case of splinters. On it were three glasses. One of them, set off from the other two, had a red flange of lipstick along the rim.

Across from the couch on the far wall against a window that looked out into the dark sky was a well-stocked, copper-covered bar that looked like it was forged from a zillion hammered-down pennies, then polished to a high gloss. There were glasses on the bar and ashtrays full of butts and half a bottle of scotch somebody had forgotten to stopper. Behind the bar the usual panoply of bottles and above them, on the next shelf up, an old-fashioned astrolabe and sextant that looked as authentic as the kind you find in maritime museums.

I went around behind the bar and saw the body of a man

sprawled on the floor. It was Matson. I killed the light and stood there, quiet and alone in the darkness, listening to myself breathe. It was real now; there is nothing more real than a dead body, especially when it's the body of someone you know. I inhaled deeply and switched the flashlight on him again, trying to be a cop once more before I went back to being a criminal. Nothing new here, I told myself, just another homicide. It was time to be objective, but my trembling hands didn't help.

I ran the beam of light up his legs, over his torso. He was lying facedown, and there was much blood under his head but no sign of a wound, which meant he'd been shot from the front. His left arm was extended over his head as though he'd been reaching for something. I moved the light forward and saw a silver-plated .38 on the floor and the cigar box where he'd obviously kept it leaning against the cabinet under the bar. He'd seen it coming, just not soon enough to stop it.

There was something sad and deserted about Matson's body, some forlorn, fruitless aspect of his humanity still lingering in his final pose of desperation. The will to live was evident in that outstretched arm, the unfulfilled and empty fingers that had reached but not grasped, a semaphore gesture broken off by a bullet. I shook my head at the sight of him and thought, Vivian, you stupid, stupid bitch.

I had stopped liking Matson a long time ago, but there had been flashes of brilliance in our friendship. There'd been times when I was sure we had something strong enough between us to preclude betrayal. I had believed that Randy Matson was a man who would bail you out of jail with a slap on the back or listen to you over a beer when the hope was gone from you. And for a time he had been just that. Looking at him now, I realized that I'd lost more than Vivian had the night I found the two of them together. I had also lost a friend.

There was a stool behind the bar, and I sat down on it and poured myself a scotch. I was in a peculiar mood, and I wanted a drink, an indulgence that, even under the circumstances, I failed to deny myself. I checked my dive watch; it was three o'clock. Time enough for a last drink with a former friend, even if he had been a prick in the end.

Men betray women and women betray men, but when one man betrays another man, something else is lost. Who knows exactly what it is? Maybe what's lost is the illusion that the basic inalienable loneliness of men might be nothing more than an illusion, a series of mirages in a desert more imagined than real; that maybe, just maybe, there were handshakes that meant something. When that's lost, the desert comes back, and you have to start crossing it all over again, this time with the burden of wondering if that illusion of loneliness you'd once believed defeated was real after all. Matson, I thought, you stupid ass.

I kept thinking of that night in that out-of-the-way bar, the expression on Matson's face when I grabbed him by the shoulder. It was a look of shock combined with a sudden penetrating regret that nothing could contradict, countermand, or set right ever again, a fine thing lost irretrievably. Randy, you son of a bitch, I said to myself without rancor, look where it got you.

I finished my drink, stood up, and went back around the bar again. I didn't like to do it, but I needed to see his face. There was nothing morbid or spiteful in it, but it's true what they say: Once a cop, always a cop, and I just couldn't bring myself to do what I was going to do without seeing his face.

Using two fingers like tweezers, I lifted his head up by the hair. A bloody paste held it to the carpeting, and I had to pull hard. The left eye was a viscous mess of red where the bullet had gone in. There is nothing heavier than a dead man's head, and I felt every ounce of it. The rest of his face had been terribly distorted from having lain for so long on a flat surface. Rigor mortis had come and gone, and the constant pressure of the floor had transformed the skin of his left cheek into what looked like a solid mass of melted wax.

Death had turned his long, sunburned neck into such an inflexible stalk that had I dropped his head, it would have slammed down onto the floor like a rock hurled by a catapult. I estimated that he'd been dead for not much more than a day and a half. It wouldn't be long before the stench would set in, but he'd be way out deep by then. That is, if everything went according to plan. I put Matson's head down as gently as I could. I didn't get up right away, though. I just knelt there next to him with the light on the back of his head for a few moments, trying to regain my focus and thinking of the time when he and I had been friends. After a while I stood up.

I went out of the cabin and up the stairs to the helm and sat down in the bucket chair in front of the controls. The keys, as I'd been told they would be, were still in the ignition. But I spent about five minutes familiarizing myself with the setup, because it had been a long time since I'd last piloted a boat this size, and I needed to jog my memory so as not to make mistakes. I used the flashlight at first, but only until I was sure where everything was. When I was satisfied, I took one last look at the sea around me and saw nothing. Just darkness everywhere, except for the soft glow of the stars and the halfhearted light of the young moon that fell softly and without effect on the water.

I turned on the engine and hit the switch that raised the anchor. It made a soft grinding sound coming up. When the red light on the dashboard stopped flashing, I opened the throttle, and the big yacht surged forward as the water boiled around the stern. I went swiftly and without lights, but I would need them farther out. My concentration was as keen as it had ever been, and I used it to open a channel through the darkness that would exclude everything except me and *The Carrousel*. In that world not even the fish were welcome. I was in a closed system, flying no colors. The coast guard cutters were out there somewhere, but there was nothing I could do about them. I was playing a lone hand against common sense, not to mention the law, and it was already too late to pass.

I needed to get out about six miles from shore, out into the deeper waters of the Gulf Stream where a sunken boat would never be found, where ancient ships and lost continents were said to rest beyond the power of memory to exhume them. At a fair speed, it would take about an hour. I found a pair of binoculars under the dash and scanned the horizon. When I turned around and looked toward land, the lights of the mansion were receding into the darkness behind me until the entire spread, seen from the distance, was no wider than a doorway and shrinking fast. Ahead of me there was nothing. I put the boat on autopilot and went below to get another drink.

I poured myself a scotch and looked out at the sea, the only sound the muted rumble of the engines, and tried not to think about Matson dead behind the bar. I checked my watch. There wasn't much time, and I was glad for that. If it's true that the spirits of the newly murdered linger in shock around the crime scene, then what I felt in that cabin was Randy's anguish and astonishment, his final betrayal. Randy—death had put us on a first-name basis again—had not expected to die.

He'd assumed he had the upper hand, the same mistake Goliath had made. Then the gun had come out. Even then he might not have believed he was a dead man. Death takes a while to sink in, especially when you think you have the world by the balls and assume immortality is your birth-right because you're young and rich and handsome and have never been shot in the head before. That is an experience from which it is very hard to extract a useful lesson. I raised my glass to Randy's ghost and wished him peace in the afterlife. I finished my drink and checked my watch again. It was time to sink the *Bismarck*.

I left the cabin and went up to the helm. It was so dark by then that I had no choice but to switch on the yacht's lights. I kept an eye out for other boats, but it seemed I had the whole ocean to myself. After about an hour, when I was sure I was out deep enough, I cut the engine and pushed the button that lowered the anchor. Then I headed for the engine room.

I have had many a teacher in my time, and some of them taught me things that I never expected to use. One of those teachers was Captain Tony, whose dangerous and dubious business, as I mentioned, was the repossession of boats, which can be even more dangerous than the repossession of cars, depending on the clientele. Occasionally, however, he also had to sink boats, sometimes for the insurance money and once for a drug dealer attempting to fake his own death on account of the fact that half the cops in North and South America were looking for him. I hadn't been with Tony on those particular occasions, but he had told me how it was done.

The method used is quite simple. Every boat has open lines, narrow pipes called sea cogs, leading from the vessel to push waste water out of the boat. They have pressure valves on them that keep the ocean from flooding into the ship. Uncork them all at once and the boat fills with water and sinks.

I opened the door that led down into the engine room, and the smell of diesel dilated my nostrils like a dose of smelling salts. I got out the flashlight, climbed down the ladder into the pit, and found the light switch.

I turned around and faced the miniature city of pumps and pipes, twisted like intestines, my eyes fanning left and right until they crossed over the body of a man slumped backward over a bilge pump. I sprang back so fast that I struck my elbow on the edge of the ladder, sending a jolt of pain into the nerve. My flashlight flew through the air and rolled across the floor, but I didn't bother to pick it up. I just stood there, crouched over, rubbing my elbow and staring at the dead man with all the adrenaline in my body now concentrated in my heart.

I took some very deep breaths and straightened up, never taking my eyes from the corpse. When my heart rate slipped under two hundred, I walked over to where the man lay and stood above him. He was wearing a pair of white Bermuda shorts and a white guayabara shirt that was no longer white because of all the blood on his chest. His arms and legs were splayed apart as though he'd been blasted by a gale-force wind. I studied his face. He was in his late thirties, deeply tanned, and as handsome as a Ken doll, with a black, neatly trimmed mustache that had flecks of gray in it. His salt-and-pepper hair was closely cropped. His brown eyes stared without sight at the low ceiling. I recognized him. He was the second man in the video, and, like Matson's, his acting days were over.

Shit, I said to myself. Nobody had mentioned anything about a two-for-one deal.

Now I knew for a fact that I'd been played. It was conceivable that Vivian might have shot Matson; crimes of passion happen all the time. But she wasn't mean and crazy enough to chase down and shoot another man. I knew somebody who was, though. For him it would have been easy.

I also thought I knew how it might have happened. Vivian had gone out to meet Matson in order to get the video and whatever else Matson was needling her and her father with.

Assuming for the moment that her father had been telling the truth about her going out there on a Jet Ski, then the only way for Williams to have made it out to the yacht without being either seen or heard would be to swim out. It wasn't that far, a few hundred yards. He might even have used diving gear. He would have climbed on board and found a place from which he could watch or at least listen to the negotiations for the tape. Whether he knew there was a second man aboard remained to be seen.

So let's say—assuming that she was even armed in the first place—that Vivian had gotten mad and, out of frustration, popped a cap into Matson's leering face. The surprise guest may have made a break for the engine room, at which point Williams would have gone after him, knowing he couldn't afford to let him get away or get to a weapon. That was one possible scenario, but there was another possibility, and I liked it a little better, not just because it exonerated Vivian of murder but because it felt right.

It may well have been that the Colonel, without telling his daughter, had come to the conclusion that Matson had to go. He would have let Vivian think she was going out to the meeting alone, without knowing that Williams was shadowing her or, more likely, that he was already out in the water, near the yacht, waiting for her to show up. Better that she not know. That way her performance with Matson would be more natural. There would be no telltale nervousness to make him suspicious. Then Williams would have made his move, catching both Matson and Vivian by surprise.

The second man may have been at the bar when the gun went off and then made a run for it, or maybe after hearing the sound of the shot he'd come running in from someplace else—possibly from one of the cabins below. If that had been the case, then too bad for bachelor number two. There could be no witnesses in order for the thing to work. Maybe he'd seen Williams and made a run for it. He hadn't made it in this second scenario either.

What happened after that was anyone's guess. Vivian might have gotten hysterical, in which case Williams would've had to bring her back on the Jet Ski himself. I could see that happening. Then there was me. It made sense now why they had brought me into it. The Colonel had been telling the truth about that much at least.

With two killings under his belt, Williams couldn't take the chance of ditching the boat himself, because getting caught would have defeated the purpose of the killings in the first place—getting rid of a blackmailer. Knowing Williams, he would've wanted to go; he'd have pleaded his case, but Colonel Patterson would come up with another idea: get Vaughn to do it. Yet there was something wrong with that, too. What if I got caught? It would have all come out anyway. They would not possibly have believed that if I got grabbed ditching the bodies, I would have gone to jail for either Vivian or a hundred thousand dollars. I might be stupid, but they knew I wasn't that stupid.

The truth was, the Colonel had needed Williams for something else tonight, but whether it was to protect him from Matson's cronies or for some other purpose I couldn't yet figure out.

I looked around but didn't see any bullet casings on the floor, not a single one. Vivian would not have thought to pick them up. I made a mental note to check the upper deck where Matson lay, but I doubted I'd find anything there either. It wouldn't make much difference, though, not without anything in the engine room to match them against. Still, it would have been nice to know that Matson and his friend had been shot by the same gun. That would have made it Williams for sure: one gun, one killer.

I got my foot under the dead man and turned him over. I

bent down and patted his pockets with the hope of finding a wallet. There was none. Since men don't often go anywhere without at least their driver's license, someone had obviously lifted it. The killer hadn't wanted his victim's identity known. Not that it mattered now. I was going to sink the boat anyway, and the extra dead man made it even more necessary that I do it quickly.

There was nothing else to do but find the sea cogs. It took me less than thirty seconds to locate them and another two minutes to open all the valves. Suddenly there was water rushing in from a dozen spots along the floor. By the time I got to the ladder, the water was already up to my ankles and rising fast. Even so, it would take two or three hours until the boat sank. It would be close, but by daylight *The Carrousel* would be on its way to the sea floor, and I would be on my way home with a lot of questions and a bad taste in my mouth.

I went back up to the stateroom and walked around with the flashlight, looking for what, I didn't know, but goaded by the elusive feeling that I had missed something. I played the narrow beam along the bar and behind it. It passed over the television screen and VCR above the bar. Then I stopped and brought the beam back. The light on the VCR was on. I had a strange and not very pleasant feeling.

I walked over and turned on the television and hit the play button on the VCR.

I watched the tape for ten or fifteen seconds just to make sure. That was enough. I had already seen it earlier that day at the Colonel's house, the house of glass you couldn't see through. It was Vivian's tape, all right: Randy Matson's last production.

I shut off the flashlight and just stood there in the dark for a while, listening to my thoughts. It wasn't likely that you would kill two men for a racy movie to begin with; it was even less likely that you would leave the tape behind if you had. Vivian might panic and forget, but not Williams, not the man who had once used human ears as cashier's receipts. So if not for the famous video, then what had it all been for? Something was missing. Then I remembered, just vaguely, that the Colonel had mentioned something about some research of his having been stolen. That didn't make any sense either, but maybe it would later on, once I got back to shore.

I thought of Vivian then with a mixture of anger, sadness, and curiosity. She must have been in pretty desperate straits to bring me into such a game. But, of course, she had just allowed herself to be used as bait to do her father's and William's dirty work. This was the Colonel's master plan, not hers, but what was the game? Two men were dead, and for what?

And as for me, the only thing that kept me from being a complete idiot in all this was the fifty grand at home under my sink and the promise of fifty more. Right then and right there, I made a promise to myself that I would get the rest of the money even if I had to break that glass house apart with a sledgehammer. Then the four of us—me, the Colonel, Williams, and Vivian—would have us a little sit-down. I looked forward to that. All I had to do was make it back.

It was time to go. The answers I needed were all on shore. I went out onto the dive deck and looked around me, but there was nothing except an endless plain of water stretching out in all directions. The only light came from the quarter moon and the stars over my head. Slender cirrus clouds slipped by like long white canoes headed west with the night and the soft, salty breeze blowing from the east. It was a beautiful night, and I was a fool.

I got the kayak loose and slipped inside. I paddled out a ways until I was a few hundred feet from the yacht. I ate a protein bar and washed it down with water from my canteen. Then I swallowed two capsules containing a mixture of ephedrine, caffeine, and ginseng. The protein bar would take two hours to digest, and when it did, the capsule would be quickly absorbed into the bloodstream, delivering a jolt of energy just when my blood sugar would be dropping. I didn't like to take them, and I could certainly make it back without them, but the night had been full of surprises, and I didn't want to come up short on juice if there were any more.

The northbound current was running smooth and strong, and there was nothing to do but go with the flow, which would mean making landfall somewhere just south of Fort Lauderdale. I was so intent on my strokes that for a long time I forgot to look back at *The Carrousel*, as though the water behind me were already part of the past. Then it came to me, and I stopped and turned the kayak around. The yacht was only a shadow now, but even in the weak, halfhearted, sidereal light, I could see that its stern was starting to list ever so slightly toward me, like some great and dying, air-breathing leviathan still unwilling to give up its life. I watched it for a few seconds, then started for home.

That's when I heard it. At first I thought it was the sound of another plane, but the engine sounded more like a boat's, possibly a speedboat, and it was to my left and very close. The engine revved, then died out again as though waiting for something. I had just started to paddle away from the noise when the wake hit me broadside and knocked me over. I was upside down in the water before I had a chance to take a breath. I gathered myself and whipped my body hard to the right, hoping for enough momentum to execute what's called an Eskimo roll, but the water was too rough and I missed it. Then I was upside down again, trying to steady myself for another attempt. The craft was right above me. A bright light illuminated the boiling water as I struggled. My lungs were empty. I had swallowed half of the ocean.

I gave my body a vicious but calculated twist, and suddenly I was right side up again, bobbing and weaving and coughing up water, struggling damned hard not to capsize again, because I knew that if I did, I might not make it. I yelled over the roar of the engine for whoever was on board to turn the goddamned thing off. I knew they could see me. The light was right on my face now. I could feel its heat, as though I had landed on the surface of the sun. The ocean danced around me as I squinted into the glare, shielding my eyes with one arm and holding the paddle with the other. I was ready to come out of the Hell Chaser and strangle somebody.

"Get that fucking light out of my eyes!" I shouted. "Your damned boat nearly killed me!"

There was no answer. Then, suddenly, the light went off.

"Who's out there?" I yelled. I began to feel around inside the kayak for the Glock, but the spill I had taken must have dislodged it from its pouch. I groped for it on the bottom of the kayak but couldn't find it. I was afraid that maybe it had gone overboard. Then, by my right thigh, just above the knee, there was something hard that shouldn't have been there. I reached down and felt the familiar outline of the gun inside the plastic bag. I got it out as quickly as I could with my shaking fingers and sat back, holding it in my lap and trying to look unarmed.

The light flashed on again and blinded me. I turned my head away. I was pretty sure who it was, and if I was right, then I was in trouble.

"Is that the fucking coast guard, or just some idiot with too much time on his hands?" I shouted. "Turn out that goddamn light!"

"It isn't the coast guard, Jack," a familiar voice called out.

"It's your old friend Williams. I guess you didn't expect to run into me out here, did you?"

"Why not?" I yelled. "Shit floats, doesn't it?"

"You've done well, Jack. You've done very well, but as you may have guessed, there's been a dramatic change in plans."

"Does the Colonel know you're doing this?"

"Who do you think sent me?"

I used my hand again to shield my eyes from the glare of the searchlight. Then Williams swung the light a little to his left so that I could see his silhouette. He was smiling broadly. Very casually, and as though he had all the time in the world, he reached down, lifted up a rifle, and calmly placed the butt end against his right shoulder. Then, still smiling, he slowly lowered his eye to the scope.

"Oh, Jackie," he said in that fake Scottish accent he sometimes used, "I'm going to miss you so."

I brought the gun up and fired at the spotlight. I would have gone for Williams, but the kayak was dancing way too much and the light made a bigger and better target. The spotlight exploded with a loud pop, and just like that it was dark again. I fired once more at where Williams had been standing, shoved the gun into my vest, paddled off a few yards, then stopped, pulled the Glock out and fired at the boat yet again. I didn't think I would hit anything, but I wanted Williams worried enough to give me some room. The reality of the situation was that it would be almost impossible to hit anything under those conditions, except by accident. My one advantage was that Williams couldn't afford to stay still long enough to get lucky.

Then there was a sudden roar as the engines of the speedboat came alive, and a white rush of water burst from beneath the bow, nearly knocking me over. The boat lifted itself out of the water like a flying wedge and zoomed off toward the east, the white foam burgeoning like the exhaust from a rocket. I waited for the wake and rode it until the water calmed.

Then the first bullet went past my cheek, hit the kayak, and took part of the front end off. The impact swung the Hell Chaser around a full 180 degrees.

I reached over my right shoulder and fired back at the darkness, hoping for a miracle. I heard him coming at me then, the engines nearly silent, slow and relentless, giving off no more noise than a blender with a towel thrown over it. I fired again, and the boat's engines flared and the speed-boat went by me and flew off into the night, fishtailing as it swerved.

There was just enough light for me to see it now, then nothing again but foam and spray in my face. The wake came up like a big paw and smacked me over. I dropped the paddle, and the Glock went flying into the wind. Then the ocean had me, and I was underwater again. The only difference this time was that I had the presence of mind to take a deep breath while there was still a chance.

There was no sense trying to stay in the kayak now, so I kicked myself free of it while I was still almost upside down. I'm thinking, This is suicide. When my legs were free, I twisted out of the life jacket, extended my arms, and swam straight down into total blackness, knowing I was dead, still not quite believing it. So this is the way I die, I thought without panic.

I went down maybe ten feet, then leveled off and swam toward what I hoped was the south. I needed desperately to surface. I was out of air. Under normal circumstances I could hold my breath for one and a half minutes, but the excitement had burned up every molecule of oxygen in my lungs. I made a deal with myself for ten more seconds and swam hard. When I had counted to ten, I made the same

deal again. I made it till twelve, and then I arched my back
and swooped for the surface.

I came up gasping at the edge of a pool of white light no
more than ten feet ahead of me. Another searchlight—not
as powerful as the one I had shot out but good enough to
catch me if I lost my luck. I took another gulp of air and dove
again, this time not as deep. Again I leveled off, but instead
of swimming away from the boat, I swam toward it, hoping
to get on the other side of him. The water above me turned
yellow-green and lingered there, and I knew if I came up too
soon, he would have me and it would be over.

The boat passed above me. I could feel myself being
sucked upward. I kicked and tried to pull myself away
but only succeeded in maintaining my position. Then the
glow was gone and the water was quiet. I played the ten-
second game again and made it to eight only with the utmost
effort. I came up facing in the wrong direction. I could see
the lights stretched north and south across the still-distant
shore. I turned around and saw the shadow of the speedboat
about fifty yards away and moving east, the light probing the
water in the general direction I had at first begun to swim. If
I hadn't turned back, he would have had me for sure.

I watched the light on the boat for a few seconds, marked
its location, not sure which way to go. If he found the life
vest, he would assume that I'd gotten rid of it because I
needed to get underwater and the vest's inherent buoyancy
would have prevented that, in which case I would still be
somewhere in the area. Or he might think that I was dead
and therefore floating on the surface of the water. In either
case he would keep looking. He would start near the place
where he had rammed me, and for a while he'd restrict himself to a fairly tight perimeter of the site. When that failed,
he would become more systematic.

I watched the light angle south, and then I turned and

swam north with the current, not that there was much choice. I swam easily, with smooth overhand strokes. I was fairly certain he had night-vision goggles, but even with them he would have to be extremely lucky to spot me. The ocean had kicked up into a light chop, so there were little swells to hide behind. Even so, I stayed under as much as I could and surfaced only when I had to. I was glad now that I'd thought to take the ephedrine; I was going to need it.

The next time I came up, I could still see the light. Williams was still out there prospecting, still fairly close to ground zero and about two hundred yards away. Now and then the light would swing unexpectedly in a different direction, as though he knew that I was in the vicinity and hoped to catch me off guard. But it never came anywhere near me, so I swam on. I didn't think I had much of a chance, but there was nothing else to do except swim.

We were the only two human beings in the vicinity, and under those conditions who's to say what strange channels open up between predator and prey? There came a time when despite the splash of the waves and the distance between us I was sure I sensed his thoughts and felt his anxiety as he scanned the water for me. I could hear him listening, and it was then that I would hold myself beneath the surface of the water and say a prayer that he wouldn't linger too long above me.

I kept swimming. My fear gave me extra strength, lengthened my endurance. The ephedrine had kicked in at last, but I was still very tired. Then, suddenly, I heard the speedboat coming closer from just to the south of me. He was getting more methodical, exactly as I'd known he would, and had begun to make concentric circles around the area. He would start wide, allowing for the possibility that I had survived the kayak and was in good enough shape to be swimming. The circles would grow smaller and smaller until I ended up at the center like a bug caught in a drain.

The searchlight nearly got me then, but the white arc faded out just a few yards ahead of me. I went under fast and swam away from the boat for as long as I could. Something brushed my leg in the dark, but I kept going. Everything depended on where Williams began his search. If I was outside the perimeter, he would be moving away from me, funneling inward, and I might have time to get away. If not, he would surely see me eventually. My arms parted the darkness in front of me as though I were a blind man moving through a curtain of water that closed and opened around me without beginning or end.

The boat went by maybe fifty feet to the east of me, then headed back out. I came up in time to see it curving back toward the beach, which meant he had underestimated me and had just completed the biggest circle. I was outside that circle, but only for the moment. It would not take long for him to funnel inward and eventually reach the conclusion that either I was dead or somehow had gotten past him. Williams would then start over, and this time he would come in even closer to shore. He could afford to be methodical. I was still miles from land, and he had the speedboat and a good two hours until dawn.

I got over onto my back and kicked with my legs, trying to conserve the strength in my arms. I'd once competed in a triathlon and thought at the time that I had reached the apex of human fatigue. I'd been wrong. I know that there are resources in the human body that can be tapped only in moments of extreme danger and excitement, and I had no doubt that I'd tapped in to them now. By all accounts I should have been too tired to move, but something kept me going. My body went from feeling waterlogged to feeling supernaturally light, as though I were not so much swimming in the water as being the water itself.

Then the heaviness would intrude, and I would be slogging away again toward the single row of lights on the shore that for the life of me never seemed to get any closer. After a while I stopped thinking altogether, as though the blood flow to my brain had ceased, and my body rallied itself and pulled me forward like a horse carrying a rider either half dead in the saddle or else far too weary to care.

When I came to myself again, it was morning. I must have opened my eyes just as my arm had lifted itself for another endless stroke, and I was all at once conscious of the heat of the sun on my back and its fierce silver glare on the surface of the sea. My tongue was swollen with thirst, and there was no strength in me. I could see the shore, now only a quarter of a mile away. But there was nothing left in me, nothing. I managed to get over onto my back, but it was too much like being in bed, and I almost gave in to the fatal luxury of letting go. I saw an orange buoy halfway to the shore and swam for it, knowing that if I could make it that far, I had a chance.

It was only three hundred yards to shore, but no matter how much I swam, the beach never came any closer, still flaunting its promise of safety with the derision of a mirage. I could see people near the shore playing in the breakers; I could hear their voices. I tried to call out to them, but my mouth made only a strange, inhuman rasping sound. Just a little farther and the incoming tide would lift me, drag me in. It seemed stupid, almost sinful, to die so close to land, and yet that was what was happening, for all at once I was no longer moving. My arms and legs had given out, and I began to sink almost gratefully. I wanted to rest even if it meant death. Just for the hell of it, I held my breath. No sense making it too easy. I went down maybe three yards when my toes touched the surface of the sandbar.

Feeling something solid beneath my feet after being in the water so long gave me a fresh surge of strength, and right then I knew for a fact that I wasn't finished, not by a long shot. I sprang to the surface and looked for the shore. It was nothing. A hundred yards at most.

Piece of cake. I could do it. I willed my empty arms and legs to move as though they were a team of recalcitrant mules in the foothills of the Andes. My limbs didn't really belong to me anymore. I had just borrowed them, and they didn't like the way I'd treated them, but they, too, must have sensed the nearing shore, because they began to obey me. That's right, boys, I told them. Don't fail me now.

I heard the speedboat coming as if from out of a dream you think you've already awakened from. It was coming in fast from my left. I stroked harder for the shore. I was sure it was Williams. I turned my head to one side and saw him standing at the helm, bearing down on me fast and hard, his bald head shining in the brittle sunlight like the helmet of a conquistador. I recalled the ears he had used for money back in Vietnam. I should not have been surprised that he'd spent the night looking for me.

It was fear that saved me then, fear that squeezed the last ounce of juice out of my adrenals. Suddenly the unbearable fatigue was gone and I was fresh again. It would not last long. But it might last long enough.

I heard the first shot but felt nothing. I took as deep a breath as I could manage and dove for the bottom and swam underwater. The boat passed over me, blocking the sun, its propellers churning madly. I had passed the sandbar, but the sea was still only about fifteen feet deep. A little farther and Williams would have to take her out again lest he beach her. But I wasn't Aquaman. He knew where I was. All he would have to do was wait for me to come up.

My lungs were bursting, begging for relief. My only chance was if Williams was looking in the wrong direction when my head broke the surface of the water. There was no other choice. I broke for the surface, knowing that I was heading for either another breath of life or a bullet in the head. I was in the same bad spot I'd been in the night before, only this time there was more light for Williams to see me with.

I decided to come up near the bow of the boat where the curvature of the hull might give me a little cover, but as I began to rise toward the darkened underbelly of the speed-boat, it turned abruptly and sped away at top speed. My head broke the surface of the water just in time to see it careening away, heading north, a spray of white foam spewing outward from its wake.

There was a roar of engines behind me. I turned and saw a coast guard cutter splitting the waves and coming in from the east, from the open ocean. It was starting to swing away after Williams when it spotted me and came about. I could see the sailors watching me through their binoculars. I waved at them, and a moment later they sent one of those small, two-man inflatable pontoons out to get me. I reached up, and the two fresh-faced sailors pulled me into the craft.

I asked for water and drank like a bedouin at an oasis. One of the sailors—a young woman—helped me to lie back and put a life jacket under my head. I struggled to sit up, but all at once my body, so long abused, failed me. I tried to speak, but not even my lips would work, so I lay back and breathed hard, and the far sun fell from the sky and crashed into my face like a meteor. After that there was only the darkness, into which I gladly allowed myself to drown.

I woke up in the infirmary at the Krome Detention Center. The sign on the wall told me that much. I was in a large room with lime green walls, barred windows, and a dozen beds, most of which were occupied. Beyond the windows the sun was still high enough to throw shadows across the white sheets that covered me from the waist down. I had an IV in my left arm, which throbbed where they had stuck in the needle, but aside from a dry mouth and a headache, I didn't feel all that bad, not considering the night I'd just lived through.

I was trying to sit up when the door opened and a nurse flanked by two men in uniform came striding purposefully toward me. The men were with the Border Patrol, and I could tell from the expressions on their faces that they hadn't come to bring me flowers. One of them was close to sixty, with the overstuffed and slightly deformed body of a bus driver. He had small blue eyes that had spent a long time trying to look hard. The other man was too tall for his weight, as though he'd been stretched artificially by machine. He was around thirty, with a mouth full of gum and hair the color of wet hay. His right eye was off center, which made him appear as if he were trying to look behind him. His expression was an imitation of his partner's, but on him it wasn't as convincing. He looked as much scared as he did mean.

Both of them had waists encircled by belts heavily laden with the standard tools of law enforcement: the guns, the cuffs, the pepper spray, and the billy clubs. They were ready for anything except a footrace, but it didn't matter, because all four of my limbs were manacled to the stainless-steel bedposts.

The older agent wore a name tag that said COOPER. He gave me a calculated glare of menace that was supposed to strike fear into the heart of any illegal alien it chanced to fall upon. He shifted his belt on his hips and spread his legs like a man bracing for a bar fight. His partner did the same. I had no doubt who led when they danced the tango together.

"Ask him his name, will you?" the older cop directed the nurse. His partner stood silently behind him with his hand on the butt of his gun, chewing his cud as though it were part of his job.

"I don't speak Spanish," the nurse said. She swabbed my arm with alcohol and slipped the needle out.

"Who are you kidding? I heard you speak it before. Your last name is Rodriguez, for crying out loud."

"*Cómo se llama,* spic?" the younger cop said.

I decided to be Hispanic until I got the lay of the land, so I told him my name was Juan. The nurse glanced at me and smiled ever so slightly, then looked away again. Then she stuck a thermometer in my mouth, for which I was grateful, because it gave me an excuse not to talk. The younger officer, whose name tag said ELLIS, sat down on the edge of the bed and smacked the side of my leg.

"You get well," he said. "You go bye-bye."

They undid my ankle and wrist bracelets and gave me an orange jumpsuit that had been washed so many times that the cloth had faded into a weary paleness. Then they cuffed my hands behind my back and led me down a narrow hallway flanked every few yards by wooden benches spaced out like dashes along the lime-colored walls. We went up a flight of steps that took all my strength to climb and came out into another hallway lined with rows of offices. We made a few turns and stopped in front of a door that had INSPECTOR RUBEN CORTEZ stenciled onto the glass in gold letters with black trim. Cooper opened the door and gave me a short, hard shove in the middle of my back that propelled me into the room.

It was a small office with a desk and a man sitting behind it. He was forty or forty-five, with dark brown hair with a gray fringe along the temples and a mustache that was all gray and needed trimming. His eyes were shiny and black, with a glint of humor in them, as though he had just recalled something vaguely amusing. He leaned back in his swivel chair as I came in.

"Who's this son of a bitch?" he asked.

"This is the guy the coast guard picked up this morning," Cooper said.

Ellis shoved me down into a chair across from Cortez. He looked me over for a long moment, then asked me in Spanish if I were Cuban.

"*Sí,*" I said.

He laughed. "*Sí?*" he repeated. "Really? Just what part of Cuba are you from?"

"Omaha, Nebraska."

He nodded and smiled. "Just as I suspected. Gentlemen," he said, pointing his finger at me, "this man is an American. I find that kind of amazing, don't you?"

Ellis spoke up. "The coast guard said there was some guy shooting at him from a speedboat."

"Is that right?" Cortez said, nonplussed. "That's very fucking exciting. Just like *Miami Vice*."

"You're a fucking American," Cooper said indignantly. He had a whiny, cartoon-character voice that had no business being in law enforcement. "You talk English."

"This is America," I said. "English is pretty popular around here."

Cortez grinned and turned his attention back to me. "What's your name?"

"Jack Vaughn."

The inspector's eyes narrowed, and his cigarette stalled in the airspace between his lips and the butt-filled ashtray on his paper-laden desk. "Jack Vaughn?" he said. "You're not a personal trainer by any chance, are you?"

"Sure I am."

"For Christ's sake," Cortez said. He spent a few more seconds reading my face, then stood up. "Take the cuffs off and leave us alone," he said. He stubbed out his cigarette and sat down on his chair again. Ellis and Cooper hadn't moved. They seemed to be in shock, but after a moment they removed the cuffs and left, looking dejected.

When we were alone, Cortez swiveled around in his chair

and opened the door of a small refrigerator behind his desk. I used the break to read a plaque on the wall to my left. Ten years before, while with the Border Patrol over in Texas, he had saved a Mexican from drowning in the Rio Grande. I wondered if that was why he'd gotten transferred. When he turned around, he had two cans of Diet Coke in his hands, one of which he set down in front of me.

He opened his and took a long sip, then held the can up before setting it down.

"You remember Tab?" he asked.

"Sure, but I don't think they make it anymore."

"Yeah, they do, but it's hard to find. You can get it in Mexico, though."

"You can get anything in Mexico."

"Yeah," he said, "especially the clap."

We laughed, but then it got quiet all of a sudden, as though a match had been snuffed out, and Cortez and I were just watching one another over the tops of our soda cans.

"You used to train my wife," Cortez said.

"You're kidding."

"No, I'm serious. About a year ago."

"Maybe so. I don't remember. In my business people come and go."

"Yeah," Cortez said. "That's the way it is around here, too."

"What's her name, your wife?"

"Susan Andrews. Blond, short hair. Kind of tall. Don't sit there and tell me you don't remember *her*."

"Oh, yeah. Sure I remember her."

"I bet you remember her ass, right?"

"That, too."

"I bet you do. Don't get cute with me, Jackie boy. There's no reason to be. We split up a long time ago."

"Sorry to hear it."

Cortez leaned forward in his chair and clasped his hands in front of him. He stared down at his mated fingers for so long that I thought he was going to start praying. Then he lifted his head suddenly, his dark eyes beaming with suspicion.

"Tell me the truth," he said in a soft voice. "Were you doing her?"

"What makes you think I was?"

"Why wouldn't you?"

I thought for a moment. "She was married to a cop. How stupid do you think I am?"

"Considering your current location," Cortez said, looking around, "pretty stupid."

"Thanks."

"Don't mention it." He lit another cigarette. "By the way, while I have you here, Jack, let me ask you a personal question. What were you doing in the water this morning, and why would somebody shoot at you? You know who it was?"

"No idea," I said.

"So let me get this straight. Some guy just pulls up out of nowhere and decides to take a few shots at you. Is that right?"

"I don't see any other explanation," I said.

"I do," Cortez answered. "Let's say the personal-training gig isn't bringing in the megabucks you had been hoping for. So you find yourself a partner with a nice fast boat and you go and get yourself a bunch of Haitians or Cubans, take their money, and dump them somewhere. Nice money in smuggling. If they had a better dental plan, I'd get into the business myself."

"You think I'm a smuggler?"

"I think you're a fucking liar. That's what I think. I think your partner decided to go solo, keep the cash for himself. So you go overboard like the sack of shit you are, and he takes a few potshots at your head, only we show up and he's got to boogey. Is that it?"

"If that's the case," I said, "where are the people we smuggled? Oh, wait, I got it now. Me and my partner forgot we were both citizens, and so we were taking turns smuggling each other into Miami. This morning was my turn. Yeah, that's it. You know, Cortez, Susan told me you were crazy. I'm just glad to see now she was wrong."

"She told you I was crazy?" Cortez asked.

"Let's just say that she mentioned you were the jealous type."

"You telling me she didn't come on to you?"

"Not to my face, no."

"What the hell does that mean, 'not to my face'? What are you, some kind of fucking leprechaun or something?"

I looked at him for a moment, confused. It had been a long time since anybody had called me a leprechaun.

"I think I need to talk to a lawyer," I said.

"What were you doing in the water?"

"Taking a swim. I'm a personal trainer. I have to stay in shape."

"What about the guy with the rifle and the speedboat? We're supposed to forget about that? Just fish you out of the drink and let you go on your way?"

"Sometimes you just have to let bygones be bygones," I told him. "Besides, this is Miami—people get shot every day. Maybe he thought I was somebody else."

He smiled thinly, picked up the old-fashioned black phone, and placed it in front of me like an offering.

"Dial away, scumbag."

I dialed a number and listened as it rang. Cortez watched me, grinning.

"Which lawyer you calling?" he asked. "If I were you, his last name would be Dershowitz."

"Can't afford him," I said. "I'm calling your ex-wife."

Cortez blinked, and then his eyes widened. He smiled broadly as he took a long drag on his cigarette. Then he exhaled. "This is going to be better than I thought," he said.

"Won't that bitch be surprised?"

Susan Andrews, formerly Susan Cortez, had been a hardworking, highly underpaid prosecutor when she was referred to me by Judge Dryer, a client of mine, who, sad to say, got sent to jail for taking bribes over on Miami Beach. Susan and Ruben—Inspector Cortez—were divorcing, and I was the centerpiece of her personal renaissance, her transformation from unhappy and unappreciated wife to unattached single. It seems she had caught Ruben coming out of the Stardust Motel on Biscayne Boulevard with her best friend, a rather curvaceous fellow attorney, at which time Susan had decided not only to get rid of Ruben but to hire herself a personal trainer and to get back into shape. I had trained her five days a week, which is a lot of time to spend with a woman who's going through a divorce and who therefore tends to see her husband's philandering face superimposed over that of any male foolish enough to get within range.

But for fifty bucks an hour, a man has to be willing to walk through a minefield now and then and trust that his charm will allow him to live long enough to make a profit. But I liked Susan. She was mean and crazy and gave off the kind of chronic bad vibes that lead to the whimsical purchase of handguns, but still, I liked her. She made it clear that she hated men and was indulging me only because of my expertise and Judge Dryer's recommendation. I, in turn, had made it clear that I didn't give a shit about her personal problems and was only in it for the money, which, of course, as a lawyer, she seemed to appreciate, at least from the standpoint of a fellow professional.

For the better part of six months, I ran with Susan, I biked with Susan, and I showed Susan how to lift weights. But what she liked most was putting on the eight-ounce gloves and going a few rounds with me in a park near her new crib in the Grove. Basically, what she liked to do was beat the shit out of me three times a week, weather permitting. Forgetting her violent frame of mind, I had insisted that she wear headgear and padding while I, being Jack Vaughn, "The Motivator" (that's what it says on my business card), wore only a smile. By the end of the second week, Susan had fractured two of my ribs and loosened an incisor with a roundhouse kick. Seems she had forgotten to mention the brown belt in tae kwon do. After the tooth incident, I wised up and started dressing a little more like the Michelin Man. I even wore a steel cup inside my jockstrap—an accessory I hadn't needed with any of my other clients, not even the Sheik.

Not being too bright, I made the mistake of introducing Susan to Vivian so as to dispel the notion I sensed percolating in the latter's jealous mind that there was anything going on between Susan and me. Vivian had started showing up at the park where Susan and I had our kickboxing sessions, and while I always pretended not to have seen her, I thought it would be a good idea to make a preemptive move before the jealousy got ugly. I made arrangements for us to meet at a bar around the corner from Susan's office. We met during a happy hour, which failed to live up to its name. Susan brought along a nice-looking fellow named Jason, a nonentity in a business suit who seemed surprised to be alive. It didn't take long before I realized I'd made a fatal mistake.

Susan and Vivian had liked one another about as much as the FBI likes the Mafia, maybe less so. They had nothing in common except their anatomy and the fact that each in her own way was beautiful. We were sitting at a small table with a red-and-white-checkered tablecloth and a candle as a centerpiece. I remember this aspect of the decor not because I'm romantic but because of the way their eyes glared in the flickering light. Almost immediately it became clear that they were looking for something to get nasty about, and needless to say they soon found a suitable subject: Chilean wine. I became the mediator while Jason did his imitation of the Invisible Man. I was so anxious to get out of the place that I paid the bill five minutes before the food appeared from the kitchen.

After that delightful evening, things begin to sour between Susan and me, and she cut her sessions from five to three, then to two, on down until it became every now and then. She let me know that she was dating Jason and had gotten into tennis. The training sessions became increasingly unpleasant and the cup protecting my balls increasingly necessary. I might be slow, but no one ever called me stupid, so I knew it had something to do with Vivian.

Maybe in some strange female way, she felt betrayed by the fact that I had a beautiful girlfriend, though I had spoken of her often enough—especially in the beginning when I was trying to convince my new emotionally labile client that she was relatively safe with me. Under those circumstances, even if Vivian hadn't existed, I would have invented her for business purposes alone. Call it Machiavellian if you will; I call it public relations. It had been a way of neutering myself without having to undergo the actual surgery, and it had worked, too—at least until the two women sat down and went to war over the seemingly insane subject of Chilean wine.

Then, as frequently happens in my business, Susan disappeared from my calendar altogether, became a name consigned to the papery wings of my dog-eared Rolodex. The last time I heard from her, she had left her old job and joined a law firm and was now defending the same money-laundering drug dealers she'd previously been charged with putting in jail. As it turns out, the dealers had a lot more money, and, in the charade that is the war on drugs, no one at her old place of employment thought the worse of her for defecting. Inspector Ruben was now nothing more than a foolish face, fading fast in life's rearview mirror. Jason had faded, too. She had a new man now, and things were, as they say, getting serious. There was no time for Jack, and I was made to understand that I, too, was part of the past. So long and thanks for the push-ups.

Now here I was, sitting across from her ex-husband, calling her at the office of one of Miami's biggest law firms, Balthazar, Epstein and Blake, with the offhanded hope that she might be of a mind to help me out. The receptionist passed me along to a secretary who passed me along to an assistant who put me on hold for so long my ear began to ache from the pressure of the receiver against it. All the while Cortez sat looking at me with a demented grin on his face, like an alligator that happened to close its jaws just as an unlucky sparrow flew by. I was nothing to him but a small snack sent by the devil to help ease him through the endless boredom of his day.

Finally Susan came to the phone. Her voice was brisk, demanding, the voice of a woman with very little time to spare. There was a long pause when she realized that it was her old friend and former personal trainer calling her, a puzzled silence that told me she was surprised, though not particularly pleased, to hear from me. I got right into it, what had happened and where I was. She let me talk. The silence deepened when she found out I was sitting across from her ex-husband. After a moment she told me to put Cortez on the line.

The inspector grinned when I handed him the phone. His first words were, "Hey, babe," and I knew immediately that they were the wrong words to use with the new and improved Susan Andrews. His grin vanished, and he shifted uneasily in his chair, as though a splinter had found its way into his ass. His face grew tighter and less self-assured by degrees, until it became a mask first of doubt, then of quiet anger. I couldn't hear her words, but I could guess their tone: cold and professional, filled with a steady refusal of all intimacy. I studied his face as he listened. I saw confidence replaced first by disbelief, then by acceptance. Cortez was nothing to her now, just the voice of a minor official with very few cards to play. At the end of their conversation, he handed the phone back to me. I hadn't liked what I'd heard him say. Susan's version wasn't any better. I was going to be stuck at Krome for a while.

"Listen to me, Jack," she said. "They're going to hold you there at Krome over the weekend. Then they'll transfer you down to federal court. They want to charge you with smuggling illegal aliens. The charge is bullshit and won't hold, but Ruben has to cover his ass on this one. Even so, under normal circumstances I could get you out on bail, but not till they send you downtown for arraignment. They're not in any hurry to do that. I can make a few calls, but it will be Monday at the earliest. That means you have to sit tight and wait."

"I can't stay here that long," I said.

"You don't have a choice. I can't do any better than Monday, and even that soon will require some maneuvering. By the way, do you have any idea how much I charge?"

"I guess food stamps are out of the question, but don't worry. I've come into a little money."

"Good," she said. "Because I bill at three hundred an hour. Listen, Jack, I have to go now. Can you behave yourself for a few days?"

"I doubt it. There's a lot of shit happening."

"I'll see you on Monday morning."

I didn't say anything. My mind was on other matters.

"I said I'll see you on Monday," Susan said.

"All right," I said. "Monday."

Susan hung up. I handed the phone to Cortez, who spoke into it for a moment before realizing she was gone. He looked disappointed, then set the phone back in its cradle.

"I guess you're going to be here for a while," he said.

"So it would seem."

"I see the bitch still holds a grudge," he said.

"What do you expect? You were screwing her friend. Women tend to take things like that personally."

"You're right. I was an asshole. I'll admit that." He stared down at the desk for a moment, as though seeking either his own reflection in the scorched mahogany or else some revelation that eluded him. He shook his head and looked up at me.

"Her voice—did you notice it? I don't know. I mean, it didn't sound quite right. Like there was something under it. You know what I mean? You used to be a cop, right? Up in New York. You tell me."

"She wasn't to glad to hear from either of us. That's for sure," I told him.

"That's not what I'm talking about. It was something else."

"I know. I caught it, too. Sounded like stress to me. Of course, she's a lawyer. That could be it."

"What could be more stressful than a hundred and fifty cases at a time as a prosecutor, and that on thirty-two five a year?"

"Divorce."

"She's past that now. I'm not even a blip on the radar screen anymore. You heard how she talked. I guess I knew it was over, but you never know how over it is until you hear it on the phone. I cremated the thing pretty good, didn't I?"

I nodded. "It sounded to me like even the ashes have blown away."

He looked at me for a moment. "Let's get back to you. What were you doing so far out from shore, and don't tell me you were swimming either, not that far out."

I told him about the kayak but omitted the sinking of *The Carrousel*. The omission was louder than the truth itself would have been. We both heard it.

"What time did you head out? In the kayak, I mean," he asked.

"About five in the morning."

"Little early to be out in a kayak, wouldn't you say? There's something else. There's always something else. You're no smuggler. But you were up to something out there. What was it? Drugs?"

"How much coke can you fit into a kayak? Come on. And where did I get it? You think maybe I paddled down to Colombia, loaded up a few kilos, then paddled back? That's a long way, Ruben."

"You were a cop once. If you still were, would you believe that story?"

"Probably not."

"I rest my case. Whatever it was, maybe it will come out, but then again maybe not. But it's there, and you know what I'm talking about. Personally, I don't give a shit. It's not in my domain. I'm just telling you man to man, cop to cop."

I sat quietly. We had a bit of a staring contest, but Cortez got bored and stood up. He turned his back to me and seemed to be reading his own commendations on the wall behind his desk. He stretched his arms above his head and turned to me again.

"You say you went into the ocean at five. We got you at seven. We get a lot of people come out of the water down here, and I've been on patrols with the coast guard. After a while you get a feel for how long a man's been in the ocean, and you were in the water for a lot longer than you say. I just want you to know that."

"All right. So now I know. Any chance I can make a phone call?"

"You just made one."

"How about a little slack for a fellow cop?"

"Ex-cop." He looked annoyed for a moment. "Okay, fuck it." He slid the phone across the desk.

"How about a little privacy?"

"Don't push it."

I punched in Vivian's cell-phone number. Everything had been screwed up, including, of course, our rendezvous. But she was out there somewhere, probably wondering what had happened to me. It was possible, however, that she already knew, that she along with her father had been part of the setup. That was something I didn't like to think about, but I had to consider it all the same. I couldn't ask very many questions with Cortez sitting across from me, but I would be able to get much from the tone of her voice, or so I believed.

Williams's voice said hello.

I started to say something, then thought the better of it and hung up. Cortez sat watching me.

"What's the matter?" he asked. "You look a little pale—even for a guy from Nebraska."

I didn't say anything.

"It's time for you to get out of here," Cortez said. "Go and meet all your new friends. The food's lousy and the weather is hot, but you'll only be here for a little while, which is more than I can say for most of them down there. Stand up.

"It's too bad I don't like you," he said. "Otherwise me and you could be friends."

He opened the door and called in Heckle and Jeckle. They

came in looking skeptical, like a couple of nervous fathers let into the delivery room. They had no idea what was going on.

Cortez put a hand on my shoulder. "Treat this guy right," he said. "Vaughn here used to be a cop up in New York. This whole thing is just a fucked-up misunderstanding. He's going to be here for a few days, so keep an eye on him."

Heckle and Jeckle were a lot friendlier to me as they escorted me out to the pen.

"How come you stopped being a cop?" Ellis asked me.

"I got tired of writing traffic tickets," I told him.

"That don't sound like a very good reason to quit your job," he said.

"You're right. Maybe I was too hasty."

The outdoor cage where they put me might have passed for a schoolyard, except for the razor wire spiraling along the top of the Cyclone fence that surrounded the compound. The sunlight pressed down on the concrete, and the dank air wriggled with the heat, but out to the west the clouds had begun to mass, collecting their strength for the late-afternoon storms that came with the summer months. It was the time of year when hurricanes are born above the coast of West Africa and speed across the ocean like demons made of wind. There was no malice in them, but they were full of destruction. Most died as soon as they were named or else wandered off and disappeared. Some, like Andrew, make it to land, where they changed history. Lay a thousand yards of sidewalk a day and the jungle rains would come again someday and try to take it all back.

But I had a more personal storm to worry about.

How had Williams gotten hold of Vivian's cell phone?

I walked through the gate and looked around and wished that a tempest would suddenly appear and scatter everything I saw to the four directions, including myself. There are places on this earth so full of distress and inertia that only chaos can set them free. Neither is it a mystery that all of those places are made by men and maintained by men, and such a place was the Krome Detention Center that day in late August. I heard the gate close behind me and felt the heat clamp down on my neck in the same instant.

No way I can stay here until Monday, I thought. I had to know what had happened to Vivian.

What was he doing with her cell phone, and why had he tried to kill me? Those thoughts kept circling in my mind like dust devils in a sandstorm, and the only way to stop their incessant whirling was clear though far-fetched. I had to get out of Krome. Two days was too long to wait for answers.

I walked across the yard toward the shadows and the promise of shade. The asphalt threatened to burn through the thin soles of the worn-down sneakers they'd given me. There was a long, dented canopy of corrugated steel that ran the length of the fence and abutted a concrete shoe box of a building. Under the canopy were wooden benches and picnic tables with canisters of water on them. Thirty or forty people sat in the shadows, some of them playing dominoes and others reading quietly in the bad light. A few merely sat staring over the expanse of the yard, watching me come. I was just another stranger walking across the desert toward them, bearing no gifts and bringing no good news.

At the west end of the yard where the clouds were closing fast, three men were playing basketball under a rim with a net made, appropriately enough, of chain. The ball refused to bounce more than a foot above the ground. The man dribbling was forced to run doubled over like a hunchback in order to stay with the ball. When he was twenty feet from the basket, he straightened up suddenly and launched the ball at the rusted rim. It sailed through the hoop and landed in a puddle without bouncing. The men came and looked down at the ball the way you look at a dead dog that belongs to somebody else. There was a brief discussion, and then the men turned and walked away, forfeiting the ball to the sun-cracked concrete.

The Haitians sat with the Haitians, and the Cubans sat with the Cubans. There was a blond man who looked like a sun-drunk German, and a small group of Central Americans with straight black hair and Mayan faces. It was like being at the United Nations, except we were all in jail, a fact that tends to kill much of the joy of the multicultural experience. Everyone was speaking either in Creole or in Spanish. The beleaguered-looking man with the blond hair stood alone by the fence, talking to himself. In his natty, beige, well-tailored if rumpled linen suit and blue bow tie, he was the best-dressed man in the compound. No one paid him any attention. His was a private club, at least until they took him off to the rubber room.

Two men, whom I assumed to be Chinese, sat with themselves. They sat so close together I thought they would merge. I could not imagine the length of their journey, and the dejection concentrated in their faces matched the storms over the swamps in the west. It is a long way back to Haiti when you've nearly died trying to escape from it, but it was not so far that you couldn't try again. The Cubans were, for the most part, home free. But China was another planet. It may have taken them months to get here, and now they were going back. They had the tired faces of men without hope and whose only luck is to endure, yet despite all this, when I smiled at them, they smiled back. Their eyes were unexpectedly kind. I gave them the thumbs-up and went past them into the shade.

There didn't seem to be an American section, so I sat with my back against the corrugated wall of a Quonset hut. A man with muscles like wrought iron dipped in black enamel walked over and asked me for a cigarette by forming a peace sign with his index and middle fingers and moving it back and forth in front of his lips. I patted my empty pockets, and he left me, looking only mildly disappointed. After all, he was in a place where disappointment was as chronic as the sunlight. I sat there and watched as six of the men marched out from under the canopy and began playing soccer with the defeated husk of a basketball.

I have to get the hell out of here, I thought. I'll go nuts if I have to sit here much longer. I glanced around, but all I saw was razor wire, low clouds, and unhappy people. Then, quite suddenly, the fatigue I had been holding at bay with fear and adrenaline swept over me, and I decided not to fight it any longer, so I tilted my head back, closed my eyes, and tried not to think.

I must have dozed off, because the next thing I knew, a guard was shaking my shoulder and telling me that my lawyer was there to see me. There was a crack of thunder in the west, and the wind picked up speed. I got quickly to my feet and followed the guard as he walked toward the main building. We had all but made it to the gate when the first heavy drops of rain began to hit the ground.

I was led into a large, rectangular room with rows of benches and tables and bars on the windows as a reminder of how things were. The guard at the door patted me down before I went in and told me I would be patted down again on my way out. His voice was devoid of inflection; it was the voice of an automaton who had repeated the same words so many times that he was no longer capable of hearing his own boredom. I would not have traded his life for my own despite the alternative. Even the prisoners were better off. They could at least go home, and home, regardless of how much a hell it may turn out to be, still possesses certain latent possibilities. The guard was just waiting for a pension to set him free; his was a life sentence, and time was a conveyor belt heading a day at a time toward the pit.

The room, which smelled of cigarettes and sweat, was nearly empty, and I saw Susan Andrews almost as soon as I walked in. She was seated at a table, her head down, reading what looked to be a brief. There was a bulging leather valise sitting on the table beside her like a mascot, and a can of soda was cupped absentmindedly in her hand. I walked over and sat on the bench across from her.

She didn't look up immediately the way most people would have in a place like Krome, and I was reminded of how fierce her concentration could be. She made one violent slash with her pen, then lifted her head and smiled at me. She had a beautiful face, but the smile ruined it, at least temporarily. The smile she flashed was thoroughly impersonal, a practiced gesture, a concession to civility, a bright coin tossed without consequence to the beggars of the world. There was nothing for Jack Vaughn in that smile, but perhaps I was hoping for too much under the circumstances.

Then the smile vanished and something human came into her expression, and I thought she looked sad and drawn out, though her beauty was still vibrant enough to hide it, except if you had met her back when I had. She smiled for real this time and shook her head as she studied me.

"You look like hell," she said.

"I didn't expect you to make it down here until Monday."

"I almost didn't. The prosecutor asked for a postponement in the case I'm trying. Seems someone down at the property room misplaced a few kilos of evidence. So here I am." She lifted the valise off the table and set it down beside her.

"How's it going?" I asked.

"*You're* asking *me* that?"

I looked her over. She looked like money. Her days as a

prosecutor were way behind her, and the drug money of her former adversaries was making her rich, one overpriced hour at a time.

"How does it feel to be making decent money for a change?" I asked.

She thought that over for a moment. "You may have trouble believing it, but in a lot of ways I liked being a prosecutor better."

"No, I'm not surprised. You're the type that likes to get her hands dirty. Money can't change that, though that is a pretty nice suit you're wearing."

"It's starting to come back to me now," she said, frowning.

"What is?"

"What it was I liked about you. Now, before we get too comfortable, tell me again how you wound up in the drink this morning with a man in a speedboat shooting at you."

I told her almost everything but left out the juicy parts. It was just me, the kayak, and some good and bad luck mixed together. As for Williams, I told her I didn't have a clue. Maybe a case of mistaken identity. Lying to your lawyer was a dead-end street, but I couldn't very well tell her the truth. She would have wanted the whole story, and I could not yet afford to give it to her—especially as there was so much of it I didn't know myself.

"A little suspicious, at least from a cop's point of view, but legally speaking it doesn't sound all that bad. Like I said on the phone, though, I can't do a thing until they bring you down to federal court for arraignment."

"For smuggling?"

"I know it's all bullshit, but they have to go through the motions."

"How long am I supposed to sit here while they figure out I didn't do anything?"

"Maybe it would help if you told them why that guy in the speedboat was shooting at you. That's really what they're after."

Before I could answer, her expression changed and she stood up abruptly, the way you stand up in a bar when the time for talking has passed. I turned around and saw Inspector Cortez walking toward us. His hands were in his pockets, and he was grinning cautiously.

I glanced back at Susan. She looked like a tomahawk about to hurl itself across the room.

"Well, now, what a surprise!" Cortez said. "Just couldn't stay away from me, could you, babe?"

Never let it be said that time heals all wounds. Whoever said that must have suffered from acute amnesia. The lids of Susan's eyes lowered ever so slightly, and the corner of her mouth twitched. She leaned over and hoisted her valise onto the table, slipped the brief she'd been reading inside, and then, with very careful movements, fastened the straps again. She looked up at me. I stood.

"I'll see you down at federal, Mr. Vaughn. Until then have a nice weekend."

Susan came out from behind the bench and went by us like a cold wind from north of the Arctic Circle. The guard at the door started to say something to her but was enough of a survivor to let her pass unmolested. It was just as well he decided to do so, as very few of us are greatly improved by a quick knee directed at the scrotum.

After she had left, Cortez turned to me. "You ever notice how some skirts make a woman's ass look bigger than it actually is?" he asked in a confidential tone.

"I guess it depends on the cut."

"She likes you. I could tell by the way she froze up when I came in. What were you two talking about?"

"About me getting out of here, what else?"

"I don't see you leaving, but don't worry, we'll take good care of you."

I didn't say anything.

They fed me a bologna sandwich and a cup of vegetable soup, after which the same guard led me back to the yard, and I walked around the perimeter of the fence for about half an hour, scoping out the barbed wire and not seeing any way through it. There was not much to like about the situation I was in. Williams was still on the loose and no doubt looking for Vivian and her brother, if indeed he hadn't already found them. Why he was after them, I didn't know. Then there was the question of the other fifty grand the Colonel owed me. If Williams had been telling the truth and he had ordered me killed, then the Colonel and I were overdue for a little chat.

I was involved in some kind of scam, and I needed answers, none of which I was going to find at Krome. The smart thing to do was to wait it out for a few days and hope for low bail. That's what I would have recommended to anyone else. The problem was, it required the kind of patience I didn't have in my DNA. There had to be another option.

Suddenly there were the sounds of sirens coming from beyond the fence. I turned and saw a crowd beginning to gather around a man lying on the ground over near the Quonset hut where I'd been sitting. It was the crazy German. He was on his back, his long, angular body possessed, it seemed, by spasms that were causing his legs to jerk and twitch every which way. The guards were blowing their whistles and trying to force the inmates away. Other guards were trying to hold the twitching man down.

The gates on the other side of the yard swung open, and a red-and-white ambulance, its lights flashing, its sirens wailing, came rushing through. I glanced around. The guards and the other inmates were all distracted. I knew I was looking at the best chance of getting out of that place I was likely to get. There would be trouble later, but later could wait. I began to walk as nonchalantly as I could toward the ambulance, just another curious man in a pale orange jumpsuit.

The paramedics were very good, very fast. People don't give them enough credit. They had the German on a gurney within a minute of jumping out of the van. No one paid any attention to me as I edged ever so slowly toward the far side of the ambulance. All eyes were focused on the mad German. They were having a hard time strapping him down. He was screaming in his native tongue and thrashing around like a lunatic.

I took a quick look around, then dropped to my knees, flattened myself out straight on the hot pavement, and rolled as quickly as I could under the ambulance.

As I said, the paramedics were very good, very fast. The van bounced as they lifted and slid the gurney up and into the ambulance. I held on to the underside of the van and kept myself off the ground as much as possible by wedging my feet alongside the transmission and by using my arms to lift my back. Otherwise someone standing a bit away from the van might see me if they happened to look down. But luckily for me the van rode rather low to the ground and cast a considerable shadow.

It was a hundred yards of hard, hot asphalt and potholes to the gate, and I knew I was going to lose some skin. If they hit a bump the wrong way, I might shake loose, but there was nothing else to do except try. I heard the driver's-side door open and close, then the same thing on the passenger side. The van sank a bit and bounced. I got ready. I reached up and got hold of a piece of the chassis and hoisted my back off the ground. The damned thing burned my hands, but I held on. The van shifted into gear and surged forward.

We were moving fast now. My forearms were starting to ache from the strain of holding myself up, and I was beginning to sag at the middle. For the briefest of moments, my shoulders touched the ground, and if I hadn't found the strength to pull myself up again, my back would have been scraped down clean to the spine.

Then we were through the gate. The muscles in my arms and legs were all used up, and I was going to have to let go whether I wanted to or not—but not at sixty-five miles an hour. What I needed was a stop sign or a traffic light or a sharp curve. Then I felt the van slow and veer slightly left, and I knew I had to let go then, before they came out of the turn. I let my feet hit the ground. My arms were over my head, and I was being dragged. Maybe we were doing thirty. I closed my eyes, let go, rolled to one side, and prayed that nothing on the chassis took my face off. Suddenly I was on my back in the middle of the road. I sat up in time to see an eighteen-wheeler coming fast. Maybe he saw me and maybe he didn't, but he didn't slow down. There was no time to stand up.

I rolled left, and the truck went by like a giant bull.

I got slowly to my feet and looked around. I was on a two-way road with nothing on either side of me except mangrove swamp. There were no streets signs, but I had a fairly good idea of where I was—in the middle of nowhere. The long day, the longest I'd had in quite a while, was heading west where the slate-colored storm clouds were massing and gathering their strength. It was still hot, but an unexpected breeze swirled through the air. It was going to rain big time, and soon.

That far south there was very little traffic on the roads. It would be mostly trucks hauling produce up from the farms in the southern part of Miami-Dade County and maybe a few vans full of migrant laborers heading home. It didn't matter much. In my orange jumpsuit, the official uniform of illegal aliens, I couldn't afford to hitchhike. That meant

I had to walk—but not along the road. The cops would be looking for me soon; that was for sure. There was also the truck driver of the eighteen-wheeler that had nearly flattened me to think about. He had probably seen me roll out of the way at the last moment, in which case he would simply be glad to have missed hitting me. Or he might decide to use his radio and call it in. Either way I had to get off the road.

I limped into the mangrove swamp and headed east. It began to rain. I had no money, no ride, and no idea what I was going to do.

It was slow going, and after an hour I began wondering if I'd made a mistake by busting out of Krome. But there was no way I could have sat still in there for days without going crazy. At least now I had a chance to get some answers. I could worry about the trouble I was in later.

I was tired, thirsty, and, despite the soup and sandwich, still a bit weak from hunger, but at least I was moving. After another mile of the swamp, I came out onto a side road across the street from a shopping mall that with its neon lights and parking lot full of cars seemed like an oasis. I had never been so glad to see and smell a Burger King in my entire life. What I wanted most was a Whopper, a Coke, and a giant order of fries, but I was broke and still dressed in orange. That was going to have to change.

I ran across the street and stood between a corrugated shed and the loading dock of a Kmart, where six or seven workers were loading boxes into the back of a trailer. A security guard appeared at the edge of the bay and looked casually in my direction. I nearly stopped walking. I wondered if he could see me from where he stood. I was almost tempted to turn around and look when he disappeared back inside the warehouse.

My next concern was clothing. The orange jumpsuit I was wearing was a police magnet, and I needed to get rid of it as soon as possible. Then, across the lot, over near the fence, I spotted one of those giant green metal bins put out by the Police Athletic League for people to donate their old clothes. I headed for it through the last of the rain.

There were only a few cars at that far end of the lot, mainly because it was exactly the kind of place where they tell you not to park if you want to avoid getting hit in the head and robbed. I was fairly certain that there were surveillance cameras covering the lot, but I was equally certain that the men watching them were not terribly observant.

I reached the bin and casually stuck my hand into the opening, like a man trying to find a bar of soap in a bathtub filled with bubbles. I couldn't afford to be too selective, but all the same I needed something that fit. The clothes were just jammed in there, and it took me a while to find a shirt I could wear. It was one of those sky blue polyester numbers out of the seventies that looked as though it were made of neon, complete with an extra-wide pimp collar and two missing buttons. I stared at it for a second and was tempted to try my luck again. Then I decided that this was no time to get picky and threw it on the ground, then reached back into the bin and tried to score a pair of pants.

I had just gotten hold of a promising pair when a police car cruised silently into the parking lot. Luckily, I was looking in that direction when it appeared; otherwise he might have caught me with my back turned. Even so, I had just enough time to get behind the bin before the cop car turned right and edged slowly around the perimeter of the lot. I crouched there for five minutes, waiting for him to complete his tortured sweep of the area, and then I heard his car's radio on the other side of the bin. He seemed to stay there a long time, but it was only because he was moving so slowly. A moment later he slid past where I was, and eventually the sound of the radio dispatcher's voice faded away.

Somebody must have found a cache of polyester in an attic somewhere, because the pants were as synthetic as the shirt I had found. The only good thing about them was that they were black. I went behind the bin and changed clothes quickly. It was only then I realized that the pants were too short by a good five inches. It was as though a levee had busted and I had just recently emerged from the flood zone. I decided I could live with them and hurriedly stuffed the jumpsuit into the bin. In five minutes time, I had gone from looking like an escaped illegal alien to looking like an escaped mental patient—not exactly the transformation I'd hoped for, but still an improvement.

Now I needed some money.

I went around to the other side of the mall and into the Winn Dixie supermarket. I didn't like what I was about to do, but I really didn't have much choice. I found the aisle with the canned meats, took a can of Spam down off the shelf, tore the little key off the top, put it in my pocket and walked out the front door. No one gave me a second look. Then I went outside and began looking for a parking meter. I had to walk a few blocks in the rain, but I finally found a row of them behind a post office. I was about to commit my third felony in twenty-four hours.

I got out the little T-shaped key and jimmied open the meter. I knew how to do it because in my rookie year as a cop I had busted a homeless guy who was using the same method up in Manhattan. He and his buddies had stolen over six thousand dollars in quarters by the time we caught them, and it had cost the borough a pretty penny to alter the meters to keep that from happening again. Five minutes and a little finagling later, I had ten dollars in quarters weighing me down. I could have taken more, but I felt bad enough taking what I did.

I went back to the mall and found myself at the rear entrance of the food court. People flashed by without looking at me. I glanced around in search of the restrooms. I had an irresistible urge to see what I looked like, mainly because I was feeling somewhat maniacal and wanted to know whether I looked that way as well.

There was no one in the men's room, so I was able to check myself out in the mirror without interruption. I was dark and windburned, like a man who has walked a long way through a desert without adequate water, and my cheekbones were getting close to the outside air. I needed a shave and my hair was sticking out in various directions, but it was my eyes that scared me the most. They were feral eyes, the eyes of a desperate man. Any cop worth his pay would just get a look at them and his radar sense would be immediately set off. If the eyes really are the windows to the soul, then I needed to find some shades pretty fast.

I washed my face in the sink and used the water to smooth down my hair, which helped some but did nothing about my expression. I went into a stall and sat down on the bowl, although not for the usual reason. The men's room in your average American mall is hardly the best place for meditating, and the smell of shit does not entice the spirit, but it was as close to an ashram as I was going to find. I shut my eyes and got my breathing under control until my heart rate was the only sound in the universe. Being tired helped, and I nearly fell asleep, but I managed to get to the place where I was floating, where the world was gone. I stayed there for ten minutes, coming out of it only when a man let himself into the stall next to mine and began farting like a Gatling gun. I looked in the mirror before I left and was pleased to see that the animal sheen had died down a bit.

I needed a glass of bourbon to brace me, but I had to settle for a pair of very thin hamburgers, some fries, and a small Pepsi. I counted out the change with the patience of a man about to be broke. I took the tray of food, sat at a small table fastened to the wall, and ate while watching the entrance with all the intensity of the fugitive I had become. A skinny black kid with his pants hanging half off his ass went by me. I read the front of his T-shirt as he approached and the back as he was going away. The front of the shirt said KILL ALL THE WHITE PEOPLE. The back said BUT BUY MY CD FIRST. Maybe it was the mood I was in, but I started laughing. In fact, I laughed a little bit too much, so much so that I started to worry about myself, as though I were both lunatic and attending physician. It was worth the worry, though, because by the time I'd stopped chuckling in my little corner, it had come to me who it was I needed to call for help.

There are people you call when you're in trouble and people you call when the trouble involves the police. The Sheik would have come or sent someone in five minutes, but he was on his way to the Bahamas on his private jet. I might have called Johnny Bingo, a Seminole Indian with his own helicopter, but I hadn't seen or heard from him in two years, besides which I didn't have his private number on permanent file in my brain. That left the Space Man. It was his T-shirt the teenager in the food court had been wearing.

I wasted money calling his house, but then the numbers to his cell phone rolled up in front of my eyes. I knew I had them right, except that the sequence of the last two digits wouldn't stay still in my head. It was either 46 or 64, and both looked equally right and equally wrong, so I spun the wheel and dialed the first pair. The phone rang ten times, and I was an inch away from hanging up when a voice out of an oaken barrel answered.

"Yo," the voice said. It was not a query but a statement.

"I need to speak with the Space Man."

"For what?"

"Business."

"Are you white?"

"Yes. Hank, is that you?"

"It might be."

"Hank, Space, come on, man, would you cut the crap for a second? It's me, Jack. I need your help."

"Unless your last name is Daniels, I don't know you."

"Come on, man," I said. "It's me, Jack, Jack Vaughn. You know, trainer to the stars."

There was a pause. "Jack, man! What's up? I thought you was one of my damned fool accountants bothering me about some credit-card shit. I should have known it was you, bro. Not too many white dudes got this number, you hear what I'm saying?"

He was referring to the fact that he had two cell-phone numbers, one for black people and one for white people, the latter being mainly business acquaintances. In the electronic age, apartheid has many forms, and his was easier to understand than most. Somehow I had become part of that small, elite group of white people entrusted with the black number. I'd been made to understand that it was an honor being bestowed on me, and I had taken it as such, especially since the only other Caucasians who had it were a couple of strippers, both of whom were a lot better-looking than I was.

"I need a lift," I told him. "I'm in a bit of trouble. Maybe you can come and get me."

"Car broke down?"

"I wouldn't call you for that."

"Your shit was in the paper today. They say you're importing niggers from Cuba. I guess the personal training didn't work out too good. It was a nice picture of you, though."

"It's more complicated than that. You remember Vivian?"

"The Chinese chick?"

"Vietnamese. Yeah. It involves her. You see what I'm saying?"

"I should have guessed that. She was a bitch and a half from the get-go. Shit. Where you at, homeboy? I'm coming like John Wayne and shit to get your monkey ass."

I told him where I was. He mumbled something to someone else. I thought I heard the sound of traffic in the background muffled by static.

"Back of the parking lot. Twenty minutes," he said. "Doors that go out by Cozzoli's Pizza. Don't make me wait, motherfucker."

Twenty-five minutes later, the car was outside. It was a stretch limousine as white as Moby-Dick and nearly as long, with tinted windows as dark as a pirate's eye patch. I would have preferred something a bit more inconspicuous—maybe an anonymous black sedan capable of dissolving in traffic, but here was the limo coming toward me. The driver coasted over a speed bump doing twenty, and even from thirty yards away I could hear the tremolo of the bass throbbing through the speakers like thunder inside a drum.

I stepped through the sliding glass doors and walked briskly toward my ride. The limousine eased to a stop just as I reached it. The door opened, and a sweet white plume of marijuana smoke rushed out to meet me like a genie lifting out of a magic lamp. A few shoppers stopped and stared as I got in. It must have looked to them as though a derelict had suddenly had a change in luck. I ducked into the darkened interior and out of range of their glances and shut the door behind me, sealing myself into the noisy confines of an alien world that was part nightclub, part traveling bong.

Besides the driver, whom I couldn't see, there were three men in the car, not counting me. All three were black, all three wore Ray-Bans, and I could tell at first glance that none of them were particularly glad to see me. I could also see that my appearance worried them. They studied me with the unabashed intensity of anthropologists who have found something strange in the mists of Borneo. The music hammered at my brain like a team of trolls armed with rubber mallets, but it didn't matter, since no one was doing any talking. I sat on the long seat across from the three men and shot them a smile that bought me nothing in return. So I tucked it away behind my teeth like a wad of gum and sat there watching them, wondering if they were debating the thought of kicking me out.

The man in the middle was Space Man, Hank Watts. He had gained back all the weight he'd lost while I was training him, right before his second CD went double platinum, but this wasn't the time to bring it up. He wore a red shirt, red pants, and red shoes, and on his head sat a small, round, red hat. Around his neck he wore a gold chain I could have melted down for retirement income, and in his right hand he held a joint that looked like an albino cigar.

Hank, a.k.a. the Space Man, took a long toke. His cheeks puffed out like a trumpet player's, and then he blew the smoke from the side of his mouth.

"Chronic," he said, smiling like a connoisseur. "A hundred dollars a quarter Z, but this shit is choice."

The other two men in the limo were hard cases. They had theirs acts down pat. One wore a black nylon stocking cap tied behind his forehead. He looked as though he weighed two-seventy, was thick-boned and massive. He wore a black sleeveless leather vest with nothing but muscle-plated skin underneath. He was wearing a silver crucifix, which made me feel a lot better, as I prefer to travel, whenever I can, with Christians.

The other man was tall and lean and wore white silk pajamas and a pair of black sandals. His hair was done up in cornrows that looked like carefully plowed fields as seen from a plane over the farmlands of Kansas. He had delicate-looking hands with long, slender fingers. And on one of those fingers sat a large gold ring with the raised image of a white skull that no doubt would make a highly memorable imprint on someone's forehead should it come to that.

Hank played his own fingers along the buttons built in to the armrest beside him, and the music went off abruptly. He reached into a pocket, brought out a silver cigarette case, and placed the joint he had just stubbed out carefully inside. All his movements were studied and precise. He clicked opened the attaché case on the floor in front of him and took out a small stenographer's notebook and a gold Cross pen.

"You're a smart motherfucker," he said to me. "I want your opinion about something."

"All right," I said. "And by the way, thanks for the ride."

"I been writin' this song for my new album, but I'm havin' some trouble with the title, if you know what I'm sayin'?"

"Sure."

"So I'm thinking," he said seriously. "Should it be, 'Your Ass Is My Destiny' or 'Your Ass Is My Destination'?"

I thought to myself, Is this my life?

I looked out through the tinted glass and up at the tinted sky and thought the tinted matter over. The Space Man took his art seriously, and a halfhearted reply would be taken as an insult.

"Well," I said. "If you ask me, I'd go with 'Your Ass Is My Destiny.'"

The Space Man looked interested. "Why's that?" he asked.

"I'm not sure, but, you know, 'destination'—it sounds like a one-shot deal, like a road trip or something. 'Destiny,' I don't know, I think it sounds a little more spiritual. You know what I mean?"

Hank nodded approvingly. "You're fucked up, Jack, but I like you. My moms said the same thing." He put the pad back into the case.

"Darin, Reginald," he said in his deep, rich voice, "this strange-looking white man here is a friend of mine. He used to be my trainer. Name's Jack. Jack is back. Hey, man, I think I'm going to write a song about you."

I bumped fists with all of them, and some of the tension seeped out of the compartment, but I could tell that I still made them uneasy, and the reason for that had nothing to do with white or black. It had to do with trouble. I was breathing it. In the mellow atmosphere of the limousine, I was the one discordant element, a human thunderhead on an otherwise sunny day. It wasn't that they didn't like me; it was just that they would all feel a lot better once I left.

I didn't blame them. There were no angels in that car, and Hank had done time for assault up in Larchmont, New York, but his story was not the one you might expect. His father had been a neurosurgeon and his mother a professor of linguistics at NYU. He had an older sister who was a lawyer and an older brother who painted pictures no one understood. But Hank had been wild and not much interested in upper-middle-class life. He had gravitated toward the streets not out of want or despair but because he was simply bored with comfort.

I knew all of this because I had arrested him for selling crack on a bombed-out corner in the South Bronx back when I was a rookie cop and he was a sixteen-year-old kid crying in the backseat. I had looked into the rearview mirror and seen him weeping. I asked him where he lived and drove him home. You can imagine how surprised I was when I saw his house. The place could have been on the cover of *Town & Country.* I had even met his parents. They were fine-looking people from another world, who couldn't understand their son.

That had been ten years ago. Now he was famous and worth $50 million. Then there were the recording studio and the clothing line. We met for the second time at a party at the Sheik's place over on Star Island. He recognized me right away and hired me to train him. He was established by then and married with two shorties, as they say, and was at that stage of things when a man is just starting to feel secure with his good luck. Now he was looking at me as though I were the reincarnation of all the trouble he'd ever had. I didn't feel good about bringing it back to him.

"The cops are after you, bro," Hank said. "Tell me why, and don't leave nothing out. My trouble days are over, and I don't need you sitting in my car looking like the goddamned Fugitive and shit unless you got a good reason to be here."

I told it. The boat, the bodies, Williams, the Colonel and the money, and of course the part about Vivian. That would be the part they would understand best.

They listened, and when I was done, Hank said, "We need to have ourselves a drink, don't you think?"

He opened a small cabinet that was deeper than it looked and brought out an ice bucket, four glasses, and a bottle of Chivas Regal. Hank and Darin opened a pair of Heinekens. The silence came back, but it wasn't vacant. There was a lot of thinking in it. They were weighing my story like a trio of diamond merchants examining a hoard of strange gems on a black velvet cloth.

"What do you think?" I asked.

"I think you fucked up," Reginald said. He was the one in white, the one with the skull on his ring.

"You should have stayed at Krome," Hank said. "Jail never suited me, but you would have been out in a few days. Now they'll be out looking for your ass."

"You wouldn't like sitting in jail if some guy was out looking for your woman, would you?"

Darin, the one with the muscles and the leather vest, cracked his knuckles and leaned forward. I hadn't noticed before, but three of his front teeth were gold-capped. "Anything else you forgot to tell us, Jack-off?"

"Chill out, Darin," Hank said. "I told you homeboy here helped me out some. I don't forget shit like that." Then he looked at me, lifting up his shades.

"You want a beer?" Hank asked.

I said I did, and he handed me a Heineken. If there was anything that tasted better right then, the Good Lord had kept it for himself.

"Where you need to be at?" Hank asked.

"How about Alaska?" I said.

"Try again."

"Coconut Grove. Take me to Miller Drive. It's near the Texaco station."

"What's there?"

"A friend of mine."

"Man or woman?" Darin asked.

"Woman."

"Sheet," Reginald said. All three laughed.

"I hope it's not that Chinese bitch," the Space Man offered.

"Vietnamese. No. It's someone else. My lawyer."

"She going to help you?"

"I hope so."

"What do you think the shit is, dude?" Darin said. "You get rid of the boat, then the old guy sends his boy out to kill you. Must be a reason for that, something you don't know about."

"Unless they just don't want to pay you the other fifty grand," Reginald said.

"I don't think it's that," I said.

"You got a plan?" Hank asked.

"I wouldn't call it a plan."

"Well, you better find one."

"She played you, man," Darin said. "Any fool can see that."

Hank, the Space Man, shook his head. "Listen to the man, Jack. You used to be all laid back and shit. You had your shit together. Now look at you. You're running loose, fucking with illegal aliens. You're dressed like a big, ugly-ass, homeless, beer-drinking John Travolta motherfucker, and to top it all off, the cops are looking for you. Damned, nigger, it's too bad your sorry ass can't sing. With a story like that, you could have been a great rapper."

"Who told you I couldn't sing?" I said.

We all laughed. Darin leaned forward and extended his hand. I took it.

"You are one crazy white man," he said with a lot of feeling. "I hope you don't get killed."

"Thank you," I said.

We were on U.S. 1 headed north. The usual franchises flashed by us in a blur of neon script. Another ten minutes of light traffic and we'd be in the Grove.

"One more thing," I said.

"What you need? Money? How much? You know I got it." Hank leaned forward and picked up his little black handbag from the floor.

"That and something else."

"Such as?"

"I don't think I can get back to my apartment just yet. So I need to borrow a gun."

The three men exchanged glances. "The white boy is high," Darin said.

"What makes you think I got a gun?" Space asked indignantly, his voice rising toward a steep falsetto. "You think all black people have guns? Is that what you're saying? That's the kind of thinking that keeps the black man down."

"Look," I said, "I didn't say you had a gun. All I meant

was that maybe you *might* have a gun. There's no reason to get psychotic about it. Besides, take a good look at me. Do I look like somebody trying to keep anybody down? Plus, dude, you've got a plane. Work with me here, man. Work with me."

All three of them chuckled. The Space Man elbowed Reginald in the ribs. "Give the nigger your gun, Reggie."

Reggie frowned and shifted his weight sideways. "What I got to be giving him my gun for? I just bought it!"

Space shook his head at me as though to say, *See what I have to deal with here?* Then he turned to Darin. "I know you're holding. Don't be giving me that Shirley Temple look, now."

The man in white silk looked like a small child reluctant to share his favorite toy. Sitting there, I suddenly had a growing sense of unreality, as though I'd just found out that the whole mad scene was a dream from which it was impossible to wake up.

"Goddamn!" Space said. "What the fuck am I paying you people for?" With that he reached under his seat and drew out the biggest nickel-plated .45 I'd ever seen and tossed it to me. I caught it, but Space must have seen my expression.

"What's wrong?" he asked.

"Jesus, Hank," I said, "don't you have anything smaller? I could kill a goddamn buffalo with this thing." I turned the gun over and balanced it in my hand. It felt as though it weighed ten pounds.

"What the fuck does this look like to you, man, Gun World or something?" Hank demanded angrily. "Do I have anything smaller? Are you out your goddamn mind? You better get real, man. The shit you're in ain't funny." He shook his head in amazement. "Do I have anything smaller? Shit!"

"All right, all right," I said. "Forget I mentioned it. Do me a favor, okay? Pull over into that lot, behind the burger place," I told him. "I've got to stick this goddamn thing down my pants."

We pulled over next to an ice machine, and I opened the door and stepped out into the dissipated heat of midevening. A stray breeze died, and with it the promise of a cooler night. After the refrigerated air of the limousine, the outside air closed around me like a choke hold. I stuffed the gun down my pants and covered it with my shirt. Space rolled down his window and handed me something. It was a CD, brand new and still wrapped in plastic.

"What's this?" I asked.

"My new CD," he said proudly.

"What's it called?" I wondered if I was actually having this conversation.

"They're Going to Extradite My Love. Maybe I'm crazy," Hank said wistfully. "But I think this shit is my magnum opus."

I glanced at the back of the CD. The names of a few of the songs caught my eye: "Let Me Be Your Pimp" was one of them. There was also a ballad: "Where Have All the White People Gone?"

"I hope you're not getting too mainstream," I said.

"Bro," he said solemnly, "once you been to the outer limits, you got to come back in. Know what I'm sayin'?"

"Better than you think."

"Hold on," Hank said. He leaned down and picked up a small leather case and unzipped it. It was stuffed with bills. "How much you need?"

"Can you spare a hundred?"

Hank looked at me over the rims of his shades and shook his head in mock disbelief. Then with two fingers he simply plucked out a half-inch slice of assorted bills and, without counting them, handed them to me through the window. I thanked him.

He flashed me the peace sign and smiled. "When you're done with the cops and shit, give me a call. You got my number. Now, chill. And remember, I ain't seen you."

I gave a wave to Reginald and Darin, and the tinted window slid upward like a dark curtain going in reverse. In a moment they were all three gone into the traffic. To tell you the truth, I was kind of sorry to see them go.

I walked away from the well-lit gas station and went east on Hibiscus Street toward the apartment building where Susan had moved after dumping Cortez. It was a quiet street with high hedges drowsing over narrow sidewalks like a row of sleepy sentries. The weight of the gun hidden under my pants made me feel more nervous than secure, and I was sorry that I had asked for it, since it confirmed in me the feeling that I had not come out of the sea the same man. I was into something else now, and the world around me seemed far too placid and self-satisfied, while in me every nerve seemed to vibrate with the dangerous possibilities alive in each moment.

Where the hedges ended, a wrought-iron fence began. It surrounded the condominium where Susan lived. The building was six stories high, set well back from the street, and looked like a green-plated icebox with row upon row of windows far too small to leap from if the mood should strike you. I walked around the fence's perimeter till I spotted her black Honda in its berth in the parking lot. I went back to the gate and rang the buzzer.

Her voice asked who it was, and when I told her, there was a very long and important silence that hung like a divide between us. Then the door buzzed, and I went through the gate and across a short path flanked by clumps of small purple flowers up to the glass door, where another buzzer on a timer went off just as I reached it. The lobby was far too bright, and the mirrors lining its walls were far too revealing. If a cop had seen me then, I would have been spread-eagled over the hood of his car in thirty seconds, and that without reference to the gun. I looked haggard and dark and hunted and hollow-faced. The elevator was a long time coming.

I turned left on the sixth floor and saw Susan at the end of the hall, standing in her doorway. She watched me coming toward her, and the closer I got, the more she frowned, and I knew my looks weren't improving as I got closer still. She stepped aside, and I stood nervously in the tiny foyer while she locked the door behind me. She was wearing a pair of faded jeans and a white tank top with her law firm's name printed in blue letters on the front. I remembered they gave them out after the 10K race they hold each year in downtown Miami.

"I guess you did the corporate run again this year. July, wasn't it?" I said.

She looked me over without approval. Her eyes lingered on my high-water bell-bottoms, the cuffs of which ended just under my calves. Then her eyes came up, and it was only then that I realized she'd been crying.

"I ran in that race once," I continued. "It's a 10K, right? You may not believe it, but I think one time I ran seven-minute miles. Of course, I was lighter then."

I smiled. Susan didn't.

"How did you get out of Krome?" she asked.

"I don't think you want me to tell you that."

"Probably not. Otherwise I'd have to call the police."

There was something a bit wrong with the way she said it. The tone was off, her voice far away from her words. She seemed distracted, enough so that the sight of me standing there in all my lack of glory was merely a mild annoyance, when in reality my just being in her place was a threat to her license to practice law. I had expected a tirade and then, if I was lucky, a little help, but not this red-eyed look of emotional distraction.

"What's wrong?" I asked. "It can't be me. I just got here."

She looked at me for a long moment. I thought she was on the verge of throwing me out, but her face softened, and she smiled.

"You know," she said, "strange as it may seem, I'm actually happy to see you."

"That may change."

She came forward and hugged me around the shoulders. That's when I really started to get scared, so much so that I forgot to hug her back and just stood there like a column holding up the ceiling. Then I woke up and held her gently, her blond hair under my chin, and I felt my shirt get wet from her tears. If it weren't for the fact that I was already a fugitive, I would have run for the hills.

Susan pulled away and looked down at my attire. "I won't ask where you got those clothes—and by the way, you need a bath. You smell like three nights in Central Park."

"Sorry, but I've been having a strange evening. Listen to me, Susan. I'm not here. We're not talking right now. None of this is happening. Okay? The last time you saw me was this afternoon."

"You busted out of Krome."

"Right."

"You're a complete ass. Come into the living room."

There was nothing fancy about the room. Hardwood floors with a faded-out Persian rug under a lacquered coffee table with a glass top. A black sectional couch, an ottoman next to it, and a tall, healthy-looking ficus standing guard by the window; a fireplace with yellow roses instead of a fire; bookshelves free of all books save for a few lonely volumes crowded in one high corner like orphans huddled on a precipice. There was also a desk with a computer, a printer, and a small lamp, and next to that a treadmill facing the window.

Even after a year, there were still unpacked boxes along

the walls. In my time I had seen many rooms like this one. It was the apartment of a young woman who worked long hours and was seldom at home. I went and sat down on the ottoman. There was so little give in the cushion that I may well have been its first customer. There was music playing, but it was turned down so low it sounded like a woman whispering to herself.

Susan returned carrying a bottle of red wine, a corkscrew, and two glasses, which she handed to me before plopping down on the sofa. I poured us each a drink. I suppose I should have been happy that I wasn't her first problem of the night, but I was a little worried now that it seemed clear she wasn't angry at my having shown up. You know you've been living wrong when even simple hospitality scares you.

"How come you're glad to see me?" I asked. "I'm not exactly helping your career by being here."

"Fuck my career, all right?"

"Mine, too." I raised my glass.

She drained hers, and I poured her another. She took a sip and set the glass down.

"You can't stay here," she said.

"I don't intend to."

"You've grown some since your mother bought you those pants."

"They were on sale."

"You lied to me this afternoon. Didn't you?"

"The part I told you was true."

"What about the part you didn't tell me? The part that made you break out of Krome when all you had to do was wait the weekend."

"I know. I left out a couple of things."

"This would be the time to put them back in."

"The less you know, the better off you'll be," I told her. "Client-attorney confidentiality goes only so far."

"Does that mean you've committed a felony?"

I hesitated for a moment. "Maybe. Maybe not."

She started to say something, then stopped and stared at me with a look of puzzlement. "Why do you keep squirming around like that? You got some kind of rash or something?"

The butt of the .45 had been digging into my groin, and no matter which way I sat, I couldn't get comfortable. Finally I gave up and just put the damned thing on the table.

Susan stared down at the gun, then looked up at me. "Have you lost your mind? Where'd you get that thing from?"

"I borrowed it from a friend. It was the only one he had."

"You have to leave now," Susan said definitively. "Really, Jack, this is too much." She stood up.

"Okay," I said. "I'll admit I'm in a little trouble. I did a favor for a friend, and it kind of backfired on me. I think they might be in trouble, too. I came here because I just needed to get inside someplace safe for a little while. Then I have to get back to the beach. I need a shave and a change of clothes. Then I'm going to try and set things right."

"How? With that?" She pointed at the gun.

"I hope not, but I'm dealing with some rough people."

"Tell me one thing: Is this about drugs?"

"No. Definitely not."

"What then? You have to tell me something."

"It's personal."

"I'm your lawyer, remember?"

"Maybe I should fire you. I'd be doing you a favor."

I could see she was angry now. Whatever was bothering her hadn't added to her limited patience.

"I need a lift back to my place. I've got to get some other clothes before I go look for Vivian."

"Vivian? I thought she ditched you for a guy named Matson."

"She did."

"What happened?"

"She got herself into some trouble, and I tried to help her out. Matson ended up being a bit more of an asshole than I thought he was."

"So did you. He was some kind of movie producer, wasn't he?"

"That's right. He was."

"What's this all about, Jack? You should have stayed at Krome."

"I should have stayed in New York."

"You can't go back to your apartment. For sure they'll have sent a man out there by now. You know how it works after that."

"I know. Anyway, I have a few stops to make first."

"Where do you think your little *girlfriend* is?" She gave the word girlfriend a nasty twist when she said it.

"I'm not sure. Probably somewhere in South Beach."

Susan sat staring at me, and judging by the expression on her face, I would say she considered me too far gone to reason with. She was right, but it wasn't just Vivian I'd be looking for. I would be looking for Williams, too.

She stood up and stretched her arms over her head and made a half turn to her right so that her joints made a cracking sound. Even under those conditions it was hard not to notice the shape she was in. Her arms looked strong, but the triceps weren't straining to break the skin. Under her jeans the slight bulge of her quadriceps told me she had kept at the wind sprints I'd prescribed for her. Those and a weight workout once a week had been all those legs of hers had required, that and trying to kick me upside the head whenever she had the chance.

"What are you looking at?" she asked.

"I did a good job on you."

"Let's go," she said. "I want you out of here in twenty minutes."

"Where are we going?"

"Come with me into the bedroom."

"Thanks, but I don't have the time right now. How about a rain check?"

Susan didn't dignify the remark with an answer.

I stood up and followed her down the hallway. So great is the sensitivity of men that they will notice a woman's ass even on their way to lethal injection. I had always considered the fact that I'd never made a pass at Susan one of my greatest accomplishments as a human being. Now I was wondering if I'd been ill.

By the time I reached the bedroom, Susan was already standing before the open door of her closet. I glanced around the room. There wasn't much to look at. A red futon mattress against the wall, the sheets swirled and swept into a whirlpool at the center of the bed. There was an old-style rocking chair that sat with the air of a departed mourner facing the louvered windows, and along the other wall there was a white dresser with framed photos across its entire length. Unpacked cardboard boxes lined white walls hung with a few diplomas and official-looking certificates, and everywhere the air of loneliness kept at bay by a life of haste. Susan's place was not so much a home as it was a pit stop between the office and the car. It was hard to believe she had lived here for as long as she said.

I watched as she tugged a pair of black trousers and a white dress shirt from their hangers. She turned and tossed them to me without a word, as though she were throwing them out the window. I felt the anger coming off her, and mixed with that anger was something else, maybe frustration. I caught the shirt and pants and laid them across my arm like a valet.

Without looking at me, Susan moved next to the dresser and began rummaging through a bottom drawer, and I began to think of the time when I'd had a drawer like that in Vivian's place and what that drawer had meant and what it had not meant. She came up holding a pair of briefs and a pair of white sweat socks and threw them my way with the air of a woman glad to be rid of things not her own, as though the clothes were visitors who had overstayed their welcome. I caught the briefs but bungled the socks. When I straightened up, she was looking at me, and when I looked at her, I could see that the tears were on their way back.

"You can take a shower in there," she said, pointing at the door to the bathroom. The door was as white as the barren walls and blended into them like snow on snow.

"Whose clothes are these?" I asked.

"My boyfriend's. Ex-boyfriend, I should say."

"Your boyfriend?"

"A lawyer at the Justice Department. About a week ago, he stopped calling. Turns out he forgot to tell me he was married."

"How'd you find out?"

"His wife was nice enough to call me. Just about an hour ago. Now you show up. Just take your shower and go, all right? I've had enough of men for one night."

I started to say that I knew that and to thank her for her trouble, but she had already turned her back and was closing the door to the bedroom behind her.

I showered with a soap that smelled of fresh-cut flowers and used two pink razors to scrape the hard days from my face and neck. I wiped the steam from the mirror and was glad to see I no longer looked quite as insane, but instead like a man who only needed a week or two of sleep. Then I went into the bedroom again and began to get dressed. Everything fit except for the pants, which were a little wide in the waist. Maybe the gun would take up the slack. I noticed a brush on the dresser and went over and had just begun brushing my hair with it when I glanced down at the framed photos I'd seen before.

There was one of Susan with her parents. It was in a gold frame, and she looked about five years old; a few more with an older boy who looked like her brother. There was one of her in a white cheerleader's outfit complete with pom-poms and a fresh-faced, sun-soaked beauty that even when you're lucky enough to be born to it only visits for a while. There was another photo of her in cap and gown in front of a stately looking building with ivy clinging to its walls, her parents beaming proudly on either side of her.

They were nice pictures, and they took some of the coldness out of the room, and I was just scanning them when my eyes froze on a framed photo hanging on the wall in an array that included her diplomas from college and law school. It was a group photo taken at some kind of presentation or awards ceremony. The people in it were standing behind a table stacked with what appeared to be packages of heroin or cocaine—your standard big-bust photo. There were seven people in the shot besides Susan. One I recognized as the former chief of police of Miami-Dade County, now retired. Another was of the mayor. There were three others: two women and a man. I glanced casually at their grinning faces. Then something registered, and I scanned backward.

The hand doing the brushing stopped in midair. I set the brush down and eased the picture frame off its mounting to get a better look at it. There was no mistake. I was just about to replace it when I felt a presence behind me.

"What are you staring at?" Susan asked.

"I was just checking out the photo. Hope you don't mind," I said. My hands were trembling.

"That's from when we busted the Falcone brothers," Susan said. "You remember them, don't you?"

"Big-time coke dealers," I said, my eyes still riveted on the man at the far right of the photo. "I remember. They got deported to Colombia, didn't they?"

"That's right. Then they mysteriously escaped and went back into business again, bigger and better than ever."

I was biding my time. I didn't want to make her suspicious.

I pointed at the last man in the photo, the man I'd seen before but whom no one would ever see again. The other dead man on the white yacht.

"Who's this guy?" I asked nonchalantly.

"Why? You know him?"

"I don't know. I might have seen him somewhere."

"His name is Duncan. Harry Duncan. He's with the DEA."

"The DEA?" I asked.

"Worked undercover. He asked me out once, but there was something about him I didn't like. What's wrong? You know him from someplace?"

"No, he just looks familiar, that's all."

She must have noticed something odd in my expression. I had a hard time looking her in the eye, but with a woman, avoiding that is the worst thing you can do. Ten years of listening to liars had sharpened her senses to an unpleasant acuteness.

"What are you not telling me, Jack?"

"Quite a bit. Anyway, I think I should be leaving now. I've been too much trouble already."

"You should have thought of that before you got here," she said.

"All right, but before I go, how about one last request?"

"Such as?"

"You wouldn't happen to have an extra banana lying around, would you?" I asked. "I haven't eaten much lately."

"There's a Denny's two blocks south of here," she said sternly.

"Thanks."

I walked into the living room, retrieved the .45 from the coffee table, tucked it under the waistband of my borrowed trousers, and started for the door. I felt old, tired, and evicted. The thought occurred to me that I should just turn myself in and get it over with, that in my present condition a quiet jail cell would seem like a retreat. I walked very slowly toward the front door. I was not sure that I could face what was on the other side of it.

"Hey, you!" Susan yelled from behind me. "Come back here."

"What's the matter?"

"Go sit in the living room," she commanded. "I'll make you a sandwich. Tuna fish. It's all I've got."

"Thanks."

I went into the living room and sat on the couch, as thankful for the brief reprieve as the condemned man who gets the governor's call at the last minute. From the kitchen came the sounds of cupboards opening and closing and then the muted whir of an electric can opener going to work. I glanced down at the coffee table, my eyes skimming over the magazine covers. There were three ancient issues of *People* and a copy of *Time*. There was also a copy of the *Miami Herald*. It was two days old, but as I hadn't done much reading lately, I picked it up and began flipping idly through the pages.

I couldn't really concentrate. A few lines here and there. Then, on page eight, something caught my eye, and just like that I was all bright light and deadly focus.

It was a story about the Colonel.

"I don't have any mayonnaise!" Susan shouted from the kitchen. "Is mustard okay?"

"Fine, that's fine," I shouted back.

I read slowly, taking it all in.

"What kind of bread?" Susan yelled. "Stale white or stale wheat?"

"Either one is fine!" I said, not paying attention.

It seemed that Pellucid Labs, the Colonel's company, was in mucho trouble, to say the least, and was under investigation by several federal agencies, including the FDA, the DEA, and, worst of all, the IRS. Someone had altered the results of the clinical trials of certain "promising" antidepressants in order to win FDA approval. The actual results, uncovered with the help of a former researcher now turned whistle-blower, were that the drugs in question produced various "undesirable side effects," contradicting the findings of the researchers cited in Pellucid Labs' initial reports. The company had also filed for bankruptcy and was seeking additional financing from an undisclosed consortium of venture capitalists who themselves were the subject of a government probe into allegations concerning the illegal transfer of funds from Pellucid's accounts into offshore banks in the Cayman Islands.

There were two interspersed paragraphs describing Patterson's military and scientific careers by way of counterpoint: the Rhodes Scholarship, West Point, Vietnam and his heroism during the Tet Offensive back in '68. There was mention of the Purple Heart and the Bronze Star he had won. Despite my having known him, it was hard not to envy his biography. In an age of myopic specialization, the Colonel had been a Renaissance man. He had walked out of obscurity with nothing but brains and a set of balls and had become a war hero and a millionaire. The gist and tone of the article were all too familiar: Someone who had achieved everything was on the verge of losing it all—another reassuring message for the mediocre who had never dared to reach beyond the meager possibilities of the next paycheck and a sure pension. Back in your place, Colonel Patterson. Who in the hell did you think you were? In the end, despite your genius (which, by the way, we always hated you for, even while we were applauding you), you turned out to be just another liar and another fraud, and we'll all sleep the better for having known it.

I finished the article and refolded the newspaper—slowly, as though it were a Christmas present opened prematurely. My head was so crowded with facts it felt like a holding cell after a riot. I closed my eyes and tried to think, but then my stomach grumbled and once again the only thing that made any sense was stale bread, tuna fish, and mustard. All the rest was babel. All the rest, including Pellucid Labs, could wait.

Then the doorbell rang.

I turned around. Susan was standing in the doorway to the kitchen.

"Are you expecting someone?" I asked.

"Not at this hour," she said, frowning.

She swept past me and opened the peephole. "Who is it?" she demanded. By that time I was standing beside the door with my back against the wall.

"Susan Andrews? Agent Hackbart, FBI. Please, this will only take a moment."

Susan glanced at me angrily. All I could do was shrug my shoulders.

"FBI?" Susan said. "What is it you want?"

"Please, Miss Andrews. It won't take long."

She glanced again at me. "I've got company," she said to the door. "Come back tomorrow."

I gave her the thumbs-up, but the hand it was attached to was trembling again.

The voice on the other side of the door sounded very solemn and full of foreboding. "We're not going away, Miss Andrews. We'll stay here all night if we have to. Let us in and we'll be gone in twenty minutes."

"Tell him to hold on," I whispered.

Susan leaned closer. "What are you going to do?"

"Hide the gun. Tell them to wait."

I ran back into the bedroom and stuffed the gun under one of the pillows on the bed. Then I came back into the living room, sat myself down on the sofa, crossed my legs, and tried to look like Cary Grant, as Cal had once suggested. We were six stories up, and I couldn't fly. The only thing I could do was look nonchalant and hope that they didn't recognize me. It was impossible to say what the odds of that were. I nodded at Susan, and she opened the door. My heart was doing its best to nail my back to the sofa.

The door swung in as Susan stepped back, and I was looking at three men in three dark suits. Three pairs of eyes found me at the same moment, froze for an instant, then fanned the room before returning to me. I sensed confusion and even disappointment, but there was no recognition in the way they looked at me. Even so, it was a moment before they took their eyes from mine, and all the while I sat there with my leg crossed over my knee with my arm extended along the back of the couch. I waited until they holstered their guns before I moved, and then it was only to sit forward with both feet on the floor.

"What's this about?" Susan asked. "Don't you know what time it is?"

Two of them were rookies, both in their late twenties. One was black, and one was white, but the academy at Quantico had somehow made them into twins. I wasn't worried about either of them, but the older man in the middle was something else. He was about fifty, the shortest of the three, and the first thing you would think when you saw him was that he was a cop.

He had the permanent tan and seared-looking skin of a sailor in the tropics, or maybe of a tennis nut who plays long sets in the middle of the day. His brown hair was fading to gray, and he had a slight stoop, as though he'd spent a lifetime looking under things. It was his eyes, however, that gave him away, and he knew how to use them. He was using them on me now, gauging my reaction to his scrutiny. I had seen a lot of eyes like that when I was on the force in New York, especially among the homicide detectives. They were the kind of eyes that would remember you.

"I'm sorry, Miss Andrews," he said, "but this is important."

"In that case let me see some ID, gentlemen."

Hackbart glanced at me, but nothing in his eyes registered recognition. I met his gaze and held it, the way you do when you've got nothing to hide. The three of them fished out their wallets, but I knew they were legit. Susan was just buying time.

Susan studied their badges. Hackbart smiled at me. It was the phoniest smile I had ever seen. "I see you have a guest after all," Hackbart said.

I stood up as they approached me, and I shook hands with all of them. It was clear that they didn't know quite what to make of me. Hackbart was still doing his staring routine, trying to see if I had any reason to be nervous. I smiled back at him.

"Are you guys really FBI?" I asked with false eagerness. No matter how dour and professional cops may like to appear, they love it when you act impressed by them. The rookies did their best to hide their smiles. Hackbart frowned, but at least now I had him thinking I was a simpleton, which is generally a good thing to do when you're talking to the police. It relaxes them.

"I'm sorry," Hackbart said. "I didn't catch your name."

"Jack Vaughn," I said, hoping that my name—at least as of yet—would mean nothing to him.

"I see. You're . . ."

"A friend. I just flew in from Rochester this afternoon. I didn't think Sue would call the FBI on me so soon though." I glanced over at Susan and grinned. "Say, you guys want a beer?"

Hackbart looked at me with an expression that was nearly sympathetic.

"None for me," he said. I had succeeded in diluting his suspicions. He turned back to Susan.

"May I sit down?" he asked.

"Of course."

Hackbart told his men to wait downstairs. After they left, he sat in one of the wicker chairs that flanked the coffee table.

"Would that be Rochester, New York?" he asked.

"No, sir, Rochester, Minnesota. You know, where the clinic is."

"Clinic?"

"Sure, the Mayo Clinic."

Susan came back and sat in the other wicker chair. Hackbart wanted me out of there, but he couldn't think of a polite way to say so. He scanned my face as though trying to assess the exact degree of my stupidity, whether I in any way posed a risk to his investigation. Then he turned his attention back to Susan.

"You know a DEA agent named Harry Duncan?" Hackbart asked.

Susan almost glanced at me then but caught herself just in time. Still, I think Hackbart sensed something. He gave me the stare treatment again. I pretended not to notice.

"We worked together when I was with the D.A.'s office," Susan told him. "What of it?"

"When was the last time you saw him?" Hackbart asked.

"That's not exactly an answer to my question."

Hackbart smiled. "I forgot. You're an attorney. You're the one who gets to ask all the questions, right? Okay, Duncan's under investigation. Your name was in his Rolodex. He also sent you a half dozen or so e-mails asking you for a date. As far as we could tell from your replies, that never happened, but even so, we need to check you out. You understand that, don't you?"

Susan took a chocolate from a box on the table and began to unwrap it. She looked over the nougat, then popped it into her mouth. She was still buying time, trying to get it together.

"You must have seized his computer to know all this," she said. "What kind of investigation are we talking about here?"

Hackbart didn't answer. He was back to giving me the once-over. The best cops are nearly psychic in their ability to catch even the slightest fluctuation in a person's demeanor, and unfortunately for me, Hackbart was of them.

"May I ask how long you'll be in Miami, Mr. Vaughn?" Hackbart asked.

"I head down to the Keys tomorrow. Gonna do a little snorkeling, a little fishing. Then I'm off to Costa Rica for some windsurfing."

"I see," he said. "You understand that everything you hear tonight is confidential? Otherwise I'll have to ask you to leave."

"Look, Hackbart," Susan said, "you can't come into my house and tell anybody what to do. Understand? You want to talk to me alone? Fine. I'll come by the Bureau tomorrow. I know where it is. If you don't know where Duncan is, then neither do I. In which case neither of us is of any use to the other. Now if you have something to ask, ask, but don't be rude to my friends."

"Uh-oh," I said, "now you've made her mad! Better get your gun out, sir!"

Hackbart was silent for a moment. "All right, I apologize. Let's start over. Did Mr. Duncan ever speak with you about his work?"

"What else do feds talk about when they're working together?"

"How long have you known him?"

"About a year. He testified in some of the cases back when I was with the D.A."

"Did he ever tell you where he was born?" Hackbart asked.

"I think he mentioned New Jersey, Union City. Maybe Newark. Someplace like that."

"I don't think that's quite correct, Miss Andrews. May I call you Susan?"

"Let's keep it formal. It's too late to make friends."

"Duncan was born in Cuba," Hackbart said.

"That's insane!" Susan said. "Duncan's no more Cuban than I am. Where are you getting this stuff from?"

"His real name is Bernardo Reyes Díaz. Small detail. I guess he forgot to mention that," Hackbart said.

"He told me he was half Irish," Susan said to no one in particular.

"Well," I said, "you know how the Irish lie."

Both of them glared at me.

"Díaz—or Duncan, as you knew him—was a lieutenant in the Cuban army," Hackbart continued. "He served in Angola during the seventies. After that he was an intelligence agent. He arrived in Miami via Spain a few years ago as far as we can tell. In other words, he's a spy."

"So much for background checks," Susan said.

"And they let him into the DEA?" I said. "Wow!"

"Not knowingly, no," Hackbart said, scowling at me.

"There was a real Harry Duncan, a student at the University of Miami who died in a motorcycle accident in 1985. Díaz stole his identity. It's easy enough to do, and besides, he had help. This town is crawling with Cuban spies. They helped him set things up. The false employment records, the good references, credit history, the whole nine yards. Then he got into the Agency. You want to know how we found all this out? Well, every now and then we catch ourselves a spy, and, as is usually the case, he gives someone up to save himself." He looked at Susan. "This time it was Duncan."

"Why'd he join the DEA?" I asked.

Hackbart glared at me. "You ask a lot of questions for a fellow from Minnesota," he said. "But the answer is, we don't know. There have been rumors for years that Castro is involved in the drug trade. If they're true, it may be he wanted someone on the inside to see if we were getting close to anything. Fidel is a first-class asshole, but he has an image to protect. He wouldn't want it to get out that he was making money off of the narcotics trade through the Caribbean. That wouldn't look too good to his friends at the United Nations."

"But Harry didn't even speak Spanish," Susan said hopelessly.

"Not to you he didn't. By the way, he also spoke Russian. Did you know that?"

"So what now?" Susan asked. "You think maybe he went back to Cuba?"

"It's possible. His cover here is blown. All we know is that he stopped using his cell phone a few days ago. That much we do know, because we've been keeping an eye on him for a while now. He had two phones. Two cell phones, that is. One he used for work. The other he didn't think anybody knew about, but we knew. By the way, do you know a man by the name of Randy Matson?"

Susan hesitated, and once again she managed to keep from jerking her head in my direction.

"I don't think so," she said. I let out a breath. "Who's he?"

"He was a friend of Duncan's," Hackbart said.

"Don't know the name. Should I?" Susan asked.

"Matson makes stag movies. Pornography, but we think that may be a cover. We've been watching him, too. Matson had a yacht named *The Carrousel*. A very nice boat. You'd have to sell a hell of a lot of dirty movies to buy a boat like that. The last time we saw it, he was anchored off Sunset Beach. We haven't figured out why it was there yet. The coast guard had it under surveillance, but the cutter assigned to the detail got called away on an emergency. They were tracking a boatload of illegals, and they didn't figure the yacht would leave in the middle of the night, but they were wrong. They're so underfunded over there it's a wonder they make payroll, let alone help us out. Now the yacht is gone."

"Man," I said, "this is just like the movies!"

Hackbart grinned. "I hope I'm not ruining your vacation, though from the look of that burn, I'd say you've already had too much sun. You've been to Miami before, haven't you?"

"Sure, lots of times."

"I know. I've seen you."

"Really? Where?"

"That I don't recall, but I've seen you." He stood up. "Doesn't matter."

"You ever go to Spurs?" I asked.

Hackbart frowned. "What's that?"

"Oh, nothing. Just a nightclub," I told him. "It's a gay place. I go there a lot. I thought maybe you had seen me there."

Hackbart looked at me in amazement and laughed. His white teeth flashed liked unmarked dice. "No, I don't think it was there." He turned to Susan, who was still sitting in the wicker chair, staring at the floor as though there were a movie playing on it.

"I'm still trying to figure out where I know you from," he said in a friendly tone of voice. I could tell it was really bugging him. I wouldn't have been surprised if he ran a check on me the moment he got back to the office.

"It'll come back to you," I said.

"Say, you don't have to answer this if you don't want, but I was just wondering. You don't by any chance have a criminal record, do you?"

"Not yet," I said, grinning. "But the night is young."

"Not for me," Hackbart said. "Well, good night, folks. I'll be in touch."

The agent gave me one last long, searching look and closed the door behind him. Neither Susan nor I said anything to one another for a few seconds. We were both enjoying the sudden pleasure of Hackbart's absence. But not for long.

"You going to tell me how you know Duncan?" Susan asked sternly. "Or should I just strangle you now?"

"Maybe Matson introduced him to me someplace. I don't remember," I said. "In my business you meet a lot of people."

Susan put her head down for a moment, then looked up. "They're not after you," she said. "Not the FBI anyway. They're a bit myopic when it comes to a case. If they do anything at all, they'll turn it over to the local cops, unless they believe that crap about you being a smuggler. That's a federal matter, but I don't care about that right now. I just want you out of here before I lose my law license."

"It's strange, that stuff about Harry," I said absentmindedly. "I mean him being a Cuban. Maybe Matson was, too. Shit, maybe we all are."

"Maybe you should leave. I'm not in the mood for you right now."

I stood up. "I need a lift to South Beach."

"The son of a bitch was a spy," she said, more to herself than to me.

"I could take a cab, but I'll need transportation once I get there."

"You think I'm stupid, don't you?" Susan asked.

"Susan, I have to head out."

"What the hell is going on here, Jack? Why are you bullshitting me? You know Duncan. Tell the truth. You were staring at his picture in my bedroom. Why? Because he's so cute? Come on! And Duncan knew Matson. Tell me you didn't know that."

"Not until fairly recently," I said. "But I can tell you this much: They're both dead."

"What?"

"They're dead. Dead and buried."

"Tell me what's going on here, Jack. Were they murdered?"

"That's right. Shot. Both of them."

Susan stared at me for a hard moment, her eyes full of doubt, perhaps even fear.

"I didn't kill them, if that's what you're thinking," I said.

"But you know who did."

"I thought I did, but now I'm not so sure. Listen to me, Susan. I was wrong to come here, but it's too late to change that. You're right: There is a lot I'm not telling you, but the less you know, the more you can deny without lying about it. Right now I just need one more favor, and then I'll be out of here."

"You've got to be kidding, right?"

"Do you still have that old BMW you used to drive? I need to borrow it."

To my surprise, Susan said nothing. She just stared at me searchingly, as though for the first time finally realizing how truly crazy I really was. Still without saying a word, she got up, fetched a set of keys from a rack by the front door, and tossed them to me.

"Take it. I'm not sure if it will start," she said. "I haven't used it in a while. It's parked way in the back of the garage with a gray plastic cover over it. "

"I was expecting an argument."

"Why bother? You'll be in jail soon enough anyhow."

I checked the peephole before opening the door. The hallway was filled with light and emptiness and the quiet of sleeping people. I opened the door and stepped out.

"You're a very stupid man," Susan informed me.

"I realize that."

"Is she worth it?"

"Maybe, maybe not. Either way, I can't leave it half done."

"I'm not sure I can be your attorney anymore, Jack, not after this."

"I understand." I showed her the key. "Thanks for the car and the clothes."

"Don't bother calling me when they catch you," Susan said before shutting the door in my face.

I stood in the hallway, staring at the peephole for a moment. Then my stomach reminded me about the famous tuna fish sandwich again. I considered ringing Susan's bell to ask for it, but something told me I had better let it ride. One more squeeze and I'd probably wind up with a black eye.

The old Beemer was where she said it would be, at the far end of the garage shrouded in form-fitting gray plastic as snug as a bodysuit. I peeled the skin off and stowed it in the small trunk, then climbed into the cockpit and prayed. I turned the key in the ignition and heard the sweet, happy purr of the engine.

Five minutes later I was on U.S. 1 heading north toward

the beach. Only three courses of action now made any sense
at all. The first was to keep driving until I hit Canada and
then get a job training Eskimos. The second was to find
Vivian and Williams, or maybe even Nick, with the hope
that the truth, whatever it turned out to be, would be better
than the chaos and uncertainty of not knowing. Of course,
there was the third alternative of turning myself in and telling everything I knew to the cops, of playing the part of
the pawn who'd gotten used like a condom on a one-night
stand.

But the more I thought about it, the less I liked that last
idea.

Maybe in the end they would give me my life back, but
not right away, and that's why I didn't do it. I couldn't see
how I could avoid doing time—and not just because I'd ille-
gally performed a burial at sea. By sinking Matson's yacht,
I had also sunk crucial evidence in an investigation, if not
the entire investigation itself, and investigations take time to
set up, especially when they involve more than one branch
of law enforcement. A big case might take years to build. A
dozen assorted careers might depend on its successful conclusion, and then I came along in a kayak and sent all that
hard work down to the bottom of the sea—not deliberately
perhaps, but permanently nonetheless.

I would have to pay for that. My ass would be grass, and
the government would be the lawn mower. It might be that
they would get me for obstruction of justice or even as an
accessory to murder, though that charge wouldn't stick. And
then there was my famous breakout from Krome. That one
was good for a couple of months. The point was that they
would do whatever they could to make my life miserable
for as long as they could, and that would mean keeping me
in jail for as long as possible. Once I was inside, it might
even be revealed that once upon a time Jack Vaughn had

been a police officer up in New York City, and then the real
fun would begin. If you think the police lack a flair for ven-
geance, then you need to hang out with them more often.

So I was in no rush to put myself in the hands of the police,
the FBI, the DEA, or even the ASPCA for that matter. Sitting
passively in the slammer waiting for fate to call my number
made no more sense to me at that moment than being free.
Jail is a lot like death in that respect: It makes sense to avoid
it for as long as possible, and I felt more than a little vengeful
myself. So since there's nothing more pathetic than a vengeful man sitting in a jail cell, I intended to stay free.

Vivian and Williams were up to something, and I intended to find out what that something was. There was no
sense in going down alone. I hit a button, and the sunroof
slid open. Orion winked at me; the wind tore at my hair.
I put the Space Man's CD into the tiny slot and turned the
music up full blast. They're going to extradite my love. I
threw my head back and laughed without reason. It was a
catchy tune, though:

> Cincinnati, New Orleans, New York City, too,
> They caught my ass in Tennessee,
> Now I'm comin' right home to you.
> They're going to extradite my love, baby,
> They're going to extradite my love.
> Now take your butt to the bondsman, baby.
> 'Cause I got shit to do. . . .

It was a good song. Double platinum at least.

Vivian owned an apartment on Michigan Avenue out in
South Beach, in a building called Tuxedo Park, just down
the street from the firehouse and a block south of Flamingo
Park, where the municipal swimming pool used to be. I
drove by the building twice but saw nothing suspicious.

The block was dark. The tall trees muted the glow from the streetlamps, and it was as quiet as a lane in a small town. On my third sweep, I pulled into a space about sixty or seventy yards up the block and across the street from her place and shut off the engine.

The flood lamps behind the hedges threw up a barrage of light that lit the sea green facade of the building and the neon letters that spelled Tuxedo Park as bright as the marquee at a Hollywood premier. I checked my watch; it was five minutes to twelve. Knowing Vivian as I did, she would be just about ready to leave for the nightclub her brother had bought with money from his trust fund, a place called Embers over on Collins. Williams, if indeed he was looking for her, too, would probably be aware of this, so the only question was whether he would try to grab her as she came out of her apartment or try to waylay her at the club. The latter would be risky. There would be too many people and too many witnesses. No, I told myself, he'll make his move here.

That meant my somehow getting into Tuxedo Park. Time was when I had a key to the place, but that time had long passed; however, there were a few other options, one of which was another felony. I was just about to exit the car when the glare from a pair of headlights bounced off my rearview mirror. I hit the recliner button on the side of my seat and slipped out of sight just as a white van slid by me, doing about ten miles an hour in a thirty-mile-an-hour zone. People in Miami don't drive like that unless they're looking for something or someone: Maybe a crackhead looking for a rock or a plumber on his way home from work looking for a hooker with a soft pair of immoral lips. But it was neither of these. It was Williams.

I turned my head just enough to catch sight of the driver's profile as the van crept by. It was Williams, all right.

He pulled up to Vivian's apartment building, and his brake lights flared as he backed into a parking space. I reached under the seat and grabbed hold of the .45. I got quickly out of the car and went around to the curb and ran along the street half crouching, knowing that if Williams happened to glance in his sideview mirror, then he would surely see me. To avoid this I ducked behind the rear end of an old Chrysler. I tucked the gun under my shirt and waited. The way I saw it, I had two choices: take him now, before he went upstairs, where he might or might not manage to get hold of Vivian, or wait for him to come downstairs and then make my move.

Williams got out of the van and started across the street. He was wearing a waist-length black leather jacket and black leather pants. That's when I decided on the second option. Still in a semi-crouch, I ran until I was just across the street from the entrance to Tuxedo Park and crouched again behind another car. Williams walked very deliberately up the flagstone steps and opened the glass door that led into the vestibule. He didn't bother with the intercom but went through the second glass door that led to the elevators.

I waited for him to disappear and went around to the driver's-side door of his van. I got the .45 out and looked around. The tree-lined street was empty, so I used the butt of the gun to break the window and opened the door and swung in behind the steering wheel. I popped the hood and a second later had ripped loose the distributor cap and the cables that led to the battery. I closed the hood with as little noise as possible and stuffed the cap and cables behind some hedges. I'd felt a wild sense of glee as I ripped the cables free; I was getting to be quite the little ninja.

Now it was time to wait. The key was whether or not he had Vivian with him. The next question was the location of his gun, for I had no doubt that he was armed. Williams was big and strong and nasty enough to be able to coerce just about anyone into his van without a firearm, but if he came out with the end of the barrel at Vivian's back, then it would be a very delicate situation indeed. If that were the case, I'd have to be close enough to surprise him. I thought through it in fast forward. He'd see the broken window. That would distract him for sure. He'd have to open the door for Vivian, then for himself. The van would not start. He would have to open the hood. He might be suspicious, but he would still have to open the hood, and that's when I would take him. Knowing that, I also knew where I would wait.

I pranced up a few cars south of where Williams's van was parked and squatted down by someone's rear fender, hoping nobody would spot me. But I wouldn't have to wait for long, because a moment later Williams came through the front door—I let out my breath. He was alone. The choice I had to make swelled up inside my chest like a Macy's Thanksgiving Day balloon. Kill him now and have one less enemy at my back or let it wait for another time. The first choice made sense. From this range I couldn't miss. Could I get away with it? Maybe. Probably. People got dead in Miami all the time. Get rid of the gun. Would I be a suspect? Maybe. Probably. Motive? What motive? Nobody knew about our intimate interlude on the high seas. After all, he had tried to kill me. Even the score. Wipe that smirk off his face now and forever.

Still, it was no easy thing to kill a man.

Not by accident, at least. Then the old video started, and I couldn't stop the tape. Going up the stairwell in the Fredrick Douglass projects. The heart's steady beating, a reminder that you at least are still alive. It sets the pace of your slow, cautious ascent up the stairs. Then the glint of metal in the almost dark and both of you firing your guns simultaneously as though in a semiautomatic dream, and for the rest of your life the burning question of every day, of every stray waking moment: What if you had waited a second longer?

Then I heard the wail of sirens far in the distance, heading away from me. The video blurred before fading completely.

As I crouched there behind the car, waiting, it came to me that the time was not yet now. Williams and I were on a collision course. Of that much I was certain. But not now. It was too soon. Or maybe I was just scared. It didn't matter. I felt the relief of knowing that the time had not yet come.

I heard Williams's muffled curse when he spotted the broken window, heard him curse again—this time more loudly—when the engine wouldn't start. Crouched in the darkness, I smiled like a fiend. I peeked up over the trunk of my perch when I heard the hood of his van open. After a second or two, he slammed it shut and cursed again. He looked around suspiciously for a moment, but there was nothing else he could do. I thought I heard him talking on a cell phone. Then he cursed yet again and started walking east toward Washington Avenue. He would be heading for Embers. I waited for him to turn the corner, then sprinted back to the car.

I made a U-turn and went north on Michigan. At the park I turned left and drove the few blocks east toward the neon playground over on Washington Avenue. I got lucky and found a parking spot right in front of an all-night grocery store, then walked the half block to the main drag, already bustling with the crowds from across the causeway, the traffic not moving and the humid air smelling like a Chinese restaurant. I had the gun under my shirt like a deadly invitation.

There are certain places on this earth that seem to rise up full-blown like Venus flytraps out of nowhere, cafés or nightclubs that flourish and prosper where other endeavors have failed and vanished almost as soon as they opened their doors. I had seen it happen in South Beach a dozen times in the years I'd been in Miami. Embers was in the first category. Nick, Matson, and a few silent partners had opened the place a few months before I met him, and from the moment the lights came on that first night, the crowds had been there at the double gold doors, buzzing with anticipation like mosquitoes after a long rain.

The Sheik had partied there, and so had the Space Man. The models that roamed there swayed like palm trees on the dance floor, and upstairs, in the VIP section, I had seen things usually reserved for motel rooms with mirrored ceilings, bedbugs, and hourly rates. I'd never expected to go back there again, just as I had assumed that I would never see Vivian again. Now it seemed I was wrong on both counts.

It was still early by South Beach standards, just twenty past midnight, but there was already a long, pulsating line of people stretching around the corner. Rain showers had swept in off the ocean, and the crowd pressed its back against the sides of the building and under the narrow ledge that girded the curtained windows of the second floor. I stood across the street beneath the awning of a tattoo parlor and watched them get wet. The rain fell with the kind of slanted fury that gives birth to jungles and howling monkeys, to floods that cover the earth. It overran the gutters and jumped the sidewalks, rolled back, then rose up and tried again.

The line moved slowly toward the door where long, tall Sidney, the gatekeeper to paradise, waited under the awning behind a lectern, checking names against the guest list like St. Peter making sure the wrong people didn't get into heaven. He wore a white sequined gown and looked like the giant bride of a man few other men would envy. The yellow wig on his head, contrasted with his black skin, failed to add to his attractiveness. It was hard to believe he had once been a karate instructor up in Detroit—that is, until you saw him drop-kick a troublemaker.

I waited for a break in the rain, then sprinted across the street and up to the lectern. The two bouncers flanking Sidney straightened up and prepared to whip my ass. Sidney glared down at me as though I were a water beetle who had swum across the surface of a lake. Even without the heels, he would have still had me by three inches; with them he had me by six or seven. I could smell his perfume from four feet away, and it filled me with the opposite of romance. As usual, he had over-done his makeup. His lipstick was the color of purple orchids, and his mascara had started to run down his face, which was dark and handsome in a Denzel Washington kind of way.

"Hey, Sidney," I said. "Don't tell me you don't remember me."

He slammed the guest book shut like a preacher closing his Bible at a revival meeting.

"Well, I'll be goddamned! Look who it is! Where the hell you been, you dried-up burden of a white man? I thought the Good Lord had called you home. Him or the devil, either one! Last time I saw you, we were playing pool at that after-hours place up behind the library. Remember that?"

"Yeah," I said. "That was the night they stole your wig."

"That's the problem with this godforsaken town, Jackie," he said. "Take off your hair for one minute and they go and steal it on you."

"The neighborhood has changed," I admitted. "By the way, is Vivian here?"

"I believe she is."

"Can I get in?"

"I believe you can't."

"Why not?"

"You ain't got on the right clothes. I let you in, I got to let in the homeless people, too."

"It's an emergency," I said. "Come on, just this one time. I'll be in and out in ten minutes."

"What's going on?"

"Somebody's after her. Somebody bad."

He looked me over for a moment. I guess he sensed my desperation, because he told his assistant to let me in.

"You must have snuck in," Sidney said. "'Cause I sure as shit didn't see you."

"That's right. I came in through the back way."

"Dressed like that, you should have."

The bouncer unclipped the rope from the brass post and lifted it past me.

"He ain't dressed right," the bouncer said.

"Shut up," Sidney said.

"Say, Sidney. Did you ever finish law school?" I asked.

"Sure did," he said, clapping me on the back. "Passed the bar exam, too—on the first try. Got some interviews coming up next month."

"They're not ready for you in the courtroom," I told him.

"They weren't ready for me here either, homeboy. Don't you worry—I dress different during the day."

I eased closer to Sidney so that no one could overhear me. He had to lean down to hear what I was saying.

"I have another favor to ask," I said.

"What you need?"

"There's a big guy trailing me. Almost as tall as you, bald head, red mustache, heavy into 'roids. Black leather. Looks crazy. If you can't keep him out, at least stall him."

"What's the deal?"

"Don't ask. Don't tell."

"I hear you. Go on in."

I went through double glass doors with the heavy brass trim, and the music and the lights hit me all at once, like the beginning of a bad trip. The bar in the anteroom was packed three deep, and the bartenders in their white tuxedo shirts and pink bow ties were gliding back and forth like a trio of ice-skaters. The cigarette smoke was so thick it made the ceiling seem much lower than it was. A mixture of perfume and sweat filled the air like the prelude to an orgy, and the women were wearing just enough to keep from getting arrested.

I went through a second set of wide-open glass doors to my left and found myself looking out over a dance floor already packed with people. I fought back a surging wave of claustrophobia and squeezed through the crowd sideways, twisting and turning my body like an eel trying to ease through muck. If I was going to find Vivian in a place like Embers, I would need an aerial view, so I pressed my way toward the stairs that led to the balcony, knowing that Williams would not be far behind.

You would have thought that with all the advances in technology they would have found a replacement for the disco ball, the cyclopean, multifaceted silver ball spinning like a miniature sun over the dance floor, but you would be mistaken. The lights were low; the speakers were throbbing; the dance floor was a quivering fresco of arms and legs, and above it all, the ball turning slowly, strafing the crowd with bars of blue and gold light. The air was so cold it was hard to smell the marijuana, but it was there, hovering, cloying, and sweet, like a red-eyed genie waiting for a wish.

The bouncer at the foot of the stairs there knew me and let me go up to the VIP section, though I could see he wasn't thrilled with my attire. Upstairs there were ten tables, but only six of them were occupied. No one paid me any attention as I crossed over to where the balcony leaned out over the dance floor like the edge of a cliff. I was standing there peering down into the crowd, completely absorbed in my search for Vivian, when I recognized the man standing against the railing with his back turned to me. I went over and tapped him on the shoulder. It was Nick.

He turned casually enough but when he saw who it was, his head jerked forward and he spit an ice cube out of his mouth. Then he began to cough. I sat on the stool next to him and waited for him to get hold of himself.

"Where's your sister?" I asked.

Nick jumped a good six inches sideways, but I grabbed him by the arm and jerked him back to earth. He shook himself free.

"Jack! My God! We all thought you were dead!" he said in a loud whisper.

"I almost was, but guess what: Jack is back, and now Jack wants to know why Williams tried to kill me last night while I was doing your father's dirty work. I'd like to hear your thoughts on that."

Nick took a nervous puff from his cigarette and leaned closer to me. "This is bad, Jack. We're all in a lot of trouble. Williams has lost his mind. I'm afraid he'll kill every one of us. He's an animal, you know."

"Where's Big Daddy? At the house?"

"No, not there. He had to leave. He couldn't stay there."

"Why not?"

Nick looked out over the crowd. "My father is in trouble," he shouted. "Big trouble. I don't know where he is, and I don't really want to know either."

"Williams is on his way here," I told him. "We don't have a lot of time to play around. You better tell me what you know fast, before I get nervous and shoot the wrong person."

"Williams is coming here? Do you have a gun?"

I pulled back my shirt so he could see the butt of the .45 that Space had given me. "Sure," I said. "Doesn't everybody? Now tell me what kind of trouble the Colonel is in. I'm not going to ask you again."

Nick glanced around nervously, like a cornered animal that didn't know which way to run. "Please, Jack. For God's sake. Let's just get my sister and get out of here. Then I'll tell you everything. I swear I will, please!"

"Where is she?"

"Down there, dancing." Nick moved closer to the railing, but warily, as though he expected me to pitch him over the side. He took his glasses off and polished the lenses with a handkerchief. Then he put them on and looked down again. After a moment he pointed. Even in the dark, he looked scared and badly in need of a suntan, like someone who had spent too many years in an office without windows.

"See her? There, in the black dress. She's dancing with another girl."

I looked down and spotted Vivian. She was dancing, all right, and I very nearly got lost in watching her. It was not the kind of dancing you learn at any decent school. I watched her for a moment, horrified and at the same time completely transfixed by the way she moved. It was as though the music had melted every bone in her body. Then she and the girl exchanged a kiss. South Beach at its finest, I thought. Nick leaned closer to me and shouted in my ear.

"We thought you were dead!" he yelled.

"You said that already. Don't act disappointed. Tell me this: Why is Williams after you and Vivian?"

"It's a long story, but he thinks we're out to double-cross him."

"Double-cross him how?" I asked.

"Please, Jack. Can't we just get out of here first? Aren't you afraid of Williams?"

"If you're so afraid of Rudolph, what are you doing here?"

"We thought we'd be safer in a crowd," Nick answered.

"Is that right?" I said. "Think again."

I took out the gun under cover of darkness and stuck it into his ribs. I looked around, but no one was watching us.

The couples at the tables were leaning into their conversations, their faces aglow with candlelight and probably cocaine, which I could have used a bit of myself at that point, it having been a longish couple of days.

"What are you doing?" Nick said desperately. "Put that away!"

"Let me ask you a question, Nick. How crazy do you think I am?"

"What kind of question is that to ask a person? I don't know. I have no idea. Personally, I never thought you were crazy. A bit stupid perhaps, but not crazy."

"Did your sister ever tell you I was crazy? Did she?" I jabbed him with the barrel of the gun.

"No! Never! She never said you were crazy. I swear to God she didn't!"

"Well, guess what? She lied! I am the craziest person here tonight! Next to me, Williams is a bishop. Do you understand what I'm saying to you? Do you? Repeat it so I can hear it: 'You are the craziest son of a bitch I ever met.' Go on!" I put the gun a little closer to his pancreas.

"You are the craziest son of a bitch I ever met," he said meekly.

"You don't sound convinced. Say it louder. Say it! Say it before I pitch you over the side!"

"You can't do that. I might land on someone!"

"That'll be their problem. They've got no business being in this hellhole anyway."

"All right, okay! You are the craziest son of a bitch I've ever met! I mean it, Jack. At first I didn't, but now I do. You're fucking insane. I think you're even crazier than Williams."

"Right now I take that as a compliment." I stuck the gun back under my shirt. Nick relaxed visibly, but I didn't want him too relaxed, so I grabbed his elbow and pushed down on the ulnar nerve with my thumb. He tried to pull away, but

I held him. "Walk ahead of me," I told him. "We're going down and get your sister. Try to run away and I'm going to kick a bone loose in your ass."

I expected him to make a break for it, but he stayed just ahead of me as we edged past the tables and toward the carpeted stairs. Maybe it was the beginning of old age, and maybe it was the mileage of the last few days, but Embers seemed like bedlam to me now, and I wanted to get out of the place as soon as possible. I needed to get Vivian and her brother to someplace quiet where we could have our long-overdue sit-down, someplace with a couple of steel chairs without cushions, a few bottles of truth serum, several pairs of handcuffs, and an overhead light that never blinked.

It was even harder to move on the ground floor than it had been on the stairwell, and it took a good five minutes to slowly weave my way to the spot on the dance floor where I had seen Vivian dancing. I went through beautiful women without seeing them. The music banged at my ears like a storm. I was as focused as a bloodhound on speed, and I had to do a fair bit of shoving. Not everybody liked it. A tall kid with a *GQ* face started to object, but something in my expression seemed to discourage him. I caught his eye and held it briefly, but in that moment I had read his mind to perfection: *This guy's a fucking cop.* Once you get that look, you never lose it.

Vivian wasn't dancing anymore when I found her. She was sitting at the horseshoe-shaped bar at the raised center of the dance floor with a drink in her hand. She had her back to me. A tall man in a black shirt and black pants was lighting her cigarette as I sat down next to her. Nick was standing beside me, looking like the Ghost of Christmas Past. I tapped her gently on the shoulder. I guess she was used to people doing that, because she didn't turn around, so I rapped on her beautiful bronze shoulder with my knuckles as though it were a door. The man in black gave me a hard look that I ignored. Vivian turned around, and her mouth fell open. She glanced at her brother, and about five different emotions went haywire on her face all at once.

She was good, at least as good as Nick, I'll say that much for her. She jumped off the stool and threw her arms around me while I glared at the man in black over her shoulder. I gave him my best lunatic glare, and his face lost some of its tan.

"Why are you lighting my wife's cigarette, you son of a bitch?" I asked.

He looked flustered. He was about thirty-five, handsome, and prematurely gray.

"Your . . . wife?" he stammered. "I didn't know anything about that. She asked me for a light. Let's just forget about it, okay?" He held up both hands in front of him like a pair of starfish. He grinned at me as though we had just signed a peace agreement at Camp David, then took his drink and entered the crowd.

Vivian kissed and hugged me like I'd just come back from Vietnam. Nick looked on grimly. I fought the urge to bite her neck and instead grabbed her by the shoulders.

"My God! I was so worried about you!" she said. "I thought you were dead!"

"That accounts for the black dress," I said, scanning the crowd. "Let's get out of here. We need to have a discussion. I don't want to hear any more crap right now."

Just as I stood up, Nick nudged me with his elbow. I followed the direction of his gaze to the other side of the bar and saw Williams there, his bald pate gleaming dully in the swirling lights. He was looking around. I grabbed Vivian by the arm, but it was too late. Williams had already spotted us. Our eyes locked across the bar, and I thought I saw a smile cross his face. It was the smile of a man who had amputated noses and ears and enjoyed every slice.

There was no hesitation in him. Almost at once he came for us, parting the crowd with his massive fullback shoulders, plowing forward, swimming through people, pushing them aside as though they were stalks of wheat in a field. There were at least a hundred bodies between us, and that should have been enough to delay almost anyone. But they didn't stop Williams.

"Let's go!" I said. "Stay with me."

I got out in front and barreled forward, not making any friends and not caring. I wasn't as big as Williams, nor as strong, but I had fear on my side. The crowd, like a beast with one mind and many faces, began to sense that a chase of some kind was in progress, and I felt the silent wave of expectation rippling around me as the dancers turned and got quickly out of our way. I looked back and saw a bouncer in his white shirt and pink bow tie cutting crossways through the grain on a collision course toward Williams. Two more of his buddies in identical getups were coming in from the rear. I pushed Vivian and Nick ahead of me. We were almost at the edge of the dance floor.

Vivian slipped and nearly stumbled. She reached down, tore off her pumps, and ran barefoot ahead of me. The crowd, partial to the prey, parted for her. I was aware of staring faces blurred by speed. Nick was way in front now. I thought for sure he would run for it on his own, but he stopped and waited for Vivian. I glanced back in time to see a bouncer with a purple Mohawk grab Williams and spin him around. Williams went with the spin and hit the man under the chin with the heel of his palm, dropping him. Then the other bouncers leaped on him, bearing him down, swinging for all they were worth. I wished them luck. They would need it.

I ran forward and herded Nick and Vivian toward the fire doors to the left of the dance floor. There was no sense trying to make it out the main entrance. The police would be sure to stop anyone attempting to leave. I hit the crash bar running with both hands out in front of me and slammed it behind me when we were through.

"Where's your car?" I yelled at Nick.

"I gave it to the valet."

"We'll take mine," I said. "It's down by the park. Come on."

I pushed them ahead of me, urging them forward. Vivian ran with her black shoes still in her hand. I kept looking back over my shoulder, expecting to see the juggernaut coming at us. We got to the Beemer and jumped in. I looked through the rearview mirror and saw a giant shadow running toward us.

Almost in a single motion, I started the car and pulled out of the spot, not switching on the lights until I made a turn at the corner.

"Where are you taking us?" Nick asked.

"To Disney World," I said. "It's time to see Mickey."

"You are crazy," Nick said. "I didn't think so before, but now I do."

"Good. You're starting to catch on."

Collins Avenue was jammed, so I headed west. At Meridian we swung north again, and it was then I started thinking about what to do now that I had two of the last three members of the Partridge Family together again.

Vivian sat up and looked back at her brother hunkered down in the rear seat. "Nick," she said, "we need to tell Jack the truth."

"That's a good idea," I said. "Start slow. I don't want you to hurt yourself."

"This is turning into something hellish," Nick said. "My life is over."

"Stop being so selfish," Vivian said.

"Okay, kids," I said. "This is how it works: Nobody's getting out of this vehicle until I find out what's going down. Got that? I have a full tank of gas and nowhere to go, so somebody better start talking before we get to Orlando."

"Are we really going to Disney World?" Nick said.

"Shut up," I said. "Vivian, what the hell is going on?"

"Go ahead, tell him," Nick said. "He's the only chance we've got against Williams."

Vivian looked straight ahead. We were on Indian Creek now, heading north, amid that long, interminable stretch of buildings called Condo Canyon, gliding under the glare of a thousand well-lit windows staring down at us from above, each filled with the promise of rest, safety, a nightcap, and a bed with clean sheets and a thin, cool pillow. I was so tired that exhaustion now seemed my natural state. I half closed my eyes just to get the feel of it, then snapped them open as Vivian started to speak.

"How much do you know about my father's company?" she asked.

"He made drugs. Got the seed money from your stepmother, now deceased. You didn't like her. The company was privately held, never went public. Why do you ask?"

Nick leaned forward in his seat. "Did you know that Pellucid Laboratories nearly went bankrupt about a year ago?"

"No. But then, as maybe you recall, that was about the time I checked out of the picture. Obviously the company survived." Then I recalled the article I'd read at Susan's.

"But you don't know how. He had to bring in some outside money," Vivian said. "Quite a bit of it."

"You're not telling it right," Nick said. "It really started years ago, about the time when all the major drug companies had jumped on the antidepressant bandwagon. Dad had had a drug in development for ten years. It was called Morphitrex. Ever hear of it?"

"Never."

Vivian lit a cigarette. She waved the match in the air and tossed it out the open window. We were in Surfside now, among the parallel rows of ratty motels where the Canadians used to stay before they got smart and took their business north to Hollywood Beach. But to me, as tired as I was, every chintzy neon sign was the entrance to the palace of sleep.

"That was the trouble," Vivian said. "No one else did either. The FDA killed it just as it was about to be approved. They found out he had faked some of the research. It turns out the drug had way too many side effects."

"That's when the money trouble started," Nick added. "The big boys like Merck and Pfizer can afford to lose huge like that, but not Dad. You know why he never took the company public?"

"Because he's a control freak," I said.

"That's right," Vivian said. "He's a control freak. But when he saw the company he'd built from nothing going under, he had to bring in the venture capitalists, the deep-pocket people. But they didn't just give him the money and then go home and take a nap. You don't borrow a hundred million dollars and not give up control. It almost killed him, but it was the only way he could save Pellucid."

"Happens all the time," I said. "What's the point?"

"Guess where the money came from?" Vivian said.

"The Tooth Fairy," I offered.

"Matson," Nick said.

"Impossible," I said. "Matson had money, but not that kind of money. He made booty movies," I told him. But then the image of *The Carrousel* and what Agent Hackbart had said at Susan's place about Matson and Duncan came back to me.

"Matson had friends," Vivian said.

"That reminds me," I said. "You forgot to mention that there was a second dead man on the boat. I know it's a minor detail, but I don't recall announcing any two-for-one-sale on dead-body disposal. He was the other lucky guy in the home movie your pops gave me to watch."

"His name was Harry Duncan. He was a friend of Matson's. Anyway, what difference does it make?" Vivian said. "They were both dead, weren't they? All you did was get rid of them."

"From what I saw on that video, you seem to have known him pretty well," I said.

"Not as well as you might think. They gave me Morphitrex. That stuff makes everybody your friend."

"Are you on it now?" I asked.

"A little."

"Is that why you were kissing that girl back at Embers?"

"Yes, but I would have kissed her anyway."

I looked at her for a moment and wondered who she was. I glanced at her half brother and noticed for the first time that they both had the same eyes. Not the same color—his were a washed-out blue, and hers were dark almond, almost black. But they had the same penetrating sheen to them, making them look like grown-up naughty children caught in the act. It came to me then that I had lived too long in a foreign country, and that country was my own. With a pair like these two riding with me, I was glad I had the gun. Too bad it wasn't loaded with silver bullets.

"If the FDA didn't approve the drug, how'd you get hold of it?" I asked.

"This is the good part," Nick said.

"They manufactured some of the pills initially, just as samples for the trials. One night I was snooping around in my father's office, not looking for anything in particular, when I came across a box of these little blue pills. Well, you know me. I just popped one down, and boy, it was fantastic, better than ecstasy, way better. Anyway, I gave one to Matson. That's when he brought Harry Duncan into it, as a partner. And that's when they made Daddy an offer."

"What kind of offer?" I asked.

"They wanted access to Daddy's research. Their idea was that Morphitrex was just the beginning. They would manufacture a whole line of designer drugs offshore for practically nothing, then bring them here and sell them at the clubs. Matson figured we could make a hundred million the first year alone."

"And your father agreed to this?" I asked.

"Yes, but the deal was just for Morphitrex," Vivian said. "The rest, Father never intended to sell. He thought that some of the other drugs he'd worked on might still be made legally in this country. He didn't want Matson to have them."

"So what soured the deal?" I asked. "How did Matson and his buddy wind up dead?"

"It was her fault," Nick said. "She was going to double-cross our father."

"That's right," Vivian countered. "And you went along with it, too. Don't pretend it was just me."

"Your father told me you shot Matson," I said.

"No," Vivian said. "It wasn't me. It was Williams. He shot Duncan, too. Father told you it was me just to get you to sink the yacht. He knew you'd never do it if you thought it was Williams who did it." She looked away. "I didn't know he was going to call you," she said. There were tears in her eyes, but they didn't mean anything to me.

"But you went along with it when he did," I said. "Tell me this: Why did Williams think he had to kill me?"

"I didn't know about that," Vivian said. "Otherwise I would have told you. Probably he thought you knew too much. I'm not even sure Father knew what he was going to do."

"You said you were going to double-cross your father," I said. "How were you going to do that?"

"Williams had her apartment bugged," Nick said. "He heard us talking."

"About what?"

"Vivian and I were going to get squeezed out of the money. That much was for sure. We could see it coming, so we made a side deal with Matson. We'd get him all of Father's papers, not just those about how to make Morphitrex. We wanted a flat fee: three million apiece. Duncan and Matson agreed to it. They put the money in an escrow account in the Cayman Islands. All we had to do was deliver. After you left to sink the yacht, Vivian called me on the phone. That's when Williams heard us talking about how we'd pulled it off. He said he was going to kill both of us. He almost caught us, too—at a restaurant. We had to run out through the kitchen."

"I lost my cell phone," Vivian said. "That man can run."

"For the first time, I agree with Williams," I said. "I'm thinking of killing you both myself. A small loss to the world you'd be, I might add."

"It was Harry who taught me how to hack into Father's computer," Nick said. "He knew a lot about computers."

"So I guess the whole thing with that juicy little video was just your father's way of softening me up," I said. "I guess it worked."

Nobody said anything.

"Are you sure it was Williams who killed Matson and Duncan?" I asked. "And one more lie, and somebody's going to have a long walk back."

There was an extended silence. As a cop I had come to know that breed of silence well, the silence of someone who has hit the wall of lies and who is too tired or too scared to think of any new ones. We were in Sunny Isles now, still heading north. I could smell Rascal's Deli before I could see its sign. It was calling me like a cup of coffee on the midnight shift up in Harlem, far away in another life. The Thunderbird Hotel summoned me sweetly from the east side of Collins as we sailed by. The sign said they even had a swimming pool. It was about all a tired man could ask for in this life.

"Williams killed both of them," Vivian said from a place I had wandered away from. "Then he dragged me back and made me confess the whole thing to Daddy, about selling the other drugs to Matson. He took my computer and all my files. He wanted to get rid of any of Daddy's research I may have stolen. Then he got hold of Nick's computer and did the same thing."

"Let me guess," I said. "You'd made backup files, probably on a disk or CD. Right? You were still in the game. What happened? Williams found out about it?"

"It was my fault," Nick said glumly. "I thought I had hidden them well enough, but Williams found them. He caught me and held a cigarette lighter under my palm. He asked if Vivian had her own set of files. I had to tell him. That's why he's after her now."

"So," I said to Vivian, "let me guess again: You've got your own little stash of stolen research. Williams found out about that, too, but he hasn't managed to locate it yet. Is that it? Tell me this: What were you planning to do with it? Your two partners are both dead. What good is that stash now?"

"I don't know," Vivian said. "All I know is I'm the one who brought the deal to Daddy, and I'm going to get my fair share. Besides, Matson introduced me to a lot of his friends. Maybe one of them can help me." She edged closer to me on the seat, so that her thigh pushed up against my own. "Maybe you can help us, too."

I let that one ride. But it gave me an idea. "Where's the stash?" I asked.

The car got quiet again. I made a left turn, pulled into the rear of an all-night gas station with a well-lit minimart, and killed the headlights.

"Tell me where the disk is or I feed you both to Williams."

"You wouldn't do that to me," Vivian said. "I know you wouldn't."

"Not to you," I told her. "But your brother back there is another story. I'm sure he's got Williams's name saved on his cell phone, and I'm also sure Williams will be very glad to see him again. What do you think?"

"Even if I tell you where it is, what are you going to do with it?" Vivian asked. "Go into business for yourself?"

"Don't worry," I said. "I'll cut you both in. I'm not greedy. But neither of you is equipped to go up against Willy Boy alone. I am, and you know it. You need an enforcer. Come on. We're wasting time, and I'm getting tired."

"Can't we stop someplace?" Vivian asked plaintively. "I haven't slept since you went out to sink the boat. Just for a little while?"

"Not until you tell me where you hid your father's stuff," I said. "That's the deal."

"It's back at the house," she said.

"Where?" Nick asked.

"In my room."

"Okay," I said. "That's enough. Let's crash. In the morning we'll head out to the mansion. All three of us, just like one big fucking family."

Ten minutes later we walked into the overly lit but nearly empty lobby of the Holiday Inn in Hollywood Beach. I knew the clerk on the midnight shift. He was a big, soft-spoken man-child named Casio Davis, whose father had paid me five grand a few years back to help his son get ready for the marines. I had to refund the money, though. The work we did by day, young Casio undid by night at the drive-through window of a Popeyes fried-chicken place. There are a lot of miles in Miami, but not as many as there are calories in a couple buckets of extra-crispy. The father wanted me to keep the money, but I gave it back to him anyway.

Despite the fact that it was off-season, the hotel, which was under partial renovation, was full, but Casio managed to squeeze a pair of rooms out for us. No one spoke on the elevator. We emerged on the sixth floor and walked along a hallway still littered with building debris and smelling like fresh paint. The deal was we would have to be gone before the day crew showed up in the morning; otherwise Casio might be out of a job.

"I'm staying with you," Vivian announced, slipping her arm through mine as though we were on our way to the prom. I didn't say anything. I was too tired to think. The thought of a bed with or without Miss Patterson in it was more than enough for me. I just wanted to close my eyes and wake up in another life. Nick didn't seem to enjoy the prospect of being alone very much, but there were limits to my concern about that. He went into his room, and I heard him put the latch on. He had good reason to be afraid. He'd seen Williams plowing through those hard boys back at Embers, and his dreams would be less than serene.

Our room was down the hall. The moment I saw the bed, I went for it as if it were the last bed on earth. I heard Vivian talking behind me, but her voice began to dissolve as I stretched out and closed my eyes. The glow from the lamp on the nightstand should have kept me awake, but I didn't even have enough energy left to shut it off. Sleep reached up for me through the mattress like a warm hand coming out of the ground, and I gave myself to it unreservedly.

Then the light was off, and I felt Vivian against me, breathing into my ear like a cat anxious to be fed. She began undoing my shirt, and I told her to just let me sleep, but I didn't push her hand away. There was no need to be nasty about it simply because I was three-quarters dead from exhaustion and needed rest far more than anyone had ever needed sex in the whole history of the world. She had lied to me, betrayed me, and nearly gotten me killed. It was enough to make a man bitter. I was bitter. I was bitter as hell. She was tugging my shirt out of my trousers; her hand felt like a roving butterfly fluttering against the hairs on my chest. Soon I began thinking that there were times in a man's life when he has to let bygones be bygones, so I kicked off my shoes and began to cooperate with the situation.

"You'll sleep better if you let me relax you," she said.

"I have been under a lot of stress lately," I told her.

"Lie back, Jack," she said

I found that fairly easy to do. After a second I sat up on my elbows and watched her black hair slide down my stomach like a retreating wave. I reached down and got a fistful of it and lifted her head. Her eyes were already as glazed over as they'd been in Matson's little movie. A thought came to me.

"You're on it, aren't you?"

"What?"

"The Morphitrex."

By way of answer, she moistened her already moist lips with her tongue and lowered her head, and I left her to her work. After a while she straddled me like a cowgirl and began to surge back and forth, her dark hair whipping around like the shadow of a condor. I held on to her hips for dear life and wondered if she was still human. I was afraid she might actually turn into something else, and I wasn't sure I wanted to be under her when it happened. She grabbed the top of the headboard and rocked and screamed and howled like a thunderstorm trying to rip itself free from the sky.

Time passed. There was a pool of sweat at the center of

my chest, and Vivian was making soft swirls in it with her index finger. The room had cooled off, and the sheets were warm and luxurious against my back. It would have been a fine way to end the night if only the day preceding it had been different. There's something about having the cops after you that puts a damper on things.

"The drug," I said. "How does it work?"

"I don't know. It's the weirdest shit I've ever taken, weirder even than peyote or mushrooms. It's like it listens to you. It knows what you want. You want something to speed you up, then that's what it does. If you want to chill out and look at a brick wall, then that wall will be the most beautiful thing in the world. I'm telling you, Jack, the stuff is unbelievable. Even Williams has taken it. I only use it for sex."

"I never thought you needed any help."

"Not with you, but even so, it just makes everything more intense. You're not complaining, are you?"

"What does Williams use it for, to grow back his hair?"

"Strength, endurance. He told me once that it was the best drug he's had since Vietnam."

"Maybe they can use that for the advertising campaign."

"There won't be one. It will all be word of mouth. That's the way ecstasy got started. The next thing you know, it's worth twenty dollars a pill—more, once people realize what it's like."

"I guess this would be a good time to talk about money," I said.

"What do you have in mind?" Vivian asked.

I ignored her question. I was almost enjoying myself. "Williams will catch on eventually that the Colonel has been squeezed out of the play, and he won't like it very much. Also, he knows I'm alive now. He won't like that either, which means he'll be coming after all three of us. I'll probably have to kill him. I'll have to be compensated for that.

I've gone through a lot of trouble for your family. It's time for the payoff."

She tensed up at that, but only for a moment. She'd told me once that her entire body was a G-spot, but the only one I had never probed was the one in her bank account. It was the one place she didn't accept visitors—especially those there to make a withdrawal.

"How much do you want?" she asked. Her eyes were bright as coins.

"Well, there's the fifty grand you still owe me for the dead-body removal. We'll have to double that because of Mr. Duncan, of course. But as the new enforcer in this little operation, I'll have to be an equal partner. I get a third of the profits. What do you say to that?"

She kissed me. "Jack," she said, "there's hope for you after all."

"More than you think. Roll over. It's my turn on top."

THREE

I AWOKE JUST BEFORE DAWN and got dressed in the dark. I was still tired but felt fairly close to form. Then I woke Vivian. She turned over onto her back and blinked her eyes, and I recalled that, like most night stalkers, she was not a particularly pleasant person in the morning. She sat up in bed and looked around.

"Where are we?" she asked.

"Up in Hollywood. The Holiday Inn. Your brother's down the hall."

"What time is it?"

"About five-thirty."

She noticed then that I was dressed. "Where are you going?"

"Not just me. You, too. We're going to the mansion to get the disk."

"It's not on a disk," she said after a yawn. "It's on one of those little portable hard drives."

"Whatever. We're going to go find it. Get dressed."

"It's too early. Come back to bed."

"Get up."

"What about Nick?" she asked.

"Let him sleep. We'll pick him up on the way back."

"I need a shower," she said. "I smell like sex."

"Later. Hurry up."

"You're worse than Williams."

"I need to be. You're worse than us both."

I sat on the edge of the bed and watched her dress, which was nearly as much fun as watching the reverse. It didn't take her long; she traveled light: a pair of black thong panties, no bra, and the black party dress so incongruous in the innocent morning light. Vivian watched me watching her and smiled like the succubus she was. She reveled in her body the way a rich man revels in gold. The smooth skin, the breasts like minarets on a mosque, the fluted ribs lined now with shadow, now with light, the flat belly with just a trace of muscle visible. The black dress went on over her head, and she moved her hips from side to side as it slid over her ass. Maybe she's right, I thought. Maybe it is too early.

It was Sunday morning, and the traffic heading south was light. The sun, in a haze of cirrus clouds, rose slowly, red-eyed and sluggish in the east, as though unsure whether daylight was worth the effort. Vivian begged me to stop for coffee, so I pulled in to the same gas station where I'd stopped the night before and got one of those giant-size cups full of java while Vivian half dozed in the front seat of the car by one of the pumps.

We made Sunset Beach in twenty minutes. A sleep-deprived young guard in a uniform with a gold braid looped around one shoulder stepped out from his little box, in which a small TV set was flickering on a counter next to a thermos. He walked over to the driver's side with his clipboard in front of his chest, leaned down, pen in hand.

"Hey, Seth," Vivian said. "Long night?"

"There's no other kind, Ms. Patterson. Not for me."

"You don't happen to know if Williams is home, do you?" she asked.

"Haven't seen Mr. Williams in two or three days, not since your father left."

"Thanks, Reggie," Vivian said, her eyes twinkling the promise of a time that would never come. "Do me a favor, okay? If Mr. Williams should come by while we're here, give me a call at the house, would you?"

"Sure."

"Thanks, I really appreciate that," she told him.

I was just about to hit the gas when Reggie thought of something else.

"Hey, I forgot to tell you: Three guys came by here last night."

"Who?" I asked. Seth looked annoyed. He'd been speaking to Vivian. Still, he answered anyway.

"They didn't say, but they looked kind of official, if you know what I mean. I told them nobody was home."

"They look like cops?" I asked.

The guard eyed me skeptically. He was wondering who the hell I was to be asking him questions. Vivian picked up on it.

"This is my bodyguard," she said.

"They might have been," Reginald said. "They had that look. Oh, and yeah, they left you a card. Hold on."

He stepped back into the guardhouse. Vivian and I exchanged glances. The sun was more cheerful-looking, having thrown off its white cloak of clouds. I took a sip of coffee. Reggie came out, reached across my body with his outstretched arm, and handed Vivian a business card. I could tell by the tightness of his mouth that he had read the name on it and was trying hard to act unimpressed.

Vivian read the card as we drove away from the gatehouse. I watched the guard through the rearview mirror, wondering if he might already be going for the phone. Vivian put the card on the dashboard.

"Agent Hackbart," she said. "FBI. Shit. What now?"

"Same as before," I said, "only quicker. I want to be in and out in ten minutes. Get your key ready."

"I don't want to go to jail, Jack."

"Why not? I thought you liked girls."

Vivian didn't say anything. She was leaning forward, looking straight ahead, as though we were on a roller coaster that was sweeping downward at full speed.

The mansion of glass had already captured the sunlight and was sitting quietly on the rise with its glistening back to the sea. The flagpole still had no flag, and the Bentley, still parked outside the garage, was covered with drops of dew. I looked over at the small guesthouse where Dominguez, the Colonel's chauffeur, lived. His little white Toyota was gone, and the windows were covered with hurricane shutters.

I parked the car behind the massive garage and killed the engine. Vivian watched me intently as I took Space's .45 out from beneath the seat. Just to be sure, I checked the clip and snapped it back in again. Despite the gun I felt vaguely unarmed, and for a moment I didn't want to get out of the car.

"Let's use the back door," I said. "The one by the pool."

Vivian followed behind me, her stiletto heels typing away on the pavement. We went quickly along the side of the house, down a path flanked by rosebushes, until we emerged in the backyard. I stopped suddenly.

"What's wrong?" Vivian asked.

I had expected to see the welcoming, jewel-blue water of

the swimming pool just as I had a few days before, but it was empty. The pool had been drained.

"I guess your father doesn't plan on doing much swimming here for a while," I said.

My heart beat out a mild version of the fandango as we stepped through the French doors and into the house. I grabbed Vivian's wrist and put my finger to my lips as I listened to the nothing there was to hear. Then, very quietly, like a pair of thieves, we scurried down the hall that led to the living room and main stairway, and I couldn't help thinking about the last time I'd raced up a staircase with a gun in my hand. There was a lot more light this time around, yet in another way just as much darkness. It occurred to me that nothing in me had changed.

I shook the thought from my head and turned back to Vivian. Her dark eyes glowed with fear. The sound of her heels clicking on the marble tiles had begun to drive me crazy.

"Take off your shoes," I said. "You're making too much damned noise."

"That gun of yours is making me nervous," she told me in a tight whisper. "Can't you put it away? There's nobody home."

"Sorry, I don't believe in concealed weapons," I said. "Sends the wrong message."

The faces in the paintings stared at us as we approached Vivian's bedroom at the end of the hall. The house of glass felt empty, but in a place that big it was hard to tell. Vivian unlocked the door while I stood facing back down the hallway.

Then we were inside. Vivian locked the door behind her while I scanned the room with eyes and gun. The closet door was open, as were most of the drawers, and there were heaps of clothing on the floor just about everywhere you looked.

The place had been gone through, no doubt by Williams. Otherwise everything looked as it had a few days earlier: The teddy bear still reigned from atop the satin pillows stacked on the waterbed and the big-bellied brass Buddha was still smoking his cigarette amid an audience of dead flowers.

"Hurry up," I said. "This place has a bad feel to it."

Vivian, still carrying her shoes by their skinny straps, darted to the bed, grabbed the teddy bear as though it were a delinquent child, and began twisting its small, brown, disbelieving head. I watched in amazement as she unscrewed the head and tossed it onto the floor next to her shoes. Then she got the decapitated bear by its leg and shook it over the white quilt.

Something that looked like a gray seedpod fell out and bounced on the quilt. It was one of those extremely compact, extremely portable minidrives with a USB connector at one end. Vivian reached down to pick it up, but I was faster and scooped it up before she could grab it. I checked it out for a second, then put it in my pocket.

"I'll hold on to this, if you don't mind. Nice trick," I said. "The bear, I mean."

"My mother gave it to me. I used to keep pot in it when I was a kid."

"Put the head back on, and let's get out of here," I said. "No need for anyone to know we were here."

We were halfway down the stairs when I heard the sound of tires crunching on the white gravel that bordered the drive. A moment later there was the sound of a car door slamming shut. Vivian froze on the steps behind me. I looked back at her. Her eyes were bright with fear.

"Who?" she asked. "Williams . . . ?"

"Maybe. Come on," I said. "Out the back."

The doorbell rang just as we hit the first floor. We ran

along the hall that led back to the pool, Vivian's bare feet padding away on the marble tiles. We sprinted past the Colonel's failed Japanese garden and headed out toward the back of the garage where I had parked. There was a space between the mansion and the garage that looked out toward the driveway. I peeked around the corner. Only a fraction of the driveway was visible, but the space was wide enough for me to spot the rear end of a black sedan. In a way I was relieved.

"It's not Williams," I said. "It's the cops."

"Now what?" Vivian demanded desperately.

"We can't take the car. They'll nail us before we hit the causeway." I looked back over my shoulder at the ripple-free expanse of the ocean behind us. Then I saw the seawall. It went beyond the house and disappeared from view behind a blockade of hedges.

"Where's that seawall go?" I asked.

"Not far. We share it with the neighbor next door, about three lots away."

"All right. That's it, then."

We ran down to where the seawall stood futile guard against the ocean. One good-size hurricane and the Colonel's glass house would be an aquarium. The cement wall, four feet high and two feet wide, made about as much sense as the stunted bonsai trees, but for now it was our only road out.

I helped Vivian onto the seawall, then climbed up after her. The hedges at the end of the Colonel's property were backed up by a wrought-iron fence that extended to the edge of the wall. The hedges were too wide to step around, so the only way to the lot next door would be to grab hold of one of the bars with my left hand. I could do it easily enough, but I wasn't sure about Vivian. I told her to stand as close to me as possible, then pressed the left side of my body as far into the hedges as I could. I reached out with my left hand and grasped a single rusty iron bar. With my right arm, I took Vivian by her waist. The plan was to swing out and around the fence to the vacant lot next door.

I stretched out my left leg as far as it would go and told Vivian to grab me around the neck. I felt her arms trembling against my chest.

"Are you sure you can do this?" she asked.

"Hold on."

I braced myself, measuring my strength. Vivian weighed about 110, and I would have to support her weight as we swung out over the ocean.

"Why don't we just give ourselves up?" she asked plaintively.

"Not yet."

I tightened the muscles in my left leg and pushed off with my right leg extended about forty-five degrees, like the pencil end of a compass, as it swung out over the water. Vivian's weight added to the swing's momentum. We did a complete 180-degree turn around the hedges, with so much force that I nearly lost my grip. My right foot swung around and down, begging for a foothold on the seawall on the other side of the fence. Vivian screamed as her legs trailed behind us in midair. My foot tapped on the far wall, slid a bit, then found traction. I twisted my body with everything I had and whipped Vivian around with such force that the arc of the swing propelled us both into the lot next door. I landed on my back in the dirt with Vivian on top of me.

After a moment of cautious silence, Vivian got up and began brushing the dirt and sand from her bare legs. I didn't get up right away. The fall and her weight had knocked the breath out of me, and I'd strained my left shoulder. I sat up and rotated the arm. There was a slight pop, and all was right with the world.

Vivian, oddly enough, was smiling with obvious delight. "That was wild," she said. "I thought you were going to drop me."

I got up slowly and winced at the pain in my lower back. "Maybe I should have."

The lot we had landed in was also owned by the Colonel, but he hadn't done much with the acreage except keep anyone else from buying it while he made up his mind what to do with it. About a hundred yards away, a solitary crane leaned over the rubble like a dinosaur looking for something to eat. To the left, near the street, a Cyclone fence stretched toward the next house, about 150 yards down the beach. Vivian couldn't run in her bare feet, and her heels were out of the question, so it took us a while to reach the fence. When we finally did, we had to follow it almost until we reached the next mansion before we found a hole someone had cut into the fence.

The traffic was light on the causeway, but with no other pedestrians around to keep us company, we were far too conspicuous. It would only be a matter of time before whoever it was who had come calling on the Colonel would head back to the mainland again, in which case we might easily be spotted. We had to get off the causeway, and fast. We walked east toward the beach, with me glancing back praying for a cab but seeing nothing. I was starting to lose all hope when I saw a yellow taxi heading our way. It was illegal to pick up passengers on the causeway, but, fortunately, for us, the Haitian driver swooped in like a hawk, did exactly what he wasn't supposed to do, and was off again even before I had the door closed.

The driver looked us over through the rearview mirror, his eyes lingering on Vivian with obvious approval.

"Where you come from?" he asked.

"West Hell, New Jersey," I said. "We need to get to the

Holiday Inn up in Hollywood. You know where it is?"

"West Hell, is this a real place?"

"Sure."

"The devil. He live there?"

"No," I said. "He moved to Miami."

"When he move?" the driver asked.

"About the same time I did."

The Haitian laughed. He thought it was funnier than I did. Vivian laid her head on my shoulder as I gazed out the window. The sun was beaming through the early morning haze, and a cruise ship was sliding toward port. A row of passengers stood outside their cabins, staring at the traffic on the causeway. Take away the cops, the FBI, and Williams trying to kill me and it would have seemed liked the beginning of a pretty nice day. I let my head fall back and allowed myself to fall asleep.

I came back to myself when the cab swerved into the driveway of the hotel. While I had dozed off, the ten miles had slipped away like a silk scarf sliding off a stripper's neck. I nudged Vivian to awaken her. I paid the driver, and he swung out of the parking lot and back into traffic without so much as a single glance in any direction.

The hotel lobby was quiet, but the little coffee stand was already opened when we walked in. Vivian insisted on some espresso, so we helped ourselves to two cups along with a crusty bar of Cuban toast slathered in salty butter, then went out to the pool and sat at a table under a green-and-white umbrella while the sky put on its makeup.

"How do you think this is all going to end, Jack?" Vivian asked. "I can't keep going on like this. I can't keep running."

"A lot depends on your father and Williams," I said. "And a lot also depends on how much the cops know or think they know. I'm betting that at this stage of the game all they care about is your father's drug business. You can be sure they've been watching him for a long time. So far as I know, the feds have no idea what happened to Matson or Duncan. Let's hope it stays that way. It'll be better for everybody."

"What about you?" Vivian asked.

"If they catch Williams and ask about the yacht . . . well, let me put it to you like this: Either Williams can tell them the truth—in which case I go down—or he can plead ignorance. If I had to put money on it, I'd pick the second choice. Not to protect me, mind you. Williams doesn't give a rat's ass about anyone except the Colonel. It would just be less complicated to say he didn't know what happened to *The Carrousel*. That's what I would do."

I took the flash drive out of my pocket and held it up for Vivian to see.

"What happens next depends on this," I said. "I'm pretty sure that once Williams gets hold of this, he and your papa—wherever he is—will disappear, fade away, go off somewhere and find a friendly Third World country that will help them manufacture Morphitrex and whatever else they can come up with. My money is on Cuba."

"Why Cuba?" Vivian asked.

I looked out past the pool and east toward the ocean just as a pelican made a nosedive into the sea.

"A couple of things. One, it's close. Two, Duncan, Matson's boat buddy, was a Cuban spy. Three, and juiciest of all, is that Cuba has a world-class biotech industry—as good as anything we have here, or damned close. A party drug like Morphitrex would mean a lot of money for Castro. Of course, he wouldn't be involved in it directly. He's too smart for that, but you can bet he'll have a hand in it, like a puppet master, from a distance."

I took one last sip of my coffee. The sugar at the bottom of the Styrofoam cup slid into my mouth as slowly as maple syrup, and I gulped a glass of water down to wash away the harsh sweetness.

"Go get your brother," I said.

"I thought you were going to go into business with Nick and me."

"You're not the only one who can lie."

"But you'd look so good in money, baby. Now you'll have to work."

She made it sound like I was doomed to a life in the tin mines of Bolivia.

"What's with you and the money thing?" I demanded. "You still have that cash in the Caymans, don't you?" I asked.

"How can I get it now, with Matson dead? It's in escrow, and besides, he never gave us the account number."

"Go up and get your brother. Forget the money. We'll be lucky if we get out of this alive."

Vivian stood up, hooked her thumbs under the spaghetti straps of her dress and straightened them out, then gave her miniskirt just enough of a downward tug to keep it from becoming a sash. Every time I looked at her, I understood once again why hell would always be crowded.

"I'm not sure I trust you anymore," she said.

"Now we're even."

When the door of the elevator closed, I walked quickly out of the lobby and across the street to the cybercafé on the corner. They had just opened up, and the sleepy-eyed kid behind the counter moved in slow motion as he set me up at a desktop near the front window. I wasn't high-tech enough to know exactly how to do what I wanted to do and had to ask him for help downloading the information on the drive we'd swiped from Vivian's room into an e-mail attachment, which I then sent to Susan with a brief explanation of its contents. All this was to buy myself a little leverage with the feds when everything hit the fan.

Ten minutes later I was back in the lobby of the Holiday Inn. I walked past the concierge toward the coffee stand, expecting to find Vivian and Nick waiting for me. My plan was simple: I would find Williams, give him the information, and try to convince him that he and the Colonel were free to go on their merry way without interference. I had no intention of trying to be a hero or of turning anybody in to the cops. As far as I could see, I was looking at a little trouble for my adventures at Krome. Eventually Hackbart might figure out that I had some connection with the Colonel, but there would not be much he could do with that. They'd put the squeeze on me for a while, but that would be the extent of it. Vivian and Nick might get away without so much as being questioned. All that mattered to me now was that Williams and the Colonel go far, far away and stay there.

The table where I'd been sitting with Vivian was empty, so I went over and pushed the button for the elevator and rode up to the sixth floor. The Do Not Disturb sign was no longer hanging from the doorknob on Nick's room, so I continued down the hallway, expecting to find them in the room I'd shared with Vivian. I didn't bother to knock and just slid the key into the lock. The green light flickered, and I went in, past the closed door of the bathroom, behind which I could hear the shower running. I could see Vivian's feet hanging over the edge of the bed. My first thought was that she'd fallen asleep again, but as I bent down to give her a shake, I spotted a thin trickle of blood at the edge of her mouth.

From behind me I heard the roar of the shower grow louder. I half turned, expecting to see Nick. I didn't even think to reach for the gun under my shirt. But it wasn't Nick. It was Williams. He smiled happily as he pointed the revolver at my chest. There was nothing I could do except stand there and listen to myself breathe.

"Throw your gun down on the bed. Nicky told me you had one, so don't say otherwise."

I tossed the gun on the bed, and Williams picked it up.

"You're a good swimmer, Jack," Williams said, still smiling. "Better than I thought. Now, just stand there and don't move."

I glanced down at Vivian. "What did you do to her?" I asked.

"Injected her with a sedative," Williams said. "Of course, I had to slap the little whore first. That's something you should have done more often. But forget that. I believe you have something that belongs to me."

"You mean to the Colonel."

"Same difference."

"Where's Nick?" I asked.

"Give it to me."

I fished the pod out of my shirt pocket and tossed it to him, but I threw it a bit wide so that he had to reach across his body with his left hand to catch it. As he reached, I lunged at him. I got hold of his wrist with one hand and his thick, muscular neck with the other. My weight carried us backward, and he slammed into the wall, causing the mirror hanging over the dresser to fall and crash onto the counter. For a moment I held him there. Then, slowly, inexorably, he began to push me back. I let go of his neck and hit him with the heel of my palm under the nose with enough force to send blood shooting out all over me.

The back of his skull bounced off the wall, and he used the momentum of the recoil to head-butt me. The pain caused me to loosen my grip on his wrist. He broke free and in the same motion hit me across the temple with the barrel of the gun. It didn't hurt much, but I instinctively tried to duck, and as I did so, Williams crouched, straightened, and drove his massive fist into my solar plexus.

Every nerve in my body fired at once as I fell to my knees, clutching my guts. Still, I had enough presence of mind to reach for my own gun, but my hand was like a blind man without a cane. Williams hit me again under the chin, and I fell backward onto the carpet. I tried to get up, but before I could even get an elbow posted on the floor, he grasped me by the throat with one hand and squeezed just enough to shut off my breathing. I instinctively grabbed both of his wrists but stopped when he put the business end of the gun against my forehead.

Then I heard the bathroom door open and click closed. Nick stepped into the room and frowned at the scene. He looked over at where Vivian still lay sprawled on the bed and frowned even harder.

Williams, still with his hand around my throat, half lifted me to my feet. A twisting blue vein in his neck pulsed like a swollen river filled with blood. I had no idea what kind of 'roids he was on, but they were working just fine. When I was upright, he gave me a shove that sent me backward onto the bed next to Vivian. He pointed the gun at my crotch and spoke to Nick without looking at him.

"You get the van?" he demanded.

"It's in the parking lot, top floor of the garage, just like you said," Nick answered eagerly, like a Boy Scout anxious to earn a merit badge.

I rubbed my throat and managed to coax my vocal cords back to life while Williams wiped the blood from his nose with an edge of the bedsheet.

"So I guess you switched sides again," I said to Nick. "Too bad. I was starting to like you."

Nick looked me up and down and smirked. "What did you expect me to do?" he asked. "Stick with a loser like you? Get real, would you?"

"Let's go," Williams said, glancing quickly at his watch

but never once moving the gun from where it was still aimed at a point between my legs. Then to me: "I know what you're thinking," he said. "You're thinking this gun doesn't have a silencer and I won't risk making that much noise in here, but think again. Get up, and get up slow."

I got up, and as I did so, Williams again pointed the gun at my forehead. "Where's the Colonel?" I asked. "I want to speak to him. He owes me some money."

"Funny you should say that," Williams responded. "He's anxious to see you, too. Now pick up the whore. We're getting out of here."

Nick glanced at his sister. "Is she all right?"

"What do you care, you little prick?" Williams boomed. "Just shut up and open the goddamned door. You two have caused enough trouble already."

"Jesus," Nick said. "You don't have to yell."

I bent down and scooped Vivian up in my arms. I was still in pain from the beating, and my legs had lost much of their spring, but I managed to straighten up. She was barely 110, but I felt like a man struggling under the gravity of Jupiter.

Williams smiled at the sight of my obvious struggle. "What's the matter, Vaughn?" he asked. "You too weak to carry her?"

I walked with difficulty past Nick and into the hallway, hoping that a maid on her rounds might spot us and call the front desk, but no such luck. Williams followed behind us as Nick opened the door to the stairs that led to the garage. Vivian felt dead in my arms, and I wasn't in much better shape myself. I had to stop twice to rest. Each time I did, Williams nudged me in the back with the gun.

Nick had parked the van next to the exit into the garage, for which I was grateful, since my back was about to crack with the effort of carrying Vivian down three flights of stairs. Nick slid the van's side door open and stood aside

while I placed his sister on the backseat. I had never been so
happy to put down a beautiful woman in my entire life.

Then Williams told me to stand with my back to him and
my hands against the van.

I don't know who jabbed me with the needle, but I jumped
as I felt the point penetrate the skin on my left shoulder. I
didn't know who was holding the gun right then, Williams
or Nick, but it didn't matter. I kicked backward with my left
foot and felt it hit something human. I spun around in time
to see Williams staggering back, his hands waving in the air
as he fought to keep from falling, and Nick looking on horrified as I made a run for it.

I ran a good twenty feet before I was back on Jupiter again.
Only this time I was running through a swamp as well. My
legs started to vanish under me as though they were being
erased while I ran. I stumbled, fell, and got up again, footsteps coming up hard behind me. Somebody grabbed me
and pulled me around hard. It was Williams. I swung at his
head with everything left in the bank, but my arms had disappeared, too, and I felt myself falling for what seemed like
forever without ever hitting the ground.

When I opened my eyes, it was night. The sky was clear,
and the stars glittered above me like peaceful angels, distant
but benign, light-years away, too far to do anything but bear
witness to the earth. I smiled up at the stars. I was glad to
see them. The constellations began to make sense. Was that
Mars with its faint rosy glow? Was that Aries rising in the
west?

I was lying on my back, and I couldn't feel my body, but it
didn't seem to matter much, not when I could float like this.
After a while somebody started to tell me a story, not with
words but with pictures. There was a beautiful black-haired
woman. Her mouth moved, but nothing came out when she
spoke. There were three men standing over me as the black-

haired woman rubbed my cheek with the palm of her hand. Everybody seemed very familiar. I smiled up at them. They weren't as pretty as the stars, but they were a lot closer.

Then one of the men—the biggest of the three—bent over, and I felt a stinging sensation across my face. And all at once I remembered who I was and that the strange dream I'd awakened into was real.

"Wake up, Jack," Vivian said. She was kneeling beside me like a nurse.

I looked up at her, then at the three men standing above us. One of them was young. That would be my buddy Nick. Check. One of them was on steroids. That would be Williams. Check.

The third man was the Colonel. Check.

The girl was Vivian. I looked her over. Not bad, I thought.

That left me. I was Jack. Jack Vaughn, personal trainer to psychos and killers. Former cop and cop killer. My hobbies were sinking yachts, finding dead bodies, and running from other cops. It's a great way to stay in shape. A lot more exciting than yoga or tai chi, I'll tell you that much. In a deranged sort of way, it was all starting to make sense.

I found my legs and got slowly to my feet. Vivian helped. I looked around. It was night, all right. We were standing on the beach about twenty yards from the ocean, next to a long wooden pier that reached into the sea. There were no houses around, but I guessed we were somewhere near Edgewater. I brushed the sand from my clothes and smiled at the Colonel. He was wearing a black, two-piece running suit and looked like a fit and trim retiree out for an evening jog. He smiled down at me benignly, as though he had just happened upon me lying there in the sand.

"We were starting to worry about you," he said. There was true compassion in his voice, which seemed odd given the fact that Williams was pointing his gun at me again. "I was afraid that Rudolph had given you an overdose."

"Yeah," I said. "That would be illegal."

There was sand on my face, and I brushed that off, too. Williams took a step back, but he needn't have bothered. I was still way too woozy to try anything even vaguely heroic.

Nick took a last drag from his cigarette and flicked the butt past my ear.

"Stupid right to the end," he said.

"Shut up," Vivian said. "He saved us all. Isn't that right, Daddy?"

"Well," I said, "I guess the Partridge Family is back together again."

"What time does the boat get here?" Nick asked. "I'm not going to stand out here all night listening to this idiot make his asinine remarks."

I looked at Williams. "You're not much without a gun in your hand, are you?" I said.

"You're not much either way," Williams said. "I proved that at the hotel."

"So what's the deal now?" I asked. "Can I go home?"

"Vivian and Nick and I have come to an agreement," the Colonel said.

"And I don't agree with it one bit," Nick said testily, scanning the ocean as he spoke. I looked with him. Far off, coming in at a good clip from the west, was some kind of boat. Williams saw it, too. He glanced quickly at his watch.

"What kind of agreement?" I asked.

"My daughter has agreed to go with the rest of us, in return for which, after we're gone, Williams will let you go. In a few weeks, once he's sure we're safe, he'll join us in our new home."

"And where's that, Andy? Havana?"

The Colonel smiled. "I'm a man of the world, Jack. One place is as good as the next—as long as you have the money to afford it. As far as you're concerned, it's really quite simple. Just keep your mouth shut. You're fifty grand ahead of the game. Keep it that way."

"Hey, do me a favor," I said. "While you're there, ask Fidel if he needs a personal trainer. He looks a little fat, if you ask me."

"I can't stand this any longer," Nick said, rolling his eyes. "I'm going down to wait for the boat." He walked slowly to the end of the pier. I followed him with my eyes for a moment and saw the lights of a cabin cruiser heading toward us.

"Suppose she decides not to go with you?" I asked.

"I have to go," Vivian said. "It's all right. As soon as we get everything set up, I'll come back, and we can be together again."

"I look forward to that," I said. "It's been so much fun lately."

The boat made a wide, sweeping turn, cut its throttle, and eased up to the pier. It wasn't a big boat, but it was big enough to reach Cuba.

"Good man," Williams said, checking his watch again. "Right on time."

At that moment a car I didn't recognize appeared above us on the ramp that led down to the sand. The Colonel and Williams must have been expecting it, because neither seemed surprised by its arrival. It was a black Chevrolet Impala circa 1968, with whitewall tires, tinted windows, and the horns of a steer for a hood ornament. Two men got out. One of them was Dominguez, the Colonel's chauffeur. The other was a longhaired man in his early twenties in a dirty white tank top that revealed a pair of shoulders festooned with tattoos. The young man opened the trunk and lifted out a pair of weather-beaten suitcases. The two newcomers embraced for a long moment, and then the younger man got back in the car and drove off.

Dominguez watched the Impala wind its way back up the ramp, then picked up his bags and walked slowly toward us. He was obviously struggling and looked even worse than when I had seen him a few days earlier.

"Where are you off to, Rafael?" I asked. "Santiago province, by any chance?"

"You talk too much," Williams said.

Dominguez studied me with his sad, sick eyes. "Goodbye, Jack. I don't think I see you again after this," he said. "I wish for you the best."

I thanked him. Dominguez nodded grimly and walked slowly toward the boat, a suitcase in either hand, like an old man balancing on a tightrope. He was going home to die.

"You had better head down to the boat now, Colonel," Williams said. "We don't want to be out here too long."

"Keep him here until we're gone," the Colonel said. "Then drive him home."

Williams smiled ever so slightly. "Sure thing," he replied. "Just like a chauffeur."

"What about the fifty grand you owe me?" I asked.

"I'm giving you your life," he said. "That should make us even."

The wind picked up. I glanced over the Colonel's shoulder and saw Nick stepping onto the boat at the end of the pier. Vivian embraced me, kissed me on the cheek, but I didn't respond. I was too busy thinking about the way Williams had smiled when his boss had told him to drive me home after they took off. I searched Vivian's dark eyes for any sign that she knew what was coming, but they told me nothing. Maybe she suspected what was about to go down, and maybe she didn't. Then, all at once, she began to cry.

"We have to go now, dear," the Colonel said in a soft

voice. Vivian brushed her eyes with the back of her wrist and walked over to where her father stood. He put his arm around her shoulders, and together they turned and walked toward the pier. They had gone only a few yards when Vivian broke away from her father and ran back to me. She threw her arms around my neck and kissed me hard on the lips. Williams looked on impassively.

"I love you," she said. "You know that, don't you?"

"Sure," I said. "Go on, now. Give me a call when you can. I'll be fine. Williams and I might even go for a beer or two. Isn't that right, Williams?" Vivian turned to look at him.

"You bet," he said, but this time he didn't smile. His blue eyes were as hard as diamond drill bits.

Vivian turned back to me. She reached up and ran her index finger over the scar on my cheek. It was a familiar gesture. I remembered the first time she'd done it—back when I first told her about the shooting up in New York. I had always taken it as her way of telling me she understood my remorse, why I'd never had it removed, and why I never would. I told her back then that there were some scars worth keeping.

I looked down toward the end of the pier. Her father was just a shadow, almost invisible against the backdrop of the boat. From that distance I could just barely make out the tall, slender silhouettes of a row of deep-sea fishing rods lined up along the stern.

"So long, kid," I said, trying to smile.

Vivian gave me one last desperate look, then turned and ran toward the boat. In a few seconds, she, too, was a shadow. A moment later, with a muted roar of its engine, the cruiser made a wide turn and headed out to sea. I watched the boat become small against the night sky. Williams didn't bother to look; he was too busy watching me.

"Let's go get that beer," I said. "I don't know about you, but I'm getting pretty thirsty."

"Yeah, that's a good idea," he said. He made a brief gesture with his gun toward the north. "Let's you and me take a walk up to those dunes over there."

"Why not shoot me here?" I asked.

He smiled. "Who said I was going to shoot you? Now, walk."

The dunes were about fifty yards away. The stalks of oat grass that covered them were waving like the hair of mermaids in the water. The sand was packed hard. Williams stayed behind me as we walked.

"Stop and turn around," he said.

I turned in time to catch his fist with my face. I fell backward onto the sand and skidded a few feet. I lay there and did a bit more stargazing before rolling onto my stomach. Judging from the blood filling my mouth, I gathered that my nose was broken.

"Get up," Williams said from behind me. "We're just getting started."

I sat up gradually. For a moment there were two Williamses, identically dressed, each one as big and as ugly as his twin. I stared at them until they merged. It was then I noticed that he wasn't holding the gun anymore, and it came to me all at once, along with the pain in my face, what he had in mind. He was going to kill me with his bare hands.

"Get up," he repeated. "I'm giving you a chance. You win, you leave. You lose, you die."

I wiped my mouth with the back of my hand; it came away as red as a prizefight in the final round.

"I've got a better idea," I said. "Suppose you just leave."

Williams didn't answer me; he stood there glaring down at where I sat as though he were looking at a body already dead. Slowly, I got to my feet. Even on my best day, I knew I couldn't have taken him, and it wasn't just the steroids either. He had been trained by the best, and he was also crazy. I, on the other hand, was beaten up, half drugged, and badly dehydrated. Still, being pummeled to death was better than being shot like a wounded animal—better, but a lot more painful.

I straightened up and faced him. The blood from my nose ran down my chin. The salty sweetness made me angry— angry, but not stupid. I took a step forward and pretended to stagger, and at that precise moment Williams charged at me from a distance of eight feet.

As he reached for me with his right hand, I spun to my left like a drunken matador, brushing his arm away with my left arm as though it were the branch of a tree. I almost fell, but as he went by me, I kicked him in the back of the knee. It wasn't a hard kick, not by a long shot, but it made him stumble and lose his balance. I guess he got it back pretty fast, but it didn't matter, because by the time he recovered, I was already running at full speed down the beach.

I waited for the sound of a gunshot, but all I heard was Williams coming hard up behind me. His fingers grazed the back of my shoulder but didn't hold, although I knew if I so much as stumbled, it would all be over. If the sand hadn't been as compressed as it was, he would've had me.

People don't realize how fast a man built like that can run for short distances. The same muscle fibers that allow a weight lifter to hoist a quarter ton over his head can power him for thirty or forty yards at a speed almost equal to that of a sprinter a hundred pounds lighter. I could hear Williams coming, closing fast and breathing hard. I felt his fingers again graze my shoulders, and at that moment I cut to the right and onto the soft, wet sand closest to the surf. I didn't have to glance back to know where he was; I could hear him coming at me from the left.

He was falling behind, but he was still close, too close. One misstep and he'd be on me. You hit top speed at thirty yards, and after that it's just a question of who slows down first. The lactic acid begins to outstrip the body's ability to clear it from the bloodstream, and the muscles lose their efficiency. They begin to tire, to cramp up, and from that point it's a basic question of chemistry. There was one other fact I was banking on: The stronger and more powerful a man is, the more he sacrifices in terms of endurance. For Williams and me it had come down to the equation between life and death.

He kept coming. It had to be the Morphitrex. Not even steroids could have allowed a man of Williams's size and age to run so fast for so long. But I had nature's own private stock of juice powering me forward. It's called adrenaline, and in moments of extreme excitement it's the best stuff in the world. The little glands that ride the kidneys were working overtime producing it, and I felt my stride evening out and my chest expanding, preparing for the inevitable switch of energy systems that would allow for the use of oxygen as a fuel source. That's the system that marathoners use. It's very efficient. You can run just about two hours before the sugar in the muscles gets used up and you hit the wall. The problem with that is by then you're no longer sprinting, and I could feel myself slowing down.

A hundred yards with the juggernaut still coming, but not as fast. Even better, I could no longer hear his breathing. I checked ahead for a smooth stretch of sand, then glanced quickly behind me. The gap between me and Williams was now sixty or seventy yards. He was still running, but he was kicking up a lot of sand and having trouble keeping a straight course. He ran with his head down, like a drunk looking for a place to collapse. I ran for another twenty yards, then slowed a bit until my breathing evened out. I needed to save something for the end.

I stopped and waited for him. When he saw me standing there, he redoubled his efforts. I picked up a chunk of
coral and threw it at him. His head jerked back, but his body
surged forward. He was almost cooked. He was mean, and
he was crazy, and he had a great deal of willpower, but the
laws of exhaustion are nonnegotiable. He was already into
oxygen debt, and his body, despite its strength, couldn't pay
it off quickly enough. I let him get within twenty yards, then
took off running again. I slowed down just enough to keep
his rabid hopes of killing me alive. Whenever I was satisfied
that he was still coming, I trotted away from him.

Again I looked back. It was well that I did so, because he
had closed to within twenty yards of me. He'd put everything into one last surge, but he was finished, used up. As I
watched, he fell forward onto his knees like a man kneeling
in prayer. I stopped and called to him. He looked up and
struggled to his feet, stumbled forward, then fell to his knees
again. I turned and faced him. He was sixty yards behind
me now, a shadow of a ruin rising up out of the sand. Say
what you will of Williams, but he had a lot of Bushido in his
bullet head.

I ran at him, full speed, or what I had left of it. The world
on either side of me blurred into a mass of incoherent light,
like a palette of watercolors smeared in a rainstorm. I
couldn't feel my feet on the sand, but I was moving fast. My
mouth was full of blood, my blood, and it made me mad.

Williams lifted his head, but it was too late, because I was
already in the air, my knees tucked into my ribs and then the
jackknife straightening of the legs as I thrust out my heels.
There was no way you could have planned it, but Williams
turned his chin to one side just as I struck him. His neck
made a sickening sound, like the mast of a ship snapping in
two. He spun half around and toppled backward. I landed
hard on my hands and belly, facing away from him, the air

knocked out of me. I must have hit a nerve when I landed, because my left arm was numb clean up to the shoulder. I got to my feet as quickly as I could, pushing up with my one good hand, and walked over to where Williams lay.

I noticed the revolver lying in the sand at his feet. He must have had it in an ankle holster. It had come loose when he fell. You tell me why he hadn't tried to shoot me with it. The .38 didn't have much range, and it would have been a tough shot in the dark with both of us running, but he might have tried, especially in the beginning when he was still close enough to have hit me. But that wasn't Williams. He had chosen to be the lion right through to the end, and that was maybe why I was alive and he was almost dead. I scooped up the gun and checked the clip. Its gold shells winked at me in the weak light.

Williams was still breathing. I stood over him with the gun pointed at his head. He looked up, but not at me. His blue eyes were peering into the vast depths of the stars and seeing nothing. There was blood all around his mouth and nose. His massive chest lifted once, twice, then dropped and stayed down. It sounds cold to say it, but under the circumstances it seemed to me like a fairly natural death, a grim fact that tells you something about the kind of territory my life had entered. I had a fresh gun, there was a dead man lying at my feet, and all I can tell you now is that it didn't shock me. I didn't feel any kind of satisfaction. I didn't feel anything at all.

I sat on the sand next to Williams's body for five minutes with the revolver still pointing at him until I was sure he wasn't faking it. Then, finally, I checked for a pulse at the carotid artery in his tree trunk of a neck. He was dead, all right. I went through his pockets, found his wallet, and buried it in the dunes under a patch of sea grass. What I needed now besides food and rest was time, and the longer it took the cops to identify the body, the better it would be for me.

There was nothing to do about Williams's body except to get away from it, so I started walking. I was just about played out, but I needed to leave the vicinity as soon as possible. Come the morning, someone taking a stroll or jogging along the beach would spot him and call the cops. They'd bring Williams to the morgue, but without identification it would be a few days before they could identify him. Probably they would have to take fingerprints. Williams didn't have a criminal record, as far as I knew, but his prints would lead the authorities to his military files. Eventually they would tie him to the Colonel, but not—I hoped—to me.

I went down to the edge of the ocean and did what I could to wash the blood from my face. I had no doubt that I looked like death on a hot plate, and it would not be a good thing if someone were to remember the sight of a man with a bloody face emerging from the beach near where a dead man was found the following day. Still, a nosebleed is hard to stop, especially when you're walking, so I had no choice but to stay on the beach until I looked a little better.

I walked south for a mile or so, my energy winking and blinking inside me like a fluorescent bulb about to flicker out. I was way too beat to go very much farther, but I pushed myself for another mile or so until I reached a place behind the dunes that held a small picnic area, complete with a rusty barbecue stand and half a dozen weather-worn wooden tables. I found a dark spot and stretched out on my back under a tree with the intention of resting for a few minutes while giving my nose a chance to stop bleeding. That was the plan anyway, but I didn't stay awake long enough to review it.

I woke up eight hours later with the sun in my eyes and the Sahara in my mouth, but at least my nose wasn't bleeding anymore. Just to make sure, I walked down to the shore and washed my face again. I touched my nose with a tentative finger. It felt a little flatter than usual, and it hurt badly, but I didn't think it was broken. I looked down the beach and saw an old man walking toward me, sweeping a metal detector in front of him as he came, his head down like a man looking for his car keys in the sand. I took off my shirt and waited for him to pass, but he didn't pay me any attention. All his hopes were buried in the sand.

From the heat and the height of the sun, I estimated it to be around seven or eight o'clock. Surely someone must have spotted Williams's body by now, and that meant it was time to go. The question was, where? It occurred to me that I had absolutely nowhere to go except home. It was the only place that made any sense, even if the cops were looking for me. It didn't matter; I was too tired to care.

I walked up to where the street flanked the beach and checked for some signage to figure out where I was, which turned out to be a bit north of a little town called Dania Beach. I walked into a diner and ordered ham, eggs, coffee, and a pitcher of water. In a booth at the end of the restaurant, a pair of middle-aged cops were eating their breakfast and ignoring me. The waitress who served me treated me as though I looked perfectly normal and even called me "sweetheart" when she refilled my coffee cup. The food brought back some of my strength, though it hurt to eat, especially when I tried gnawing through the slab of ham that came with the eggs. By the time I finished my third cup of coffee, I began to think I might actually make it home without collapsing.

A half hour later I was on U.S. 1, walking south and feeling vaguely human and looking for a pay phone so that I could call a cab. Finally, at a gas station, I found one that actually worked, and ten minutes later I was sailing toward

Miami Beach. I was well fed, poorly rested, and ready to go to jail. I must have fallen asleep, because the next thing I knew, the driver was waking me up.

"Rough night, huh?" he said. His Russian accent was as thick as herring in cream sauce.

"Very rough," I told him. My face was hurting again, and I was thinking about having it amputated when I got the time. I handed the driver a twenty-dollar bill and told him to keep the change.

"I hope she is worth it," he said. "My friend, you look like hell."

"People keep telling me that. I'm beginning to take it personally. Was she worth it? Ask me in a month. I'll tell you then."

Sternfeld, the landlord, was standing on the front step when I hauled my body out of the cab. As usual, he was braced inside the chromium bay of his walker. He was nearsighted, and so I was almost in front him before he realized who it was. He squinted at me and frowned.

"You look like the walking dead," he said.

"Coming from you," I said, "that's hard to take."

"Where the hell have you been? I saw you on television the other night. There's some people looking for you, kid."

I put my foot on the first step and looked over my shoulder. "It was all a big misunderstanding. Everything's okay now." I heard myself saying it, but I had trouble believing that it was true. It was as though some divine law were being violated, a law that says there must be a wake created by our actions that will surely wash back on us no matter how long it takes. I looked up at the cracked façade of the Lancaster Arms as if it were the Wailing Wall. It had taken a long, hard night to make the place look good to me, but then, like I said, every paradise is relative.

"You're late with the rent again," Sternfeld said. "Nothing new there."

"Anybody come by to look for me recently?" I asked.

"The cops, a few days ago. Suits with badges. I told them you had skipped. They didn't seem that disappointed."

"They search my room?" I asked. I was thinking about the fifty grand under the kitchen sink. That might be hard to explain.

"They searched the one I showed them—204," Stern-feld said, smiling slyly. "Right next door to yours. Vacant, though." He shrugged. "What can I tell you? I guess maybe I got the Alzheimer's."

"Why'd you do that for? You might get yourself in trouble."

"I did it because I liked them even less than I like you."

"Anyone else besides the cops stop by?" I asked.

Sternfeld surged forward in his walker so that the back legs came off the ground like those of a horse about to buck its rider.

"Do I look like some kind of goddamn concierge to you or something? And you ignored me when I said you were late with your rent. Don't think I didn't notice that, Mr. Wise Guy."

"Come on, Sternfeld," I said. "Us New Yorkers have to stick together, right? Just tell me. You'll get your money."

"All right, asshole. A couple of days ago, a big guy stopped by asking for you, but I didn't like the look of him, so I told him you had moved out. Looked like a fucking Nazi. He a pal of yours?"

"Not even close."

I gazed at Sternfeld. He was two years older than water and had every disease this side of leprosy, but time was still having a hard time pinning him to the ground. He'd been a cabdriver in New York and had saved enough money over the years to buy first his own cab and then nine more. He'd bought the Lancaster Arms and retired to Florida after his wife died ten years ago. He'd been in North Africa during World War II and had the shrapnel in his right shoulder to prove it, and if you think he was gruff with me, you should only hear how he spoke to people he *didn't* like.

"What the hell are you looking at?" he asked.

"Nothing. How are you feeling these days?"

He spit into the hedges to his right. "Swell. My youngest daughter just called to tell me she's a lesbian now, but at my age I could give a flying fuck. Besides which, I got enough grandchildren anyway—every single goddamn one a half-wit. Other than that, though, everything's jake."

"Look," I told him, "I'm just going upstairs and sleep for a week or two. After that maybe you and I will take the red-eye out to Las Vegas and hit the buffets and the blackjack tables. You must be tired of playing bingo by now."

Sternfeld perked up. "That sounds pretty good. Hey," he said with a grin, "wouldn't it be a riot if anybody I used to know in Vegas was still alive? And hey, by the way, you prick, your rent is due."

"I heard you. Tomorrow, okay? I just need to sleep."

"So sleep. See if I care. Just don't die before you pay me." With that he wheeled his walker around and *tap-tap-tapped* away.

I found the spare key I kept under the air-conditioning unit and opened the door to 206. It looked the same, and I was glad to be there, glad really to be anywhere. The books on the shelves looked down at me like the old friends they were: Montaigne and Dante and Shakespeare and Mickey Spillane—all the classics. I walked into the tiny kitchen and stared benignly at the dirty dishes in the sink. They were a welcome sight for some strange reason, a sign of human business left undone but still within reach of completion. I found a six-pack of beer in the fridge, and it seemed to me that I had indeed reached my own personal promised land, even if it was going to be a very brief oasis.

I went back into the living room, unplugged the phone, and closed the blinds. I turned on the A/C and set the ceiling fan on a light, breezy spin that swirled the air around like a straw swirling cold lemonade in a glass. I sat on the sofa, opened a beer, and waited for the room to get comfortable. I felt good. The whole trick was in not thinking too much. I put Williams's gun under the sofa cushion and sat back and waited for something to shatter my peace. Let them come, I thought, not really caring whether they came or not, but holding out the hope that it would not be today or tomorrow, that I could finish this beer and possibly the next. I wasn't ready for any more trouble yet, but the hell with that. The long, crazy summer was over, and I was too weary to care. Let them come.

I stayed fairly drunk for a day and a half and ordered take-out over the phone. I must have still looked a little crazy, because none of the delivery people would meet my eyes after their first sight of me, and one of them ran off without his tip. That's what happens when you get behind in your shaving. Then, on Tuesday night, I came down with a bad case of cabin fever and realized I had to get out, so I put on my Nikes and a pair of shorts and opened the back door. The air had dried out, and there was an unexpectedly cool breeze blowing down from the north. It was nine o'clock, and the southbound traffic was light. I stepped through the door and waited for someone to shoot me. When no one did, I went for a run. Usually I ran on the beach, but I'd had enough of running in the sand for a while. Besides that, it was pretty dark down by the water's edge, and there was no sense in pushing my luck.

Susan called me at seven o'clock the next morning. Her

voice had nothing in it to hold on to, just words strung together in formation without emotion or excitement. She said she'd be there to pick me up at eight-thirty, and that was about it. You would not have believed she knew me at all. Maybe she didn't. I took a shower and got my only suit out of the closet. It was a khaki number I'd worn only once, and it looked a bit wrinkled, but it wasn't like I was going on a job interview, so I put it on over a light blue shirt and wrapped up the package with a black tie located only after the greatest of difficulties.

Susan's car was already there when I went outside. It was cloudy, and the streets were wet. She didn't say anything when I got in beside her, and from this alone I knew it was not going to be a jubilant morning. I wasn't exactly unhappy with the silence, as I was contemplating dark thoughts of going to the slammer, something I'd told my mother I would always try to avoid. That wasn't the only area where I'd disappointed her. She had told me once that I should try to make a new friend every day, but a cursory review of the recent past revealed that I had fallen a bit behind schedule on that mission, too.

"What do you think is on today's agenda?" I asked.

"Your ass, what else?"

A few minutes later, we were in a conference room on the sixth floor of the federal building in a room with an Arthurian-style round table, floor-to-ceiling windows, worn gray carpeting, and about ten cops of all persuasions, none of whom looked particularly glad to see me. Hackbart was there, too. He was standing by the window drinking coffee out of a Styrofoam cup. He saw me come in and gave me his best scowl, perhaps the first of the day. Over his shoulder I watched a squadron of turkey buzzards flying lazy circles around the Freedom Tower to the north and hoped it wasn't an omen.

Hackbart smiled at Susan and handed her a cup of coffee. I got my own. Then we all sat down around the table. The atmosphere in the room was thick with solemnity and, from my side, fear. We were introduced. There were CIA, FBI, DEA, Customs, coast guard, cops from the city of Miami, and cops from Miami Beach. There were cops of every make and model, and I knew at that moment without a doubt that I was the safest man in the world. I didn't see anybody from the Justice League of America, however, but for all I knew, Batman was under the table with a tape recorder.

The murmur of voices died down all at once, and every eye turned toward the head of the table, where the district attorney sat. He was a tall, lean black man in his midfifties, with salt-and-pepper hair. His name was Lloyd Caldwell, and his somber face was locked into the deliberate expression of someone who puts people in jail for a living. Caldwell coughed into his fist and pushed the wire-rimmed glasses he wore farther up the bridge of his nose. He studied me for a long moment and nodded. There was a crimson folder in front of him and next to it a yellow envelope. He opened the folder and scanned quickly through the contents, all the while drumming softly on the table with the longest set of fingers I'd ever seen. They were fingers for Chopin. After a few seconds, he closed the folder and leaned back in his chair.

"For those of you who don't know me," he said, "my name is Lloyd Caldwell, and I'm the district attorney who's been asked to preside over this meeting. I want to remind everyone here that what's said in this room this morning does not go beyond the door." He looked at me, then at Susan. "Does Mr. Vaughn understand that, Miss Andrews?"

"He does."

"Good," Caldwell said. "Clarity is very important, especially in such delicate matters, matters which if they became known to the public could further compromise an already seriously compromised investigation."

"I understand completely," I assured him.

Caldwell held up one of those square white envelopes used to protect CDs. "Your attorney was kind enough to provide us with some information you sent her a few days ago. The information came from the computer files of a man currently under investigation, a former client of yours, Colonel Andrew Patterson."

Caldwell never took his eyes off mine, but I just gave him the cold, blank stare of a confirmed idiot and didn't say anything. The best thing to do when the cops are quizzing you and the stakes are high is not to give them anything they don't already know, unless you know that what you tell them can't hurt you.

"We've had the Colonel's house under surveillance for some time now. You were seen there last week. What was the nature of your visit?"

"He asked me to come out to see him," I said. "He was looking for his daughter. Her name is Vivian. We used to date about a year ago. He wanted me to help find her."

"There was a white yacht anchored a few hundred yards out from the Colonel's mansion. He mention anything about that?" Caldwell asked.

"Not that I can recall," I said.

"But you do remember seeing it?"

"Yeah, I saw it. Is it important?"

He slid a photograph over to me. "This was taken from a plane the night before your visit to the Colonel," Caldwell said.

I picked up the photo and examined it more thoroughly than I needed to. It was an aerial shot of *The Carrousel*.

"Is this the yacht you were talking about?" I asked innocently enough.

He slid another photo over to me, and I examined that, too. There was not much to see, just a shot of open water.

"This was taken at the same location two nights later. As you may notice," Caldwell said, "the yacht is nowhere to be seen."

"Where'd it go?" I asked. My pulse had picked up considerably, and I could feel Hackbart staring at me from his side of the desk.

"We were hoping you might shed some light on that for us, Mr. Vaughn," Caldwell said.

"Call me Jack," I said. "Sorry. I have no idea what happened to it. Whose was it?"

Caldwell seemed to be getting impatient. "It belonged to Randy Matson, another client of yours. Funny thing though," he said, "it's registered in the name of a phony corporation in the Cayman Islands."

"I know Randy," I said. "He made porno movies. He didn't have the money for a boat like that, not even close."

"Someone he knew did. Tell me this: Did you know a man named Harry Duncan?"

"Never heard of him," I said. "Oh, wait a minute. Agent Hackbart mentioned his name the other night when I was at Ms. Andrew's place. Wasn't that his name, Agent Hackbart?"

"Cut the crap, Vaughn," Hackbart snarled. "Everything leads back to you. What the hell did you do with that boat?"

"I sold it on eBay, what else? Now, listen to me. If you can't find the boat you're looking for, then I'm sorry. But I have no idea what happened to it."

"Bullshit!" Hackbart barked.

"Please, gentlemen," Susan said. "Let's keep it civil."

"You were pulled out of the Atlantic Ocean a few days ago by the crew of a coast guard cutter after a man in a speedboat was spotted firing at you with what appeared to be a rifle," Caldwell said. "You claim to have no idea who it was doing the shooting. Is that correct, Mr. Vaughn?"

"That's right," I said. "Just another psycho. You get them all the time."

"And you stand by that story now?" Caldwell asked.

"That's right."

"What about this? The Edgewater police found the body of a Sergeant Rudolph Williams on the beach a few days ago. He was an assistant to Colonel Patterson. I suppose you knew him."

"Rudy? Sure, I knew him," I said. "Nice guy, quiet type. Never said very much. What happened to him?"

"He had a broken neck," Hackbart said testily. "As if you didn't already know that."

"My client is prepared to cooperate with you, Mr. Hackbart. You don't have to try to intimidate him."

"Intimidate him?" Hackbart said. "Lady, you haven't seen anything yet."

"Mr. Caldwell," Susan said, "the smuggling charge against my client won't stick. He's no more of a smuggler than you or I. Aside from that, are you prepared at this time to charge Mr. Vaughn with any other offense?"

Caldwell didn't answer her directly. He was back to looking at me again, and it was obvious from his expression that he wasn't too thrilled with what he was seeing. After a moment of serious staring, he held up the envelope with the CD again.

"How did you come by this information, Mr. Vaughn?" he asked.

"Vivian gave it to me."

"The Colonel's daughter?"

"That's right."

"Why would she hand this over to you?"

"I have no idea."

"Do you know where the girl is now?" Caldwell asked.

"No." The lies were stacking up like a house of cards and one wrong move would send them all scattering across the big mahogany desk.

Hackbart leaned forward in his chair like a man about to dive out an open window. "Just how stupid do you think we are?" he asked.

I had an answer for that, but the ice was too thin for comedy.

"Mr. Caldwell," Susan said, "from what I've heard here this morning, you don't have enough evidence to implicate my client in any way in your investigation. On the other hand, he's provided you with what is, by your admission, some very valuable evidence in the Patterson case, a case far more important to everyone in this room than my client's breaking out of the Krome Detention Center the other day. No one here is interested in Mr. Vaughn, and the fact that he has connections with several of the players is due to the nature of his job, which brings him into contact with a good many people, including, I might add, myself."

"Lucky you," Hackbart said.

Caldwell was silent for a long moment. I could see the set of scales inside his mind doing a seesaw act, with my ass in one pan and his investigation in the other. At last he looked up. He stared at me and almost smiled. Then he turned to Susan.

"Very well," Caldwell said. "We'll proceed, then. We have here a very strange situation, Mr. Vaughn, but my colleagues and I, as well as other government officials, believe that the situation can be resolved with a minimum of difficulty, depending on what you say here today. By all rights, Mr. Vaughn, you should now be sitting in a jail cell for any one of several serious offenses, including obstruction of justice, and that's just the beginning. These are all serious charges, and under normal circumstances you would most certainly be indicted. As you no doubt realize, Mr. Vaughn, you could spend the better part of the next ten years in prison. Are we clear on that, Mr. Vaughn?"

"Very clear," I said. I happened to glance outside through the floor-length window. The overgrown turkey buzzards with the serrated wings that fly around the courthouse were still circling in the bright morning sky, but I was no longer sure they were looking for me.

Caldwell threw me one last hard stare, picked up the crimson folder and showed it to me, then set it down again. "We've assembled a little dossier on you, Mr. Vaughn. For the benefit of the others, I'd like to review certain aspects of your biography. You have a problem with that?"

"My life is an open book, sir," I said.

Susan kicked me hard enough to make me wince. Caldwell saw it and allowed himself the slightest of smiles.

"You were born in Ithaca, New York, after which your family moved to Manhattan. Married once, divorced once. You attended St. John's University on a partial football scholarship and majored, oddly enough, in comparative literature. Your older brother, Matt, was shot down over Laos in 1972. For a time you taught English at a private school in Manhattan. In 1995 you became a police officer. You received a whole slew of commendations, were generally well liked by your superiors, but were prone to flippancy. Despite that, you were on the fast track to detective when you shot another officer in a stairwell up in the projects. He fired first. It was dark, and he was working undercover. A tragic accident. You were cleared of all culpability, received the mandatory counseling, and were returned to active duty. Six weeks later you resigned. Where'd you go after that?"

"Nowhere in particular," I said. "I bought a car and just drove around a lot. I drove all over the country. I even drove to Alaska. Then I got tired of the cold and came south. That's how I ended up in Miami."

"And now you work as a personal trainer?" Caldwell asked.

"That's correct, sir."

"You were a good cop," he said.

"Thank you."

"You could be again. Even with all this," he said, tapping the red folder. "It's not beyond the realm of possibility."

"I don't think so," I said.

"Why not?"

"Too dangerous."

Even Hackbart had to laugh at that. Susan kicked me under the table, but not as hard as the first time.

"Miss Andrews and I," Caldwell began, "have reached an agreement—an agreement, I might add, in which your record as a former officer of the law plays no small part." He picked up the envelope and showed it to me. "This is a sealed indictment with your name on it, Mr. Vaughn. Whether or not it remains sealed depends entirely on you. It all comes down to this: Can you keep your mouth shut?"

"Sir," I told him, "I've got the worst case of amnesia you've ever seen, and it's getting worse by the day. By the time I get downstairs, I won't even remember this meeting. Is that good enough for you?"

"I'm starting to like you, Mr. Vaughn. We understand each other very well. It's a pity we never met prior to this occasion. Now, before you go, we have a few things we need you to sign—and yes, one last thing. It would be better for you if none of us ever sees you again. I hope you don't take offense at that."

"None at all. I hope I don't see you either. I've had enough of cops to last a lifetime."

"I've heard that said before," Hackbart said. "But it never lasts."

An hour later Susan and I were at the Bayfront Market-place. We were sitting at a café called the Lost Lagoon, watching a line of tourists filing on board a fake pirate ship that was moored in a wreath of floating garbage. We had finished eating, and I was drinking an early scotch while Susan sipped her cappuccino. A crescent of foam had found purchase on her upper lip, but I didn't mention it. I thought it made for a nice accessory to the tailored blue pinstriped suit she was wearing.

"Let me ask you a question," she said.

"Go ahead, Counselor."

"Vivian aside, Cortez aside, how come you never made a pass at me in all the time we trained together?"

The question caught me by surprise, and I knew I had to be careful about how I answered it. I was edging back toward her good side, and I wanted to keep it that way.

"That one's easy," I said. "I told you before. I'm a professional. All personal trainers have to take an oath when they get certified, and getting mixed up with clients is a no-no. Anyway, one woman at a time is enough."

"Is that the truth? Not the part about the oath, the rest."

"Mostly. But there's more. I'm just not sure you want to hear it."

"Come on, tell me. You're not going to hurt my feelings. Lawyers don't have any. You know that."

"Maybe that's part of it. You're a little on the hard side, Susan. You've got that damned force field around you not even a rhino could get through."

"What are you talking about? What force field?"

"I don't know. It's like some kind of invisible padding you wear. You like men—at least from the waist down you like them—and you like them to look at you, except that the moment they do, it's like they've shown their hand, and you get disgusted."

"That's not true," she said indignantly.

"Okay, then. I take it back. Besides, I couldn't have handled both you and Vivian at same time even if it had come down to that."

"I doubt you could handle me at all."

"About the only thing I can handle right now is another glass of scotch."

"Well," Susan said, "look on the bright side. At least you're rid of that little bitch."

"Yeah," I said. "One down and one to go."

So much for staying on her good side.

A week later I came home from the gym and found an envelope under my door. It had no return address on it, but the scent of perfume told me who it was from. The letter had a postmark from Bimini and had been sent three days after Vivian and the Colonel left Williams and me standing on the beach up in Edgewater. I looked over my shoulder to see if Hackbart was sneaking up on me with a lasso, but there was no one there, so I locked the door behind me and opened the letter. It was written on stationery from a hotel named the Beachcomber.

Dear Jack:

Please write back to me as soon as you receive this letter. I am so worried about you. I know you don't believe me, but I really do love you. I hope you can come and see me someday. What happened to Williams? My father is very concerned that he was picked up by the police. Please contact me as soon as possible.

Love always,
Vivian

I read the note again a couple of times just for effect, then
tore it up and flushed it down the toilet. Then I sat at the
little table in the kitchen and wrote a reply.

Dear Vivian:
  I'm doing fine, and business is great. I'm even train-
ing Susan again. You remember her, don't you? Tell
Dad I said hello and how's his old hammer hangin'?
Williams? I'm afraid his health has taken a turn for
the worse. Tell your dad he'd better start looking for
a replacement. Try the ape cage at the Havana Zoo.
You might find somebody there with the right quali-
fications. Stay in touch, but not by phone—the cops
may not be through with me yet.

Love,
Jack

After things had settled down and nobody showed up to
kill or arrest me, I decided to take a trip to New York, just
to get out of Miami for a while before business picked up
again. I decided to drive. I could have flown, of course, but I
wanted to feel the distance. It had been five years, and while
hardly anybody thinks of New York as a holy city, anyplace
is holy if that's where you were born, if that's the first place
your spirit will fly to when you die. I had the feeling that
when my time came, mine would fly to New York, but now
I had business there. I was going home, and I wanted it to
take a while. As it turned out, it took longer than I figured,
because somewhere in the middle of Georgia, the T-Bird
snapped a fan belt. That set me back a day, but I didn't care.

It was early in September, and most of my clients—rich, traveling bastards that they were—were still out of town.

Despite the continuing protests of the Thunderbird, I made it to New York about eight o'clock on a Friday night, in the middle of a thunderstorm that would have done justice to Miami, so I checked in to a motel out in Queens, ate dinner at an all-night Greek diner that I remembered from the old days, and later on fell asleep watching the Jets give the Dolphins a good preseason whipping. Some things never change.

I spent the next day visiting a few old friends, some of them from the college days and a few from the cop days. I went to a bar named Chauncey's in the West Village where police and firefighters used to hang out and sat at the bar and drank one drink too many. All the old guys from my other life were still there, and they treated me like the prodigal son. The bartender still remembered me, and that's always a good sign. Still, when I left the bar that night and walked through what's left now of Little Italy, I understood for certain that I really didn't belong there anymore. Sure, you can go home again. You just can't stay there for very long.

I wandered around Manhattan for a while looking for the New York I had known, but I couldn't quite find it. It seemed always just out of reach, always a potential, a remembered scent, lingering maybe just around the next corner. Oh, most of the places were still there. The noise was the same, and the crowds and the pigeons were all there, but somehow I felt like a ghost. I walked a lot. I walked looking for a sense of nostalgia I couldn't find, and I felt, finally, somehow traitorous for not having found it. I walked uptown to Fifty-ninth Street where Central Park begins, then turned east and walked over to the Plaza Hotel. There I sat on the edge of the fountain and watched the people go by. After a while I came to the conclusion that there were a few too many of them. Soon there would be one less.

The next day I put on the khaki suit again, along with my one good tie, and drove straight up Queens Boulevard into the neighborhood called Jamaica. There was one last thing to do. I was nervous and a little scared, and part of me thought for sure that I was being stupid. Let sleeping dogs lie, they say, but maybe there are some dogs that need to be awakened when the time comes, when their sleep has done as much good as it's likely to do. I wasn't sure, but I kept driving.

The cop I shot was named Edward Stuart. It was a good English name with the sound of royalty to it, but Stuart was a black man, all of twenty-nine at the time I shot him, and he had grown up in the same projects where he died. I'd been warned not to go to his funeral, but, being me, I went anyway and got the crap beat out of me by a half dozen or so of his relatives, along with one white guy, another cop, who decided he didn't like me much either. It was a biracial beating, which shows that people can work together. I hadn't even fought back that hard. I did just enough not to get beaten too badly. I don't have full recall of the evening's festivities, but I do believe it was one of Ed Stuart's brothers who eventually drove me home.

A few weeks later I left town.

I got the Stuarts' phone number and address from information and made the call from a phone outside a Shell station on Jamaica Avenue, half hoping that no one would be home and that I'd be able to drive home with the coward's comfort of having tried. But still, there were some pretty good reasons for not contacting the widow of the man I had shot. Two years is not a long time, and there was no telling how far she had moved on in her life, but no matter what the answer to that question was, I would still be a sorry reminder of a terrible time. There was another question that bothered me as well: Had I come all this long, stubborn, disastrous way for Beth Stuart and her son or for Jack Vaughn?

A boy answered the phone, and I almost hung up, but then I heard a voice that didn't quite sound like me ask if Mrs. Stuart was in. He yelled for his mother, and a woman's agitated voice came back and asked who it was. I told him, and he shouted my name so loud it embarrassed me to be Jack Vaughn. Then I heard a silence so wide I thought I might never reach the other side of it, then the sound of footsteps.

"Hello. Who's this?" asked Beth Stuart.

"Jack Vaughn," a voice said.

"What can I do for you, Mr. Vaughn?"

"I'm in town for a few days. I was wondering if I could stop by for a couple of minutes."

"What for?"

"Look, I've come a long way for a few minutes of your time. It won't take long."

"What? To apologize again? Mr. Vaughn, listen to me. I just put flowers on my husband's grave. What can you say to that?"

"I know," I said. "I saw them: yellow roses. I put mine next to them."

She let out a long breath. "All right, Mr. Vaughn," she said wearily. "You come on by."

Beth Stuart met me at the door of her little house on a tree-lined street with a face that held more suspicion than mercy. She was a tall, good-looking woman in her early thirties, with a high forehead and bright, intelligent eyes, and she was dressed for church. She invited me into a small living room overflowing with furniture. A football sat perched in a black recliner across from a television set. I picked it up and sat down and glanced around. There were a lot of pictures on the wall, but I didn't want to look at them. Instead I studied the football just to give my eyes something to do.

"That belongs to my son."

"That would be Robert, right?" I said.

Beth Stuart looked at me as though I'd said something in a strange language. She was very gracious under the circumstances, but I got the feeling of some great force being held at bay by a wall of well-worn civility. She went into the kitchen and came back with a pitcher of iced tea and watched me intently as I filled first her glass and then my own.

"What can I do for you, Mr. Vaughn?" she asked. Neither of us touched our tea. The glasses were just a pair of witnesses. I put the football down next to the recliner, then reached into my pocket and got out the cashier's check for forty grand and put it on the table.

"I would have put it in the trust fund, but the woman at the bank told me it had been transferred someplace else. She didn't know where. Anyway, I figured it might come in handy for the boy's college or something."

She picked up the check, studied it for a moment, then slid it back to me across the polished teak surface of the coffee table. Her face was hard, but it wasn't anything I hadn't expected. It wasn't as hard as the lid of a coffin.

"That's all right, Mr. Vaughn. We're doing just fine. We don't need any of your money. I've already forgiven you, as the Lord says we must. If you can't forgive yourself, then there's not a blessed thing I can do for you."

I took a sip of iced tea and set the glass on the table. I stared down at the carpet for a moment and tried to think of something else to say. When I looked up, Beth Stuart was staring at me defiantly.

"You're right, Mrs. Stuart," I said. "I'll be going now. Sorry to interrupt your day. Thanks for the tea."

"You're most welcome."

She stood up. The message was clear: Hit the road, Jack.

I started to reach for the check, but instead I sat back.

"Look," I said. "Maybe you can help me out. I don't know. I'm trying to do something here. Can you understand what I'm saying?"

She met my eyes, and her lips started to tremble, but she'd had much practice in being tough, and the tremor vanished without a trace. I don't know what she was seeing. Maybe she saw a man at the end of his rope, because something changed in her face. And then, as though driven by a force of nature, the front door flew open and a boy of about ten with a basketball under one arm burst into the living room. He started to run up the stairs but stopped short when he saw me. I stood up.

"Who are you?" he asked boldly. He was tall for his age. He wore the baggy satin shorts of a basketball player. I could see his father in him.

I glanced at his mother. Our eyes locked.

"This is Mr. Vaughn," Beth Stuart said. She hesitated for a moment, then said, "He knew your father."

The boy's eyes widened, and he came slowly down the stairs and studied me intently for a moment, as though I were an unexpected statue in a strange city. I looked at his mother in confusion. She nodded. The boy and I shook hands. I didn't know what to do or what to say.

"You knew my father?" he asked incredulously, as though his father had been some great hero out of antiquity, some Hercules so powerful and remote that anyone who had known him was lifted automatically to the level of myth, to legend. It took everything I had in me to keep my bearings.

"Sure I knew him," I said. "Anyway, I was just stopping by to give my regards."

"You're a police officer?" the boy asked. This, too, was incredible.

"I was. I'm retired now."

"You're too young to be retired," he said.

"Maybe you're right," I said.

"You better go get cleaned up for church, Mr. Robert," his mother said. "Mr. Vaughn is coming with us. Isn't that right, Mr. Vaughn?"

Our eyes met again, and I nodded. "Whatever you say, Mrs. Stuart."

Two hours later, after the service, Beth Stuart and her son walked me out to where the Thunderbird sat waiting in a light rain. Robert had already loosened his tie and seemed anxious to shed his suit and become a basketball player again. He said good-bye and ran off toward the house, shedding his jacket before he reached the front door. I watched him go with a mixture of relief and sadness. I didn't think I would ever see him again. Of course, you see people every day whom you won't ever see again, but it's different when you know it.

"I guess you'll be heading home now, Mr. Vaughn," Beth Stuart said, her hand over her head to shield it from the rain. "You think this old rustbucket will make it back to Florida?"

"I don't know," I said. "Maybe you ought to pray for it."

"I don't pray for cars, Mr. Vaughn, only for people."

I nodded. The rain was urging me to go.

"Thanks for the church," I said. "Thanks for everything."

I started to walk toward the car. When I turned back, Mrs. Stuart was still standing there watching me.

"You're going to have to tell him the truth one day," I said to her. "I mean, about what happened and all."

"I know," she said. "But not yet, not here, and not today. He's got some years left before he has to know everything. Childhood needs to have some mercy in it." Her eyes were glistening, but maybe it was the rain.

"Okay," I said.

"You take care now, Jack Vaughn. My hair's getting wet. I never thought you were a bad man. Now I know for sure, but just the same, a little church now and then won't do you any harm either."

"That's for sure," I told her, thinking of Williams, of Matson, of everything. "That's for sure."

Then I turned the car south, and the rain escorted me out of the city and onto the highway toward home—or at least Miami. It was still hard to say if they were both the same thing.

ACKNOWLEDGMENTS

A special thanks to the creative writing department at Florida International University for their help in the writing of this book.

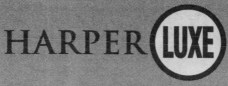